HOPE

THE SHACKLEFORD SISTERS

BOOK FOUR

BEVERLEY WATTS

Cover art by Midnight Muse
Typography by Covers By Karen

CHAPTER 1

*J*f truth be told, Hope Shackleford did not relish spending the festive season under the same roof as her entire family, even though the roof beneath which the gathering was to take place belonged to the Earl of Ravenstone and was far grander than the modest vicarage in which she'd spent her whole life.

Indeed, given that her two eldest sisters were married to influential members of the *ton,* it had to be said that her family were becoming increasingly accustomed to indulgences entirely above their station.

Hope, on the other hand, despite possessing a head of flaming red hair giving indication to the contrary, was a practical young woman who eschewed both whimsy and optimism, unlike the rest of her eccentric family - in particular her father whose calling as a man of the cloth seemed in recent years to play a secondary role to his passion for meddling in affairs that, in Hope's view, were entirely none of his business.

Thus, the chances of their Christmas festivities being wholly focused on the simple joys of the season were, in Hope's opinion, slim to none.

While the rest of her family had already departed for Ravenstone in a comfortable fleet of carriages sent by the Earl the day before, Reverend Shackleford naturally had his duties as the spiritual mentor of his flock to perform before he would be free to take part in more frivolous pursuits.

As usual, her stepmother Agnes had decided it would be far too much strain on her delicate sensibilities to remain behind in support of her husband, and given the speed at which the Reverend had agreed, Hope suspected he had no wish to spend any more time alone with his wife than she did him.

It had therefore summarily been decided that she, being the eldest child living at home, would remain to provide succour to her father until after the service on Christmas morning when they would depart for Ravenstone to join in the festivities.

Still, it meant that now, after a more than passable dinner provided by their cook Mrs Tomlinson, Hope was able to spend a quiet contemplative Christmas Eve with a good book while her father readied himself for the midnight service to come.

Indeed, with the parlour so cosy and warm, a fire roaring in the hearth and Freddy, her father's foxhound snoring contentedly at her feet, Hope was persuaded that she had indeed been given a fortuitous reprieve from the foolish games and ridiculous diversions she was sure were even now being indulged in by her sisters and brother. Naturally, she would attend the midnight service along with most of the villagers, but for the next couple of hours she intended to make the most of her rare solitude.

∞∞∞

Gabriel Atwood, one time Viscount Northwood, couldn't help wondering if he would ever manage to thaw out, or possibly more importantly whether he would actually survive the night.

Being Christmas Eve, the only conveyance he could find that would take him from the port of Dartmouth to the village of Blackmore was a farmer's wagon. The farmer in question had been visiting with his sister, and after being almost flung from the cart for the umpteenth time due to his saviour's erratic driving, Gabriel very much feared the man was mauled.

Gripping the slatted bench beneath him, Gabriel gritted his teeth as he shifted with difficulty and suddenly found himself focused on his nether regions. God's teeth, he wasn't sure his arse would ever recover. He glanced over at the silent, surly man beside him. Clearly, the bumpkin was not a cheerful drunk.

Grimacing, he hunkered down into his flimsy coat and tried to ignore the gnawing in his stomach. He couldn't actually remember the last time he'd eaten. Grimacing he looked down at his filthy hands and stained britches. He had no fear that anyone would recognise him as a member of England's Upper Ten Thousand. In his current state, he looked more like a gallows bird, and he suspected that had his companion not been in his cups, greed would not have overcome his common sense.

The fact of the matter was that everyone who knew him or of him currently believed him dead. The bastards who'd betrayed him would have made sure of that.

His only hope was to seek aid from Nicholas Sinclair, the current Duke of Blackmore before his enemies realised that news of his demise had been greatly exaggerated.

∞∞∞

At just after eleven o'clock, Hope reluctantly laid aside her book and rose to ready herself for the first service of Christmas Day.

She left Freddy in the kitchen after letting him out to do his business. The dog had wasted no time in speedily cocking his leg up the nearest object before hastening back into the warmth of the silent kitchen and curling himself up in front of the embers still burning merrily in the large fireplace.

After checking that the greedy hound was not able to help himself to the plate of cold meats and cheese kindly left by Mrs. Tomlinson to refresh them after the service, Hope donned her warmest cloak and ventured out into the night. The weather was unusually cold for South Devon, and shivering, she wondered whether they might even be in for some snow. The ground was crisp underfoot, and she took care picking her way towards the shadowed outline of the church just as the bells began to ring.

As she neared the entrance, the hazards of falling over something nasty in the dark gradually lessened due to the soft candlelight shining from inside, and eventually she joined the queue of villagers devout enough to brave more than one sermon written by her father's curate in a twenty-four-hour period. Whilst she smiled and shook excited hands though, she suspected it might well have been nosiness rather than piety that had brought most of Blackmore's residents out on such a cold evening, as it was generally accepted that one never knew what Reverend Shackleford would get up to next and no one wanted to miss out.

As it was, those who had believed sleep more important would undoubtedly later bemoan the fact that they missed the Christmas Eve service of eighteen ten, although the telling of it would undoubtedly be embellished until the actual events were entirely lost in translation.

But then, as the Reverend always said, 'One should never let the truth get in the way of a good story.'

∞∞∞∞

It was nearing midnight by the time Gabriel Atwood finally reached his destination, but as he stood at the foot of the steps leading up to the imposing front door of the Duke's magnificent Seat, he felt sick to his stomach. Blackmore was shrouded in darkness. Which could only mean that Nicholas Sinclair was not in residence. Why the bloody hell hadn't he considered the possibility that his former commanding officer might actually be spending the festive season in one of his other bloody houses?

Despairingly, Gabriel climbed the steps and hammered on the front door. Surely, there must be servants who'd remained to watch over such a valuable property. After ten minutes he kicked at the door in frustration. *Imbecile* he fumed to himself. He'd placed all his eggs in one bloody basket, and he didn't know what the devil to do next.

He was just about to begin hammering again when he suddenly heard church bells. He paused listening. Mayhap the staff were attending the midnight service. With a small sliver of hope, he started back down the steps and wearily made his way down the shadowed drive towards the festive ringing. He had no illusions that Nicholas might also be there - the house behind him had clearly been shut up for the season. Nevertheless, there was a good chance there would be someone in the church privy to where the Duke had gone.

God help him if there wasn't.

∞∞∞∞

Reverend Augustus Shackleford glanced down at the sermon in front of him. Why, oh why hadn't he gone over it before now? There were twenty pages for pity's sake. He had no excuse. Certainly not one that would satisfy the Almighty that he'd been doing his deuced job properly. He looked over at his congregation stoically waiting for the address to begin. They might be accustomed to Percy's fire and brimstone narrative, but they were expecting at least a little Christmas cheer, not a fifty-step guide to avoid spending next Christmas downstairs with Old Nick.

5

The truth was he'd been neglecting his duties of late, and this was Percy's way of telling him so. God only knew what tomorrow's sermon consisted of. The Reverend sighed and shook his head. He couldn't deny that the expectations of his parishioners had increased tenfold since he solved the mystery of Redstone House the year before. In fact, sometimes he felt as if the villagers regarded him less as a spiritual advisor and more as a resident mummer.

He glanced up once more. He certainly had to say something, but he couldn't keep his flock from their beds for another two deuced hours. Sighing again, he opened his mouth. Just as the main door was flung open causing the candlelight to waver in fantastical patterns. Surprised, he stared over his flock who collectively turned to see what had caught their Reverend's interest.

The newcomer was a tall slender man dressed completely inadequately for the weather. To the Reverend's less than perfect eyesight, he actually resembled a scarecrow used by the local farmers to protect their crops. Wordlessly, the man limped down the central aisle, his whole bearing a testament to overwhelming exhaustion. The congregation simply sat and followed his progress, sensing something important could well be about to happen.

On reaching the pulpit, the man stopped and spoke, his voice low and hoarse with desperation.

'Tell me you know where Nicholas Sinclair has gone.' As the Reverend merely stared back at him in astonishment, he turned back to face the silent congregation and suddenly thundered, 'For the love of God, does anyone here know the whereabouts of the Duke of Blackmore this night?'

Then he slowly crumpled to the floor in a dead faint.

∞∞∞∞

It took four villagers to carry the unconscious stranger to the vicarage, where he was unceremoniously put to bed still fully clothed. The local apothecary proclaimed him simply suffering from exhaustion and determined that a good night's sleep in a proper bed would likely see him back to full strength by the morrow when they would undoubtedly discover exactly why the man was looking for their Duke.

Naturally, Reverend Shackleford was torn between doing his Christian duty (it was Christmas Day after all, and well … no room at the inn, stables and all that…) and concern that either he, Hope or Percy, or possibly all three of them might be murdered in their beds overnight.

After leaving the oblivious stranger to his dreams, the three of them sat mulling over the problem in the kitchen whilst partaking of Mrs Tomlinson's excellent light repast. It had to be said that after a couple of brandies, the Reverend was much more inclined to view the whole episode as a bit of a reprieve since in the uproar that followed the stranger's dramatic announcement and subsequent swoon, he hadn't had to give the address at all.

'Whilst we are unsure as to the stranger's motives,' Hope was saying as she took a small sip of her sherry, 'we cannot deny that his distress was very real. For some reason, he was desperate to get word to Nicholas.' She paused and frowned. She was about to say something that for her was entirely out of character, but there was something about the stranger that both pulled at her heartstrings and imparted a sense of urgency she was unable to shake. Taking a deep breath, she continued. 'Despite the fact that he is dressed like a vagabond, he has the bearing of a man of quality and has undoubtedly come a long way to speak with his grace.' She drew herself up before declaring defiantly, 'I think we should take him with us tomorrow.'

To her astonishment, neither of her companions disputed her statement. The sense of need conveyed by the stranger had clearly affected them all in a similar manner.

'I'm not sure Nicholas is going to be very happy about us foisting an unknown man on him on Christmas Day,' was all the Reverend commented with a sniff.

'We don't know that he is unknown to his grace,' retorted Hope. 'Remember, Nicholas was in the Royal Navy for many years before he inherited the title from his father. Mayhap this man is known to him from his days at sea.'

'That as may be,' interrupted Percy warily, 'but we must consider the possibility that we might also unwittingly be bringing an enemy into his grace's household.'

'I am no enemy of Nicholas Sinclair.' The deep voice came from the kitchen door which had opened without any of them noticing. Hope stood up with a gasp before looking accusingly at the still comatose foxhound whose only contribution to the unexpected entrance of a total stranger was a slight thump of his tail.

'You should be in bed, sir,' she commented hoping that the tremor in her voice was not noticeable.

'There is no time,' came the whispered response as the man limped painfully into the room. 'I must speak with the Duke of Blackmore. Do you know where he is?'

Without answering, the Reverend stood and pulled out another chair. 'Sit down, man, before you fall down,' he declared. 'And deuced well eat something. You look as though a puff of wind might blow you away.'

The man hesitated, then swayed slightly. Finally, he inclined his head in an approximation of a bow. 'Gabriel Atwood, at your service,' he murmured hoarsely before finally giving in and collapsing into the proffered chair.

Hope pushed the remains of their repast towards him, and after a small hesitation, he began to eat. 'Percy, fetch some more brandy,' ordered Reverend Shackleford watching as their guest pushed food into his mouth as though there would be none tomorrow. Clearly, Mr Atwood had not eaten in some time.

Rising to fetch a fresh loaf of bread, Hope put it in front of the man with a pot of honey. 'Why do you wish to speak with the Duke of Blackmore?' she asked, wincing as she watched him unceremoniously tear the loaf apart.

Before he could answer, Percy returned with a decanter of brandy and another glass. The Reverend poured three generous measures as they waited for their unexpected guest to finally stop eating. At length, Gabriel Atwood leaned back with a sigh and picked up the snifter of brandy, staring into its amber depths as though it contained the secrets of the world.

Finally losing patience, Hope repeated her question.

Gabriel looked over at her before tilting his head back and swallowing the fiery liquid in one mouthful.

'I cannot say,' he bit out, doing little to conceal his frustration at their refusal to tell him the Duke of Blackmore's whereabouts.

'You'll have to do better than that,' responded the Reverend flatly.

'If I tell you more, your lives may be in danger,' he shot back savagely, throwing his hands up in the air at their obstinacy.

Hope narrowed her eyes, refusing to be intimidated by their visitor's dramatic declaration. 'If, as you say, our lives could be at risk should you favour us with such knowledge,' she snapped, 'then it stands to reason that the Duke of Blackmore's will also be threatened should we take you to him.'

'You need not take me to him,' retorted Gabriel. 'I do not need a nursemaid. Simply point me in the right direction, and your part in the matter will be finished.'

For a few seconds the only sound that could be heard in the kitchen was Freddy's gentle snoring, then the Reverend shook his head in regret. 'I'm afraid that's not possible, Mr Atwood, or whoever you are.

'The Duke of Blackmore just happens to be my son-in-law, and he is currently spending the festive season at a house party together with the rest of my family.'

CHAPTER 2

*G*abriel did not feel any of the expected pleasure at the feel of a comfortable bed underneath his aching limbs. Despite his exhaustion, his mind refused to shut down. His frustration at the stubbornness of his host warred with the total surprise that his one-time friend and mentor had actually wed. And a commoner at that.

The Nicholas Sinclair he'd known in the Royal Navy was a stern, solemn man not disposed to much laughter - understandable given the personal tragedies he'd experienced. However, despite Sinclair's serious nature, he was known to be scrupulously fair, honest and above all compassionate. Indeed, his crew would have followed him to the ends of the earth.

But married? Gabriel could not imagine his erstwhile Captain leg shackled at all. Since leaving the Navy, Gabriel had spent as little time as possible in England, and none at all embroiled in the endless merry-go-round that composed the London Season, so had heard none of the gossip. He shook his head in the darkness. Mayhap the Duke's demeanour had changed since they last met. God knew, the man deserved some happiness. He only hoped that the Reverend's daughter possessed the qualities to provide it.

Unfortunately, Gabriel very much feared that whatever hard-won peace Nick had found was about to be thrown out of the window. But while he bitterly regretted bringing his troubles to a man he considered a friend, there really was no one else he could trust.

Grunting, he turned over and plumped up his pillow. While Gabriel knew Nicholas would not refuse aid to his former First Lieutenant, things had changed. The Duke of Blackmore had other responsibilities now. Other loyalties. Sighing, he flung himself back onto his back. At this rate, he was never going to get any sleep. He thought back to the conversation in the kitchen earlier. The striking red-haired chit - what was her name? Hope. Just before he'd entered the kitchen, he'd heard her bold assertion that they should help him, but her manner when she spoke to him directly had been wary, even distrustful. Inexplicably, he found himself disappointed that her defence of him had seemed to waver once she'd had the opportunity to speak with him face to face.

Chuckling grimly to himself, he marvelled at the ridiculousness of his thoughts. Here he was, running for his life, and he was actually bemoaning the fact that an admittedly tempting armful had not swooned over his pretty face. He lifted his arm to rub at his sore eyes, then winced at the smell. God's teeth, if she'd gotten a whiff of him, he wasn't surprised she turned her nose up. Ripe didn't begin to describe the unpleasant odour radiating from his armpits. He could only hope that the Reverend's charity ran to a bucket of water and some clean clothes.

∞∞∞∞

Hope tossed and turned for what remained of the night, going over and over the earlier conversation with the enigmatic Mr Gabriel

Atwood. Shivering, she remembered the desperate intensity in his eyes and her belief that he was more than his appearance suggested.

Unexpectedly, she found herself wondering what he'd thought of her, which was entirely ridiculous, since it was possible, given his desperate actions, that the man was in mortal danger. In such a situation, he was hardly likely to have taken any note of her at all.

And if she was being truthful, he would be unlikely to have taken note of her in more normal circumstances either. Hope was honest enough to accept she was no raving beauty and possibly lacked the more *sparkling* personalities enjoyed by her older sisters. Even her twin, Faith, had more wit than she.

In truth, the only talent she possessed was a singularly loud voice, and even then, it wasn't at all a melodious one. Naturally, being described as possessing a deafening pair of lungs was not a gift she was particularly proud of, though her sisters had thought it a great advantage when they were children. Indeed, Hope had spent most of her time alone on lookout duty during their childhood escapades. It was most likely the sheer amount of time she spent waiting and watching that taught her to value her own company over that of her more boisterous siblings.

Sighing at the absurd direction her thoughts had taken, Hope finally abandoned her attempts to sleep and climbed out of bed, though it was still well before dawn. Shivering uncontrollably, she hastily dressed in the freezing chamber whilst lamenting the supposed peaceful contemplative Christmas Eve and morning she'd envisioned.

Hurrying downstairs to the kitchen, she found Mrs Tomlinson already up and about as the cook set about packing them enough food to sustain them on their journey to Ravenstone. Hope grabbed a freshly baked scone and took her bounty to sit by the already roaring fire, juggling the hot cake as she warmed her hands next to the crackling flames. Taking small nibbles, her thoughts returned to the strange events of the night before.

Their unexpected guest had infuriatingly refused to tell them anything further and just as stubbornly, her father had refused to tell him where the Duke of Blackmore was currently residing. After such a stalemate, Gabriel Atwood was finally persuaded to return to his bed only after the Reverend promised him that they would personally escort him to Nicholas at first light. And now, despite dawn being at least an hour away, she was unsurprised when Gabriel Atwood appeared only minutes behind her.

Thankfully, Hope did not have to introduce him to Mrs Tomlinson. The cook had been present at the midnight service and only eyed the stranger curiously as she handed him a bowl of porridge.

There was no sign of either her father or Percy, and Hope guessed they would already be preparing for the first service of Christmas Day. Given the unusual circumstances, it was also likely to be the only Yuletide service as it was now crucial they leave at the earliest opportunity to ensure they reached Ravenstone in a single day.

Covertly, she watched as their guest ate his porridge in silence, hugging the fire much as she. He ate with polite precision, emphasising her belief that he was not the vagrant he resembled. Indeed, once finished, he thanked Mrs Tomlinson courteously before standing. After a few seconds, she realised he hadn't moved. When she looked up at him enquiringly, he gruffly enquired if there was a possibility he could wash. 'A bucket of water in the stable will do,' he added quickly, no doubt lest she consider his request to be overly presumptuous.

Hope rose and tutted, irritated with herself. 'I'll have some hot water sent to your bedchamber,' she stated nodding towards Mrs Tomlinson. He bent his head in thanks and turned to go.

'And some clean clothes,' she added tartly to his back.

∞∞∞

In fact, the Reverend's first and only sermon of Christmas Day was the shortest he'd ever given and contained none of Percy's usual dire warnings. Under normal circumstances, the early service was rarely attended by more than a handful of villagers; however, on this occasion the church was packed to bursting with parishioners eager to get a peek at last night's dramatic interloper. Consequently, Reverend Shackleford went through the Eucharist at breakneck speed, secure in the knowledge that God undoubtedly approved of their quick departure as evidenced by the fact that almost the entire village had risen so early to get it over and done with.

By seven thirty am, they were cosily ensconced inside the Earl of Ravenstone's luxurious carriage and on their way to Cranborne Chase, the location of Adam Colbourne's Estate on the borders of Wiltshire.

While the carriage was undeniably a little small for four adults and a large dog, the press of bodies generated enough heat to ward off the bitter chill of the early morning. And for Hope, a cloth-wrapped brick stayed warm against her feet until they were well out of Devon and into Somerset.

The Reverend made no bones about his relief that their guest no longer smelled worse than Freddy, but despite gritting his teeth, Gabriel did not rise to the bait. In fact, whoever the clothes he was wearing had previously belonged to, the foxhound clearly approved, and lost no time in jumping up on to the seat and snuggling into the newcomer with a contented sigh. After a startled grunt as the dog leapt on him, Gabriel was grateful for the additional furry warmth and finally, for the first time in what felt like forever, managed to close his eyes and actually sleep.

Sitting opposite, Hope watched with a mixture of surprise and amusement as Freddy climbed all over their unexpected passenger. Indeed, for one ridiculous moment, she found herself wishing she could do the same. With an almost audible gasp at the absurd direction her thoughts had taken for the second time, however briefly, Hope felt her face suffuse with colour. What the deuce was wrong with her? Granted, there had not been a surfeit of attractive men passing through the vicarage of late… Her ponderings screeched to an abrupt halt, and she couldn't prevent a small chuckle escaping. The truth was there had *never* been a surfeit of men, attractive or otherwise, passing through the vicarage. Indeed, especially given their unruly behaviour growing up (and sadly she had to include herself in this), it was a miracle that three of her sisters had married and married well. It certainly hadn't been due to the machinations of their father. From both Tempy's and Faith's accounts, it appeared they both may have gone as far as *hoodwinking* their lovers into marriage. Hope pursed her lips. A scandalous state of affairs that she had no intention of emulating. Faith might be her twin sister, but in truth, they were like chalk and cheese, and Hope could not imagine herself taking such a wanton tack with a would-be suitor.

That's if there ever was one.

Sighing, she turned her attention back to the handsome stranger. And he was handsome, despite his pallor and being swamped in her father's castoffs. In repose, he looked younger, although there were a few flecks of grey in his black curls. His hair was long, much longer than current fashion dictated, and although relatively clean shaven, it was obvious his last attempt had been done without a mirror. She tried to remember what colour his eyes were and was almost frustrated that they were shut. Until suddenly they weren't.

They were grey, almost silver she realised as they regarded her drowsily. For some foolish reason, she returned his gaze and was instantly aware the minute he came fully awake. His expression was impassive, almost guarded, and she felt her face redden for the second time in as many minutes. Hurriedly, she lowered her eyes and stared down at the book in her lap. Gabriel Atwood was clearly a man accustomed to giving nothing away. She wondered how he'd ended up in his current situation.

'Tare an' hounds, it's started snowing.' Her father's muttered observation brought Hope back to the present, and she glanced out of the carriage window, viewing the drifting flakes anxiously.

'We've been travelling for nearly six hours,' she guessed. 'Ravenstone can't be much farther now.'

'I deuced well hope not,' retorted her father. 'It'll be getting dark in another hour or two, and we've already passed the only inn on this road.'

'So, Nicholas is staying with Adam Colbourne,' Gabriel determined. 'I wasn't aware they were acquainted.' Reverend Shackleford eyed him narrowly, realising that this was the first time he'd given the man any indication of their destination.

'Pray tell me how a man dressed like a damned vagrant has any idea of the comings and goings of high society?' he questioned flatly.

Gabriel looked over at him and raised his eyebrows. 'Good question,' was all he murmured with a faint smile.

Hope was about to comment, when Percy, who up to now had been entirely uncommunicative, suddenly leaned forward with a frown. 'I can hear horses,' he blurted.

'Well, of course you can,' retorted the Reverend, 'we've got four of them pulling this damned carriage.'

The curate shook his head. 'You don't understand, I think there are horses coming up behind us.'

One year earlier

Gabriel Atwood, the fifth Viscount of Northwood, stared at himself in the mirror. What the deuce did it matter whether his cravat was tied in a waterfall or a bloody mathematical? The whole consideration was absurd. Abruptly, he nodded at the reflection of his valet who was currently hovering anxiously behind him. 'That will be all, Heavers,' he advised abruptly, finally unable to stand any more of the man's fussing. Turning away from the mirror, he softened his brusqueness with a nod and a smile as he picked up his cloak.

Why the devil his uncle would drag him up from Northwood and choose a Christmas ball to brief him, he had no idea - the opportunity to speak privately would be practically nonexistent given the inevitable crush that would no doubt accompany such a gathering at Albany House. Sighing, he headed out of the front door of his little-used Belgravia townhouse and stepped into his waiting carriage.

He had only been in London a night, and already, he was chafing at the ridiculousness of it all. It seemed to Gabriel as though the vast majority of the *ton* existed in a bubble that bore no semblance to reality. Their cares and concerns appeared only to focus on the latest *on dit* or scandal or marriage or the myriad of other mindless pursuits that made up the London Season, and under normal circumstances, he would have none of it.

Grimacing, Gabriel glanced out of the window into the dark. He hated London and spent as little time as possible there. When not travelling at his uncle's behest, he preferred to spend his time on his Estate in Hampshire - unlike his late father who'd much preferred the bustle of Belgravia to his Country Seat. Northwood Court had never really been home to David Atwood, since his wife had died in the birthing of his only son and heir there, and for as long as Gabriel could remember, the old Viscount had spent most of his time in Town indulging in all manner of reckless pursuits, from gambling to horse racing.

For the most part, Gabriel was far closer in disposition to his father's younger brother. Benjamin Atwood had led an almost charmed career in the Royal Navy, rising to the rank of Admiral whilst still relatively young. Naturally, the adolescent impressionable viscount-in-waiting dreamed of following in his uncle's illustrious footsteps.

On reaching his majority, Gabriel eagerly sought his father's blessing, but perhaps unsurprisingly, the Viscount's only reaction was a callous indifference. Indeed, once he'd purchased his son's commission, David Atwood appeared to lack even the remotest curiosity in his offspring's career, and Gabriel saw his father on only one occasion before Lord Northwood's recklessness saw him thrown from his horse whilst racing across Hampstead Heath. He was fifty-three.

Gabriel's sudden elevation to the title had been as unwelcome as it was unexpected. Indeed, Gabriel had only recently been promoted to First Lieutenant when the news of his father's death reached him, and his burgeoning naval career skidded to an inevitable halt.

After being forced to resign his commission and return home, everyone expected the new Viscount to take up the same pursuits as his father, but Gabriel simply wasn't interested. At first the Estate took up most of his time, but he had not entirely lost his burning desire to serve King and Country, and when his uncle approached him with certain *clandestine* proposals, Gabriel threw himself into the role of undercover envoy with alacrity. He could come and go from his estate with no one really the wiser. Spain was the destination of most of his assignments, and while he hated the ever-present heat and dust that seemed to seep into his very pores, he could not deny that he felt more alive than at any time since he'd resigned his commission to take up his father's mantle at Northwood.

Gabriel's musings came to an abrupt end as he realised the carriage was slowing down, and five minutes later he was surrounded by a multitude of peacocks as they jostled to join the throng already perspiring in the Duke and Duchess of Albany's ballroom. Once inside, Gabriel helped himself to a glass of lukewarm Champagne and looked around for his uncle, finally catching sight of him at the other side of the room. Determinedly ignoring the sidelong glances cast his way from the current crop of debutantes shopping for a husband, Gabriel eventually managed to push and shove his way to Admiral Atwood.

Benjamin Atwood had always been more politically aware than his older brother. Indeed, it was occasionally and very quietly professed a shame that he had not been the one to inherit the Northwood title. That aside, it came as no surprise to anyone that Atwood achieved the rank of Admiral before his fiftieth birthday. In truth, his ambition had always been such that most people were more surprised he'd had the time or the inclination to father a son of his own. Predictably, his wife was an heiress whose family could trace their naval roots back to the Tudors. On the triumphant production of their only offspring whom she named Henry after her father, Caroline Atwood was content to remain in the background, preferring to spend the majority of her time at their manor house near to Portsmouth.

'Good evening, Sir.' Gabriel gave a slight bow and spoke with the deference due to a man of a higher rank than himself, even though in such a civilian setting, the Viscount was possessed of the loftier station.

But then, few people knew that Benjamin Atwood's nephew was still on His Majesty's payroll.

The Admiral seemed unusually out of sorts, appearing reluctant to even look at his nephew. Gabriel frowned. It wasn't like his uncle at all. Usually, the two had much to talk about and enjoyed the brief periods they spent together. Mayhap the very public situation they were in was concerning the older man.

When his uncle finally spoke, he was still staring straight ahead. 'I have no doubt you are wondering why the deuce I have brought you here this evening,' he remarked levelly.

'Indeed, Sir, it had crossed my mind that it's very difficult to have anything approaching a serious conversation in such a crush.'

Ben shook his head. 'Now there you are wrong,' he argued, seeming to relax slightly. 'In a situation such as this, we are much less likely to be overheard or even taken note of.' He waved his hand surreptitiously around, proving to Gabriel that any interest shown in the Viscount had entirely waned when it was obvious to the matchmaking mothers present that he had no intention of being accosted.

'I wish you to return to Spain,' the Admiral declared suddenly. His voice was low and intense while his gaze continued to peruse their surrounding guests. Gabriel glanced up in surprise as he'd returned only a month earlier. 'You will sail on the morning tide a week hence aboard the *Seahorse* which will take you to Cadiz…' The Admiral paused and at last looked down at Gabriel before he continued. 'You must be in the city before the new year. Your orders will be waiting for you in your cabin.' Unusually, Gabriel noticed a bead of sweat dotted across his uncle's brow. 'Is the Captain of the *Seahorse* aware of my mission?' the Viscount asked with a frown.

The Admiral looked away again, smiling and inclining his head towards an attractive widow as she passed, eying him coquettishly. He waited until she was out of earshot before answering. 'Her Captain is Henry.' The older man's level tone of voice gave no indication of the lightning bolt he'd just delivered.

The last time Gabriel had seen Henry Atwood, his cousin had been pointing a gun at him.

CHAPTER 3

*T*he snow continued to fall, already beginning to coat the ground in a thick white blanket and making it almost impossible to see anything beyond a few feet of the carriage.

The four human occupants sat motionless, listening for the telltale sound of hooves.

'I can't hear a deuced thing,' declared the Reverend after a few seconds. 'I think you've been reading too many of Agnes's periodicals Percy.'

Gabriel twisted in his seat and strived to see through the curtain of white outlined in the small window. As yet, there didn't appear to be any signs of any pursuit - equestrian or otherwise. 'Is this road well used?' he asked.

The Reverend frowned. 'It's not the main route to Salisbury, but it has its fair share of vehicles. Farmers mostly, I suppose.'

Gabriel continued to stare through the window. 'I should tell you that Percy's hearing is probably better than any of us.' He glanced back at Hope's low-voiced comment. It was obvious from her tone that she feared the worst. He made a decision. Pushing himself up from his seat next to the curate, he steadied himself by pressing his hand against the roof of the swaying coach.

'I'm going to join the coachman on the box,' he stated flatly. 'If there are any other travellers in the vicinity, I want to be ready for them.' Putting his hand inside the front of his breeches, he pulled out a pistol, causing Hope to gasp and shrink away.

'Thunder an' turf,' growled the Reverend, 'what the devil are you doing with that monstrosity? It's a wonder you haven't shot off your ballocks. Put the blasted thing away. If anyone's catching us up, they have as much right to the deuced road as we do.'

'If they wish us no harm, then none will come to them either,' Gabriel replied coldly. 'Believe me, I have no wish to shed blood on the Lord's birthday.'

And with that, he tucked the weapon back into his waistband and pushed open the door, grabbing hold of the railing decorating the edge of the carriage roof to lever himself up. White flakes swirled through the open door, bringing winter into the stuffy warmth of the coach. The only one who appeared to enjoy the sudden frigid influx of snow was Freddy, who lifted his muzzle to woof in excitement.

Cursing, the Reverend climbed to his feet with the intention of pulling the door shut, but Percy beat him to it. In an uncharacteristically daring manoeuvre, the curate held on to the door frame with one hand and leaned out to grab the handle. Unfortunately, his intrepid deed didn't quite go according to plan as Gabriel, now firmly established next to a bewildered coach driver, leaned over the side of the carriage at the same time to slam the door shut, causing Percy to go down like a sack of potatoes.

Hope yelped as the small man landed in her lap, following it with a most unladylike curse as she shoved him off. 'Deuced men,' she muttered, turning to the curate who was now squashed in a daze between her and her father.

'Percy,' yelled the Reverend in a panic, 'can you hear me?'

'I should think the whole of Somerset can hear you, Father,' commented Hope waspishly. 'I think it might be better if we give him some space.'

'Splendid idea,' responded the Reverend without moving. After waiting a few seconds, Hope sighed and got to her feet, intending to shuffle into the seat opposite. Just as she was about to subside next to a delighted Freddy, she finally spied through the small rear window what looked like moving shadows behind them. Her heart thundered in her chest. Not for one second did she believe the shapes to be harmless travellers. As the figures gradually materialised through the veil of snow, she could see there were approximately four people, and all were riding low over their mounts with the clear intention of catching up with the carriage.

Unhappily, Percy chose precisely that moment to cast up his account.

One year earlier

Despite his concerns over his cousin's previously murderous intentions, Gabriel presented himself at Portsmouth Harbour on the appointed day and time. The weather was cold, grey and blustery, causing him no little concern at the prospect of seasickness once they were out at sea. There was no sign of Henry as he was quickly hurried aboard the skiff ready and waiting to receive him, and as he huddled inside the small cockpit, he couldn't help but reflect on his uncle's less than detailed instructions.

Under normal circumstances, Gabriel would be briefed extensively before being sent off to risk his life, but on this occasion, he recognised the Admiral was being deliberately obtuse. Whether that had anything to do with his son, or the sensitivity of the mission, Gabriel had no idea. He'd been informed that his orders would be waiting for him. Was Henry aware of what they contained? He shook his head, frustrated at the lack of answers, and stared towards the looming thirty-eight-gun frigate rolling lazily at anchor outside the harbour. As he understood it, *HMS Seahorse* was his cousin's first command.

Their dual not long after Gabriel had inherited had been hushed up, especially the part where Henry had turned to shoot before the required number of paces had been taken. The only saving grace was that the debacle had taken place far away from the gossipmongers in town. The whole farce certainly hadn't been on Gabriel's instigation. Indeed, he'd done his very best to talk Henry out of it - as had the man's second. Notwithstanding the fact that duelling was against the law, the female Henry was fighting over was a local chit who certainly had no reputation worth salvaging. Indeed, she'd washed her hands of the whole affair. Gabriel had had no idea that Henry had set his sights on his cousin's light-skirt. If the idiot had simply enlightened him, the whole unsavoury business would never have taken place.

Fortunately, Henry Atwood was a terrible shot - a fact that may have contributed towards his enrolment in the Royal Navy rather than the Army. Despite his cheating, he missed Gabriel by a mile. Naturally, afterwards, he had argued that his failure to hit his intended target had been intentional, but as Henry had been swiftly bundled away by his father and the whole sordid escapade quickly buried, Gabriel had not had the opportunity to actually speak with the numbskull. Instead, since then, he'd done his damnedest to avoid his cousin entirely on the off chance that Henry decided to have another go.

And now, here he was at the mercy of the man he last saw looking at him down the barrel of a pistol.

Clearly, the Admiral had wanted to believe his son's version of events. Indeed, up until the Albany Ball, they had not spoken of the contretemps at all. Gabriel was aware that his uncle had coerced Henry into joining the Navy, ensuring his son remained at sea until the whole possibility of the scandal getting out had been entirely put to bed. While Henry appeared to stay out of trouble, Gabriel had heard nothing about his promotion to Captain. However, perhaps that was unsurprising given that the Viscount rarely ventured far from his estate unless it was to undertake another mission.

Gabriel's musings were cut short as they arrived at the Port side of *HMS Seahorse* and his attention focused on climbing the swinging ladder without either bashing his brains out on the hull or falling ignominiously into the crashing waves beneath him. He couldn't help but reflect as he finally found himself on the heaving deck, that his sea legs were not returning quite as quickly since he'd resigned his commission four years earlier.

Picking up his ditty bag, he staggered slightly as he turned to see his elusive cousin watching him in amusement. Gritting his teeth and doing his best to swallow his ire, Gabriel nodded his head affably. 'Good to see you, Henry,' he lied for the benefit of those watching.

Captain Atwood stepped forward and gave a small bow. 'Lord North-wood,' he acknowledged formally. 'Welcome aboard. My steward will show you to your cabin where I trust you will find everything in order.' Gabriel raised his eyebrows and stared back nonplussed for a few seconds, before briefly bending his head in acknowledgement. If his cousin wished to keep their association formal for the duration of the voyage, then he was happy to play along. Indeed, it would make things easier if there were no recriminations or rehashing of past indiscretions. And given that Gabriel was of the mind that the whole debacle had not entirely been Henry's fault, he was more than willing to keep his distance. Also, a knife in the back should Henry still be harbouring a grudge, would be much less likely if they did not have to go over old ground.

Ten minutes later, he was alone in his cabin staring at an envelope with his name written in flowering letters. This was his fourth covert mission at the behest of his uncle, but he'd never felt this level of fore-boding at the thought of what the envelope contained, and for the first time, he wondered if he had already pushed his luck too far.

Mayhap it was finally time to stop trying to save the world and settle down with a biddable wife to sire an heir for Northwood.

Sighing, he shook his head, and picking up a letter opener, slit open the envelope. Now was not the time to be getting cold feet.

∞∞∞

Hope groaned at the mess on the carriage floor. This was not the first time in the last couple of years that Percy had taken a nasty knock to the head. Any more and the poor man was likely to be addled for the rest of his life. But now was not the time to reflect on the curate's mental state. They had more immediate problems to deal with. The riders were definitely getting closer. She could not imagine that Gabriel had failed to notice them. Indeed, it appeared as if the carriage was travelling faster, so she had to assume the increase in speed was deliberate.

Her father was muttering to himself as he did his best to mop both himself and Percy down, showing surprising care as he endeavoured to make the small man as comfortable as possible. The unpleasant stink was making even Freddy bury his nose in his paws.

Casting a quick glance through the window, she let out an involuntary whimper, realising the riders were almost upon them. Desperately, she cast around for something to use as a weapon should their pursuers attempt to gain entry.

The Reverend looked up. 'Well, providing we don't all end up celebrating the Lord's birthday in person, courtesy of those deuced rogues on our tails, I think the chucklehead will recover.'

'How can you be so calm, Father?' Hope quizzed, her voice almost inaudible with fear. 'We have nothing at all to defend ourselves with.'

'I don't imagine it's us they're looking for,' responded the Reverend staring out of the window, 'but I don't believe the Almighty would wish us to throw our guest to the wolves without at least putting up some kind of a fight. What have you got in your reticule?'

'Well, I'm not carrying a weapon if that's what you were hoping,' snapped Hope, nevertheless picking up her fallen purse and tipping it upside down. The contents fell to the floor of the carriage. A comb, a kerchief and a small pot of rouge, courtesy of her sister Temperance. 'Mayhap we can colour them to death,' she mocked, then suddenly paused, staring first at the small round pot and then at Percy who was drooping in the corner.

Getting to her feet, she stumbled over to the curate. 'Hold him upright for me father,' she ordered to the bewildered Reverend. Then getting to her knees, she opened the pot and quickly dotted small red pinpricks all over Percy's face and neck.

'What the dickens are you doing?' her father demanded. 'He looks like he's got deuced smallpox.'

'Exactly,' panted Hope, glancing over at the Reverend as under-standing dawned. She climbed back to her feet. 'Quickly, lay him across my lap,' she hissed as the carriage began to slow. Clearly, Gabriel had realised they stood no chance of outrunning their pursuers. While almost scared to death, she was glad he hadn't yet elected to use his pistol. Perhaps they could yet talk themselves out of their hobble. She looked out of the window as her father manhandled a still largely insensible Percy onto the seat next to her. The carriage was now encircled on both sides as the coach drew to a stop.

'Wot the bloody 'ell d'yer think yer doin?' Gabriel called down from the box, his voice almost unrecognisable.

Hope grabbed hold of Freddy's lead as the hound began to growl threateningly. 'We need to help him,' she quaked in a low voice, grip-ping the lead whilst trying not to tip the unfortunate curate to the floor. Her father stared back at her wordlessly for a few seconds, then at her nod, he pushed open the door. 'What is the meaning of this?' he demanded in his most strident tones.

The horses surrounding them continued to dance around, steam from their nostrils pluming in the cold. The faces of all four men were ominously concealed with thick headscarves.

'Get out o' the carriage ol' man.' Reverend Shackleford couldn't tell which of the men had issued the order, but after stiffening slightly at the highhanded tone, he gave a last glance backwards and climbed out of the carriage.

'Father, who are these people?' came Hope's querulous voice from inside, equally unrecognisable in its desperation, which the Reverend was sure was only half-feigned. 'We need to get Percy inside. The rash is spreading.'

Frowning behind his scarf, the probable leader demanded to know how many occupants were in the coach.

'Just myself, my son and my daughter,' responded the Reverend in what he hoped was a suitably obsequious tone. 'The two men on the box are our coachmen.'

'You don't look like bloody aristocracy to me,' commented another of the men. 'How is it you're travelling in such luxury?'

'They coulda nicked the carriage from the last coaching inn.'

'A bit bloody old to be a knight of the road, I'd have thought.'

The Reverend could see Gabriel shifting on the box, undoubtedly ready to use his pistol should the situation deteriorate further.

'We are being conveyed to deliver my dying son to his wife and children,' improvised the Reverend hastily, hoping to head off any bloodshed. 'The carriage belongs to the Earl of Ravenstone. It is under his charity that we travel. I pray you let us continue lest my son perish before he has had chance to make his peace with his family.'

'You say this coach belongs to Ravenstone,' commented the leader. 'Show me the crest.' Hurriedly, Reverend Shackleford pushed the door closed and brushed the clinging snow away from Adam's family crest.

'That's the Earl's alright,' confirmed the third man, speaking for the first time. 'Blackmore's crest looks nothin' like it. Northwood's not 'ere.'

The name meant nothing to the Reverend, but he saw Gabriel stiffen slightly at its mention. Clearly, whoever Northwood was, he was known to their passenger.

'Father, please,' came Hope's wavering voice from inside.

'What's wrong with 'im?' asked the leader, dismounting and striding over to pull the door back open.

The Reverend's heart thudded sickeningly as the man went to stick his head inside, ignoring the foxhound whose growling was getting louder by the second.

'Shut the bloody dog up, or I'll put him out of his misery,' snapped the man, standing back.

Hope leaned forward and handed the lead to her father. They shared a worried glance as the Reverend pulled the reluctant hound out into the cold.

'If you let go of the cur, my man'll shoot 'im,' remarked the leader coldly as he climbed inside the carriage. Augustus Shackleford swallowed anxiously. Would the man realise they were shamming it? If he touched Percy's face, he would surely recognise their deception.

'I asked you what was wrong with 'im?' the man repeated impatiently.

As her father described later, Hope's response was a consummate piece of playacting. If the Reverend hadn't known better, he himself would have been convinced that Percy was truly about to pop his clogs.

'I... I...' she began, only to pause, gulping back a realistic sob. 'It's our belief he has...' Hope's voice was lowered to a whisper as she leaned forward, almost as if she couldn't bear to say the word, 'smallpox,' she stammered finally, pulling back the kerchief to reveal Percy's pox-marked face.

'Blast and bugger yer eyes,' shouted the man, rearing back at the sight of the myriad of red pin pricks covering the curate's deathly pale face.

'Wha...' began Percy, trying to sit up, only to be shoved ruthlessly back as Hope bent her now convincingly snot-streaked face and wailed almost directly up his nose. Percy began to struggle in earnest, possibly thinking he was about to be smothered, but luckily the leader was too busy clambering out of the carriage to notice.

'This ain't Blackmore's carriage,' he shouted to his men, hurriedly remounting his horse. 'Leave 'em be. I doubt any of 'em will still be alive to see in the new year anyway.' And with that he pulled on his horse's reins and began galloping back down the road, clearly eager to put as much distance as he could between him and the plague-ridden coach. Startled, the other three looked over towards the now howling occupant for a moment before crossing themselves and hightailing back the way they came.

CHAPTER 4

One year earlier

The voyage through the Bay of Biscay went without any major incidents, and within ten days they were approaching Cadiz. It had been a long, tedious voyage as far as the Viscount was concerned, given that he'd deemed the wisest course of action was to spend as much time as he could in his cabin.

But now, standing in the bow, Gabriel stared over the water towards the shimmering fortress city. This was the first time he'd visited the former Moorish stronghold, but even from here, its Arabic roots were apparent, and he recognised that any force wishing to take the city would not find it easy. Cadiz was located on the northwest tip of Isla de Leon, which in turn was separated from mainland Spain by a narrow saltwater channel. The city itself was protected by a four-mile-long sandy peninsula on which he could clearly see the continuous line of the Cortadura fortifications.

As the ship rounded the fortress of Santa Catalina on its way to the inner harbour, he pondered the unlikely alliance Britain had formed with Spain.

Three years earlier, Napoleon had sent a full twenty-eight thousand men over the Pyrenees, marching through Spain and into Portugal. His decision to then turn on the country that had stood with him in the Battle of Trafalgar had been a surprise, not least to the Spanish. But he could not have anticipated the backlash his decision to place his brother on the throne would have. That, together with the bloody reprisals after the taking of Madrid, had prompted the Spanish to rebel. Naturally, the British saw the Spanish revolt as a way of putting a rub in the way of Napoleon's plans, and the unofficial alliance between Spain and Britain began.

Gabriel chuckled grimly at Napoleon's description of his campaign waged in the Iberian Peninsula. The Spanish Ulcer he'd called it according to the broadsheets. But it looked as though the self-styled emperor's determination to finally crush the Spanish into submission might well be about to come to fruition.

Gabriel had been in the north of Spain during the devastating defeat suffered by the Spanish in Ocaña mere weeks ago and had only narrowly escaped with his life. Undoubtedly, after their victory, the French believed Andalusia ripe for the picking.

He watched as the ship sailed slowly nearer to the harbour. There were only a small number of Spanish ships at anchor, and the city itself, by all accounts, was virtually ungarrisoned as the Spanish forces were massing along the northern border of Andalusia as they attempted to stop the French from marching south.

Gabriel was painfully aware that if the French army continued its unrelenting advance, he was already on borrowed time if he wished to avoid becoming trapped again.

The shouts of the crew as the first pair of anchors were dropped put an end to his uneasy musings, and he headed down into his cabin to gather his belongings. The envelope with his orders remained in his bag where he'd left it.

Seating himself on the small bunk, Gabriel stared down at the brief message. He was to report to a Captain Ortiga at the Castillo de Puntales where he would receive further instructions. He had no idea why his uncle was being so ambiguous, but the only reason that made sense was that the Admiral was trying to protect something. But what that something was, and why, Gabriel had no clue, which was frustrating in the extreme - not least because of the implied lack of trust. But if that was the case, why the devil send him in the first place? Mayhap he'd have been better to give the deuced mission to Henry.

But then he was more likely to risk his nephew's skin than that of his only son, despite their mutual regard. And mayhap Henry was only here to keep a watchful eye on him. Gabriel frowned as a sudden thought occurred to him. Had this mission been officially authorised or was it unsanctioned?

And if it was the latter, was there anyone, aside from his uncle, his cousin and a small number of the *Seahorse's* crew, who actually knew he was here?

∞∞∞∞

As soon as the riders were out of sight, Gabriel quickly climbed down from the box. 'We need to keep moving,' he stated. 'At this rate, we'll never reach Ravenstone before dark.'

'Who were those varmints?' asked the Reverend bluntly, ignoring the younger man's urgent words. 'And don't give me any deuced Banbury story about putting us in danger, that ship sailed about ten minutes ago.'

Before Gabriel could respond, Hope climbed out of the carriage, her face white as the surrounding snow. 'I've wrapped Percy in a blanket, but he seems much more himself,' she offered shivering.

'Well, that's a deuced relief. He already had more hair than wit even before the extra knock on his head,' groused the Reverend, turning his attention back to Gabriel who was staring at them, clearly nonplussed by the conversation.

'Mr Atwood,' snapped Hope finally, stamping her foot in vexation. 'No more shilly-shallying. You need to tell us what in blazes is going on.'

Gabriel sighed, impatience showing in every line of his body. 'At least let us continue the journey. I don't know what caused those men to turn tail, but they may yet get some pluck to their backbone and choose to finish what they started.'

'Which I assume is putting you to bed with a deuced mattock,' returned the Reverend darkly.

'I don't know wot the bloody 'ell is goin on, or who those gallows birds were, but why the bloody hell are you lot still standing around in the snow?' came an exasperated shout from the box. 'It's cold enough to freeze the balls off a brass monkey out 'ere, and Nelson mightn't need 'em anymore, God rest 'im, but I for one would like to keep my stones for me once yearly.' There was a pause as they all stared up at the coachman open mouthed. 'And at this rate, I might not even survive the bloody night, let alone have a quick strum, so if'n you don't mind, could you please get yer arses back in the bloody carriage, so we can be gone afore they come back?'

'I couldn't have put it better myself,' snapped Gabriel after a last incredulous look up at the coachman.

'Hmph,' muttered the Reverend, ushering Hope back into the warmth. 'He's got to be one of Blackmore's.'

Five minutes later, they were off again. Gabriel eyed Percy with concern. 'What the devil's wrong with him?' he asked pointing to the red dots decorating the curate's face.

'That's what sent the varmints packing,' chuckled the Reverend. 'You should have seen that fellow's face when he thought it was smallpox.'

'I am actually here, you know,' protested Percy weakly, 'and a little bit of warning might have been beneficial.'

'We had no time, I'm afraid,' responded Hope, leaning forward to pat the curate's knee in sympathy. 'When you sustained the bump on your hea...'

'When did he take a bump on his head?' interrupted Gabriel.

'When you slammed the carriage door on it,' declared the Reverend.

'I ... what...?' Gabriel shook his head, clearly thinking them all addled. 'So how ... or when did he develop deuced smallpox?'

The Reverend sighed. 'He didn't, and he hasn't.'

'It's rouge,' added Hope, pulling out a small pot from her reticule.

Gabriel frowned for a second before their explanation sank in, then he shook his head and gave a shout of disbelieving laughter. 'God's teeth, I could have done with you in Spain,' he chuckled. 'Are you always this quick thinking?'

'If you're referring to me,' stated Hope, 'I like to think I generally have my wits about me. And speaking of intellect, now that we have established that none in this carriage are entirely bacon brained, mayhap you'd be kind enough to finally enlighten us as to the circumstances that led up to your presence in this conveyance. I suggest as you've already let it slip, that you start with Spain.'

In the event, their carriage finally turned into the long sweeping approach to Ravenstone just as full dark descended. The occupants of the house had clearly been waiting for their arrival, because no sooner had the horses pulled up, blowing and snuffling in the cold air, than the imposing front door was thrown open, and a whirlwind of bodies rushed down the steps shouting.

'Merry Christmas...'

'It's snowing...'

'Freddy…'

'We thought you'd never get here…'

'We supposed you'd been murdered…'

'Or kidnapped…'

'Mother forgot her salts…'

'Or lying in a ditch, mortally wounded…'

'And she swooned headfirst into the syllabub…'

'Nicholas and Adam were coming to look for you…'

'So, Felicity made her lie down…'

'Who's he…?'

'Has Percy got the plague…?'

'ENOUGH' thundered the Reverend, finally managing to extricate himself from the throng of bodies competing for his attention. 'Where's Grace?'

'I'm here father.' His eldest daughter's voice came serenely from the top of the steps. Unlike their younger siblings, both the Duchess of Blackmore and the Countess of Ravenstone had paused to don fur capes before venturing out into the cold night air. Grace's hand was tucked into that of her husband and as etiquette dictated, their graces lingered in the doorway as the Earl and Countess of Ravenstone preceded them down the steps to welcome the remainder of the party into their home.

'We were terribly worried about you.' Temperance gave her father a quick hug, before enveloping Hope in a fervent embrace.

'Undoubtedly, some more than others,' muttered the Reverend with a sniff.

'I can assure you my wife has destroyed a suitable number of kerchiefs in her concern for your welfare, Reverend,' Adam commented tactfully before waving his hand towards a footman who had accompanied them down the stairs with trays of hot mulled wine. 'Help yourself to refreshment. Believe me, Augustus, it's very good to see all three of you. Nick and I were about to come galloping to your rescue.' He paused slightly, eying the tall form of Gabriel as he stepped into the ring of light created by the lanterns at the foot of the steps.

'Forgive me, but I don't think we are acquainted, sir,' the Earl commented mildly.

Gabriel bent low at the waist. 'Viscount Northwood, at your service, my lord,' he murmured formally.

Adam frowned and was just about to speak when Nicholas came up behind him.

'Gabriel, what the devil are you doing here? They said you were dead.'

One year earlier

It was early afternoon before Gabriel was allowed to disembark. Pettily, he decided to leave without informing Captain Atwood of his intentions. His orders had told him to report immediately to the Castillo de Puntales. However, he decided to leave that particular pleasure until the following morning to give him time to get a feel for his surroundings.

His cousin had made no bones about the fact that Gabriel had been expected to remain on board the *Seahorse* prior to his meeting with Captain Ortiga, but since the last he heard, Henry Atwood was not his keeper, Gabriel elected to go ashore to look for lodgings. Primarily, he had to admit, because it put a rub in the way of his cousin's wishes, but also because his instincts continued to clamour that there was something smoky about this particular mission. His uncle had never before insisted his whereabouts be known at all times. Indeed, the Admiral had always appeared to trust his nephew implicitly, and that trust had been entirely mutual. Gabriel had never failed to accomplish his purpose, however dangerous. But this time, he'd been given a watchdog. That was the only way to describe Henry's involvement.

To put it bluntly, the whole business stank. Gabriel thought it safe to assume Henry would put a tail on him, and under normal circumstances, it would have made no real difference if his cousin knew where he was lodging, but on this occasion, Gabriel was determined to elude whoever Henry sent as a watchdog.

Distancing himself from the seamier area surrounding the docks, Gabriel made his way into the maze of narrow streets that made up the old city. His Spanish was passable, and after spending an hour or so getting his bearings and ensuring he was no longer being followed, he was quickly able to get directions to a reasonably respectable pensione situated within walking distance of the Castillo. The city's inhabitants he spoke to did not seem to have any particular grievance against the British, given that the two nations had been on opposite sides of the war only months ago, although mayhap that would change once there were more of his countrymen garrisoned in Cadiz. In all honesty, he'd been surprised to note that the *Seahorse* was currently the only British ship at anchor in such a strategically important city.

The pensione was at the end of a narrow alley and entered by a plain door with no sign outside. Indeed, without help, he would never have found it. Nodding politely at the elderly toothless woman who showed him to the small sparce room, he couldn't entirely shake the fear that someone might endeavour to murder him in the middle of the night. Still, he was here now, and once the door closed behind his stout landlady, he jammed a chair up underneath its handle. Satisfied that no one would enter without him knowing, Gabriel looked out of the small window. Set deep into a thick stone wall, it opened wide enough for him to climb through but was much too high up for him to reach the ground without a decent rope. However, looking over towards the next roof, he thought that mayhap he would be able to jump the gap without too much difficulty. Where it would lead him, there was no way of knowing, but at least he'd established a means of escape should he need it.

Content that he'd done everything he could to secure his safety, he decided an early night was in order. He stripped off his outer clothing and lay back on the top of the threadbare blanket. The weather was unusually warm for the time of year - even in southern Spain, a few weeks of colder weather could normally be relied upon during the winter months, but instead, it was decidedly agreeable. After taking the precaution of placing his pistol underneath his pillow and tucking his belongings under his arm, Gabriel closed his eyes and quickly fell asleep.

He rose early the next day, a habit he'd adopted since joining his uncle's covert payroll. The fact that he was almost certainly sharing the mattress with a few extra bedfellows undoubtedly contributed.

After splashing his face and hands in a small bowl of water, and using the bucket provided, he pulled on a relatively clean shirt. Although he'd got used to packing light, he still missed the exquisitely starched, not to mention beautifully clean, shirts handed to him at home every morning by his valet. Quickly tying his cravat without the benefit of a mirror, he reflected that Heavers would have a fit of the vapours if he could see him now. Chuckling at the thought, he rescued his pistol and tucked it in his breeches. As he picked up his bag and removed the chair from the door handle, he suddenly wondered whether there were any public baths in the old town. With its Moorish influence, he certainly hoped so. It had to be said, he was beginning to smell rather ripe. Mayhap he would get the opportunity to bathe after he'd met with Captain Ortiga. Providing he was still breathing of course.

CHAPTER 5

*A*lthough the latecomers were given the opportunity to freshen up, there was no occasion for private conversation with the remainder of Christmas evening devoted to the younger Shacklefords. While Gabriel was grateful the Earl had not summarily had him thrown out, he couldn't help chafing at the delay in speaking with Nicholas. Indeed, he was under no illusion that only the Duke of Blackmore vouching for him had ensured him a decent bed and the opportunity to partake of an excellent goose at the Earl's table.

The ladies had not left the gentlemen to their port as he'd hoped and all in all, by the time the younger siblings finally went off to bed, Gabriel felt entirely wrung out. He'd been travelling anonymously for months, slowly making his way through Spain until finally a stroke of luck saw him succeed in securing passage on a British merchant vessel on its way to Plymouth.

In truth, he was weary unto death, even more so as he was well aware that it was now his problems would really start. They had been watching for him. Had Henry somehow discovered he was still alive? He remembered the vagrant's comments about the Blackmore crest.

Clearly, his uncle and cousin had suspected that if he lived, he would seek out his old captain and mentor. His mind whirled, and the thought that they may yet come after him choked his gut. And mayhap not only him…

Strangely, the only balm to his fractured soul during the evening was Hope Shackleford. Although they were seated at opposite ends of the table, he found his eyes continuously searching for her. The difference between this Hope Shackleford and the one he'd spent the last eighteen hours with was marked. Here in the company of her siblings, she was relaxed, smiling often. Her hair, tied back in a simple ribbon was the red of autumn berries, and it gleamed like burnished copper in the candlelight. He found himself almost spellbound, which was entirely ridiculous given that he was three years over thirty and not unaccustomed to attractive women desiring his attention. But the thought of this particular female throwing herself at him left him unexpectedly hard and aching. He sucked in his breath in surprise. God's teeth, where the bloody hell had that come from?

It had been over a year since he'd last been with a woman, and in truth, he'd not even thought about it until this moment - it had to be said that living with constant fear and dread was very effective at quelling lustful urges. He took a sip of his wine, endeavouring to get his previously quiescent cock under control before someone noticed and possibly tossed him out on his ear.

Taking a deep breath, he turned his attention to the other Shacklefords seated at the table. A quick count informed him that the Reverend appeared to have eight children, of which seven were female. He winced at the thought - his carnal urges thankfully beginning to take flight at such a prospect, but as he eyed Mrs Shackleford, he was surprised to see her tuck into her supper with an enthusiastic appetite. Clearly, she could not have borne all eight children. His sympathy increased towards the Reverend who'd had to put up with seven offspring of the supposed fairer sex and possibly more than one wife. Indeed, he intimated as much to a Miss Felicity Beaumont who was seated next to him and who was evidently a good friend of the family. The lady had grinned at him before saying it was no more than the Reverend deserved, and that there were actually eight girls in all. Hope's twin sister Faith was apparently arriving on the morrow with her husband. Oh, and there had been three wives...

By the time the younger children were finally dispatched to bed, Gabriel was more than half-sprung and in no way prepared for what might be the most crucial conversation of his life. Despite the earlier demands in the carriage, he had refused to enlighten his travelling companions further. In truth, he had been hoping the explanation for his presence would be for the Duke's ears only, but he was disabused of that notion as soon as he entered the Earl's sitting room and stopped dead. Fiend seize it, the information he possessed was not only sensitive, it was potentially life threatening to any who became embroiled. And here he was involving a room full of strangers. Unfortunately, it looked as though the whole deuced family was determined to know what he was doing here.

He blinked as Nicholas came forward and offered him a brandy. 'Augustus has explained the circumstances surrounding your unexpected arrival at his door, Gabriel,' he declared, 'as well as the alarming incident during your journey here.' He sighed and placed a sympathetic hand on the Viscount's shoulder before adding dryly, 'I understand it was your desire to speak with me alone, but if I attempt to exclude my wife's relatives from your account, I suspect at the very least, I would be spending the next year sleeping on the couch. You may rest assured that whatever you have to say will not go beyond this room unless you wish it.'

He moved back to his chair by the fire and invited Gabriel to sit on the only other spare seat. Gritting his teeth in frustration, Gabriel finally acquiesced, glancing around at his audience as he took a sip of the fiery liquid.

'You undoubtedly have me at a disadvantage, your grace,' he eventually commented brusquely. 'I have risked much to speak with you privately, yet it seems I have no choice but to share my words with your entire family. If I tell you my intelligence might well put them in danger, will you reconsider their presence here?'

'Seems to me laddie that the lives of three members of this family have already been put at risk.' Gabriel frowned at the speaker, a small wiry man standing by the window. After a few seconds, he jumped up. 'Malcolm,' he exclaimed, the delight in his voice unfeigned.

The Duke's valet grinned, and moving forward, pulled the younger man into a rough embrace. 'We thought ye dead, laddie,' he said gruffly once he'd let Gabriel go, 'but I'm sure I speak for both of us when I say we're more than happy te find the reports were rudely exaggerated.'

'This is all very well, but mayhap you could enlighten the rest of us as to how you are acquainted,' interrupted Grace, glancing between the three men.

'Gabriel Atwood was the best First Lieutenant I ever had,' Nicholas clarified. 'He had a very promising future in the Royal Navy but unfortunately was forced to resign his commission to take up the mantle of Viscount on the untimely death of his father.' He shook his head and frowned. 'I thought you were enjoying the life of a country gentleman at Northwood Court,' he continued, 'until six months ago when I suddenly received news of your unexpected demise. It was mooted as some kind of accident, though the details were sketchy at best.'

'As you can see, the reports were a little premature,' snapped Gabriel sitting down again. 'I assume you received such tidings from my uncle, Admiral Atwood?'

The Duke nodded. 'I believe he has been installed as the new incumbent of your title.'

Gabriel grimaced before swallowing the rest of his brandy and briefly closing his eyes, clearly furious at the turn of events that had seen his uncle installed as the new Viscount Northwood. The room was entirely silent as he struggled to master his anger, and strangely, the first eyes he sought as he battled to get himself under control were Hope's. She was regarding him steadily, the sympathy in her eyes tempered by curiosity. For some reason, her level gaze helped him centre himself, and letting out a breath he didn't realise he'd been holding, he spoke again.

'Whatever sadness my uncle exhibited in the reporting of my *fatal accident*,' he ground out, 'was entirely contrived. Predominantly because he was the one responsible for trying to kill me.'

One year earlier

Gabriel did not bother taking a roundabout route to the Castillo de Puntales. Henry would undoubtedly have been expecting him to meet with Captain Ortiga as soon as he rose, so if anyone did spy him, they would simply report back that he was following orders. The narrow alleyways were already busy with traders, and the Viscount broke his fast with a sweet pastry filled with almonds and some kind of sugary liquid. Ten minutes later, after rinsing his hands in a convenient fountain, he turned a corner and suddenly found himself in the plaza fronting the imposing Castillo.

He paused before approaching the guard lounging at the entrance, obviously enjoying the early morning sun. Hopefully, whoever Ortiga was, he was expecting a visit from an Englishman. However, Gabriel didn't know whether the Captain had been informed of his visitor's identity and determined to keep the knowledge to himself if possible.

As Gabriel approached the entrance, the guard straightened up and eyed him suspiciously. Plainly, he did not believe the stranger to be Spanish, and he had almost certainly *not* been briefed to expect a visit from an Inglés. Holding his hands open in a universally nonthreatening gesture, Gabriel smiled encouragingly and informed the guard that the Capitán was expecting him.

The soldier, at least, had no interest in his identity but simply confirmed, 'Inglés?' Gabriel nodded, and the guard directed a quick volley of rapid Spanish towards an unseen person before indicating the Viscount should wait.

Gabriel seated himself on a convenient mounting block. In truth, he was surprised at the lack of military activity surrounding the Castillo and in Cadiz in general, especially given that the French were currently on the verge of marching into Andalucía. It had been a very different story in Ocaña in the north of Spain.

Mayhap the Junta in Seville did not believe Napoleon's army would get this far south. If that was the case, he hoped they were right, but did not share such optimism.

He waited ten minutes before another guard arrived and ordered him to, 'Sígueme.' Understanding the Spanish for *follow me*, Gabriel rose and nodded to the first guard as he passed, only receiving a suspicious glower in return.

Captain Ortiga turned out to be a small olive-skinned man like so many of his compatriots. The only impressive thing about him in the Viscount's opinion was a large bushy moustache which he twirled rapidly as he regarded the Inglés through narrowed eyes. The Captain pointed at the seat facing his enormous mahogany desk. *Compensating? Quite possibly*, Gabriel thought with an inward chuckle as he nodded and seated himself.

The silence descended once more as the man continued to stare at him. Gabriel wondered at the suspicion in his eyes. Had the Captain been expecting someone else perchance? At length, just when the quiet started to become oppressive, Captain Ortiga spoke, giving weight to Gabriel's uneasiness that he had not been expecting a visit from an Englishman.

'Why are you here?' the Captain demanded without warning. They stared at each other, Gabriel searching vainly for the correct answer - if indeed there was one. Admiral Atwood had given him no clue and neither had his good-for-nothing cousin. Not for the first time, the Viscount felt his life could be in danger if he did not answer the question correctly. Was this whole deuced trip some kind of red herring designed to …. what? He narrowed his eyes, his outward calm giving no clue to his inner turmoil.

'It was my belief you were expecting me,' he said at length, making a concerted effort to keep his tone pleasant. 'I was told to report to a Captain Ortiga on my arrival in Cadiz. I believe you, sir, to be that man.' He held out his hands in an attitude of surrender. 'I was given no more information than that. Indeed, given the lack of intelligence, I assumed I was here to collect something.' He noted that the Captain had not asked his name and Gabriel was careful to leave out the names of his uncle and cousin, at least initially. He did not know whether such name-dropping would help or hinder him.

'I not Capitán Ortiga.' The small man's shrugged response sent chills up Gabriel's spine. 'There is no Ortiga. You are mistaken.'

They stared at each other for a few seconds, then the Spanish Captain grunted and tapped his head. 'English estúpido?' he commented before pointing to himself. 'Capitán Pérez. Non Ortiga.'

Gabriel stared back at the arrogant man in front of him, his mind spinning. There was no Ortiga. Was the error an accident? Every instinct he had was clamouring for him to leave. Now.

'But you are expecting a visit from an Englishman.' His voice when he finally managed to speak was gratifyingly impassive.

The Captain shook his head, then tipping it to one side, regarded Gabriel narrowly. 'Why you here, Inglés?' he questioned abruptly.

The Viscount felt the sweat gather in the small of his back. He had to get out. He still had no clue as to why he'd been sent here, but whatever patience the Captain had was very obviously wearing thin. And not every Spaniard was happy with the current British interference.

Gabriel stood abruptly and gave a small bow, resisting the urge to wipe the beads of sweat now trickling into his eyes. 'It appears I have made an error,' he offered politely, hoping the hoarseness in his voice was attributed to the heat and dust. 'Forgive me for wasting your time, señor.' Every sense Gabriel had was screaming at him to run.

After a pause that seemed to last forever, the Captain rose from his chair and inclined his head in turn. Trying not to show his relief, Gabriel took the action as a dismissal. With another polite nod, he turned and strode from the room, shutting the door behind him. Then quickly lengthening his strides, the Viscount urgently sought the quickest way out of the Castillo, the back of his neck prickling with an overwhelming awareness of his vulnerability.

He almost expected to be arrested, or worse, feel a bullet in his back, but he found his way out unmolested. Without pausing, he strode along the edge of the plaza and swiftly made his way back into the narrow alleyways of the old city, walking randomly until he was sure there was no chance he was being followed. Finally, he stopped, and leaning gratefully against the cool stone, closed his eyes and exhaled with relief.

However, his mind would not allow him much of a respite, and after a few minutes, he began replaying the events of the last two weeks in his head. What the devil was going on? The orders provided by his uncle were sketchy at best, totally unlike the usual instructions given to him at the start of a mission. The vague directives gave him absolutely no insight into why he'd been sent to southern Spain.

What to do now? He sensed he was running out of time. Should he simply return to the *Seahorse*? Clearly, that was what he was expected to do.

Or was he?

Gabriel felt his heart begin to beat erratically as his sense of danger overwhelmed him. He'd been sent to see a captain who didn't exist which meant he'd been played for a fool. But who would go to such lengths if their only purpose was to make him look beef-witted?

Unless it wasn't. Unless whoever it was simply wanted him out of the way. Permanently.

And there were only two people who would benefit from his demise.

Admiral Benjamin Atwood and his son Henry.

CHAPTER 6

*G*abriel felt sick. He had no illusions about his cousin. Henry hated him, always had. But had he misjudged his uncle? There were many who believed Benjamin Atwood should have inherited the Northwood title. Was the Admiral among them? He'd never given Gabriel any reason to think so.

But no, it was ridiculous to suppose his uncle had gone to such lengths just to be rid of him. There were far easier ways to dispose of an unwanted relative.

But then the demise of Viscount Northwood whilst in the service of King and Country would undoubtedly silence any gossip.

That's if, in truth, he was in the service of King and Country.

Gabriel's mind went round and round until he felt like planting a facer on someone. He had no answers, but until he did, he realised he dare not step foot back aboard the *Seahorse*.

Gabriel ran his hands through his hair in frustration. He couldn't believe he was even contemplating the possibility that his cousin was a cold-blooded killer. And if Henry's plan was to see him dead, was there a chance that the Admiral was unaware?

The Viscount had always believed that his uncle held him in affection. Indeed, they were extremely close during Gabriel's formative years, when he'd viewed his uncle with nothing but admiration. However, it was difficult to argue the fact that the Admiral had clearly sent him on a fool's errand. Sighing, Gabriel picked up his bag and slung it over his shoulder. Somehow, he had to leave the city without Henry knowing.

By now, the treacherous little weasel would expect him to realise he'd been duped. How long before he came looking? Or would he simply wait for Gabriel to return to challenge him onboard his ship? The Viscount had no way of knowing, and it was clearly a waste of time to try and second guess. Somehow, he had to find passage off the Isla de Leon without being spotted by any of the *Seahorse's* crew. Not an easy task he knew. He could only hope that Henry was not actually expecting him to run, and indeed, there was nowhere to run to. For a second, Gabriel paused.

Was he being foolish? Seeing shadows and conspiracies where there were none? If he ran now, his only option would be to try and make it to British secured Portugal and purchase passage home from there. But with the French marching inexorably south, it would not be an easy journey. And what the bloody hell would he say when he returned home? Was he taking a coward's way out? He had no proof that his closest relatives wanted his blood, just his gut, and on the surface of it, a simple mistaken identity. And while his gut had never let him down before, he could not just accuse either his uncle or his cousin of bringing him so far simply to have him murdered. He would be a laughingstock at the very least. At worst, he might end up being committed. He had no illusions about the Admiral's connections.

Gabriel shook his head with a sigh and stood irresolute for valuable moments. Moments that could well cost him his life if his suspicions were true.

'I've been looking for you, cousin.' The familiar voice sounded behind him.

Slowly, Gabriel turned to regard his grinning relative and knew he'd run out of time.

'I was just breaking my fast before returning to the ship,' he responded evenly.

'I see no breakfast in your hand,' answered Henry, the smirk still on his face. Gabriel gritted his teeth and pulled out the cloth in which his pastry had been wrapped. 'You're welcome to the crumbs if you're that hungry,' he mocked, holding out the package.

Henry's eyes narrowed, sensing the insult behind Gabriel's words, but in the end, all he said was, 'If you must eat in the street like a vagrant, you will forgive me for not joining you.' Gabriel shrugged and tucked the cloth back into his breeches, enjoying his cousin's ill-concealed annoyance.

However, Henry's next words put an end to his pettiness. 'Given that it's obvious you've finished, I suggest we return to the *Seahorse* together.' Gabriel felt his heart plummet.

'I am not actually ready to return onboard,' he countered casually. 'I was thinking to find a public bath to wash off the brine and dust.'

I will arrange for a bath to be filled in your cabin,' was the disdainful response. 'I wouldn't want your lordship to … horror of horrors … smell.'

Gabriel did not rise to the bait. 'I think not,' he responded mildly. 'I will return to the ship later on this afternoon after I've had the opportunity to see a little more of the city. I trust you will not set sail until the morrow?' The two men stared at each other for a few seconds. It was not lost on Gabriel that his cousin had not asked about the meeting with Ortiga. There had clearly been no mistake. The Viscount's suspicion that his life was forfeit rose to a certainty. He felt the sweat begin to trickle down his back.

'I would prefer that you return with me now.' The answer was soft but was clearly not a request, and Gabriel knew the charade was over. If he returned to the ship with his cousin, he would never make it back to England alive. Henry made no effort to conceal the malicious triumph in his eyes. If he was going to make a run for it, it would have to be now. With luck, he could lose himself in the narrow streets. He hitched his bag higher onto his shoulder in preparation just as two more sailors appeared, one at each end of the alleyway, effectively cutting off any escape.

Gabriel swore softly. 'Come along, Gabe,' his cousin called jovially. 'There'll be plenty of water for you when you're back on board. In fact, I'd be surprised if your sleep tonight isn't the longest you've ever had.' There it was. The acknowledgement that he would not live to see another day. Henry just couldn't help himself. Gabriel shook his head wearily then eyed the two approaching sailors.

'Tell me, how did it go with Captain Ortiga?' Henry was laughing openly now. Gabriel gritted his teeth. 'There is no Captain Ortiga, as you well know.'

'I was actually surprised you made it as far as the Castillo,' his cousin went on conversationally as the two sailors took hold of Gabriel's arms. 'After all, a strange city in the midst of a war, well, anything could have happened to you.' He shuddered theatrically before grinning again.

Gabriel simply glared back. There was no escape for him now. But it was a long way to the *Seahorse*. The opportunity would present itself.

His chance came sooner than expected. As Gabriel, surrounded by his three *escorts* entered another plaza, they were jostled by a group of giggling women inadvertently bumping into their tightknit group. 'Pardon, señors,' apologised one as she struggled to extract herself and her numerous purchases.

The Viscount wasted no time. Sticking out his foot, he elbowed Henry causing the *Seahorse's* captain to stumble forward, directly into the lady's many bags which she promptly dropped with a cry. The provisions spilled out onto the ground, and Gabriel took advantage of the mayhem to slip in between the two confused sailors. Once free, he didn't look back but simply ran into the nearest alleyway like the devil himself was chasing him. Now all he needed to do was hire a boat.

Unhappily, nearly five hours later, he was still no closer to getting out of the city. His initial euphoria had faded away replaced by a gnawing anxiety. The only way off the damned island was guarded by Henry's men, and it was beginning to look as though his only option was to swim. He shook his head ruefully. His cousin might yet get his wish. There was no doubt he'd underestimated the *Seahorse's* Captain. The scapegrace he'd grown up with had been replaced by a ruthless opportunist.

Gabriel was hidden in the bell tower of the Church of Santiago, almost overshadowed now by the nearly completed magnificent Cathedral in the same plaza. He'd entered at the start of the noon service, and it had been easy enough to slip away during the mass. His intention was to wait until dark, then sneak out the same way he'd come in. Hopefully, he would less likely be spotted by one of Henry's jack tars once the sun had gone down. He was painfully aware that it was a terrible plan, but it was the only one he had. Especially as he needed to be well away before they began ringing the bells, otherwise the noise could well burst his eardrums. He leaned back against the wall. The lack of sunlight, together with the stiff breeze through the uncovered openings, made the small circular room much colder than at ground level. He hugged his arms around his legs in an effort to generate some warmth. His stomach was also growling in protest. His last meal had been several hours ago. Mayhap he was getting too old for such havey-cavey business. Despite his discomfort, he slipped into a light doze, only to be woken by a sudden vicious pain to his chest.

'Do you think me so stupid, Northwood?' ground a voice directly in his ear. Gabriel instinctively kicked out and rolled away. Disoriented, he didn't know what his foot connected with, but he heard a satisfying grunt. Blinking, he stared up into the glittering eyes of his cousin, who this time stood over him with a pistol pointed directly at his head.

Again, he'd underestimated Henry Atwood, and the malice in his cousin's eyes told him this time it would cost him his life.

'Why are you doing this, Henry,' he rasped, struggling to breathe after the blow to his chest.

'The high and mighty Viscount Northwood at a loss. Now there's something I'd kill to see... Oh wait, I will very shortly.' Henry sniggered and leaned back against the circular wall. 'Wait for me downstairs,' he said without taking his eyes from Gabriel's.

'Gladly,' the Viscount responded.

'Funny,' was the snapped response. 'I was talking to him.' He nodded his head towards the man groaning near the stairwell, and Gabriel had the satisfaction of knowing his foot had connected with a couple of ribs.

The sailor didn't speak, but after throwing a last scowl at the man on the floor, he stumbled down the stairs.

'Tell me,' Gabriel wheezed as soon as they were alone, 'what the bloody hell is this all about?'

Henry put his head on one side and regarded Gabriel almost curiously. 'You know you're a particularly hard man to kill, cousin. You were never supposed to make it here, but you never spent long enough on deck for me to throw you overboard, so I was forced to sail all the way to bloody *Cadiz* to finish you off. Couldn't do it in Portugal - too many of Wellesley's men might have smelled a bloody rat.

'Still, improvisation and all that, and there was always the thought of sweet ripe little Marta in the city who, believe me, cousin, is truly worth sailing halfway round the world for.' He chuckled at his own joke as Gabriel continued watching him silently.

'Once we anchored, I'd intended to wait until the crew had gone ashore to finish you off, but you decided to go bloody sightseeing.' He shook his head in disbelief. 'By the time my man caught up with you again, you'd actually made it as far as the bloody Castillo. Clearly, you're not a complete imbecile.' He gave a small grin before adding, 'I was hoping they'd do me a favour and lock you up. Certainly would have speeded things up a bit. But being the slippery bastard you are, you escaped again.' His grin widened. 'Don't worry cousin, when my father takes over as Viscount Northwood, he'll ensure everyone knows you died a noble death. So sad, but there we go - they'll say you were reckless, just like your foolish father.'

Devil take it, this whole escapade was all about his bloody title. 'Hellishly long way to bring me simply to put a bullet in my head,' drawled Gabriel forcing down his anxiety.

'What better way for you to die than in the service of King and Country, far, *far* away from any prying eyes,' Henry sneered, 'except, of course, at this particular moment in time, you're not in the service of anything. In fact, nobody knows where the hell you are - well, nobody who cares anyway.' He chuckled again at the flare of panic Gabriel couldn't suppress and continued, 'I promise I'll lay it on thick. By the time I've finished, you'll have a hero's funeral. Of course, there won't be a body, but that's a small matter. I'll testify that you died the bravest of men. How does being shot by a French musket as Bony's army enters Cadiz sound to you? Plausible? After all's said and done, the idiots here aren't going to stop them. The damn city's ripe for the taking.'

Gabriel stared back at him in contemptuous silence.

'What about my uncle,' he demanded at length. 'I refuse to believe he is party to this madness.'

Henry laughed out loud, and the Viscount went cold. 'Whose idea do you think it was to take you for such a long *one-way* trip *Lord Northwood*? Your father was an irresponsible imbecile. The title should never have gone to him. Your death will simply make things as they should be.'

Gabriel glared at his grinning cousin wordlessly. What else was there to say? He'd been betrayed by a man he thought cared for him. He would die, and no one would ever know the truth. He watched Henry lift the pistol, his whole body in shock. The shot when it came seemed distanced, but the pain in his chest took his breath away. Another blast, and the top of his thigh was on fire.

Numbly, he watched Henry step towards him. His nemesis did not speak, but hefted Gabriel onto his shoulder and simply tipped him out of the window.

CHAPTER 7

'*D*ear God, how are you alive?' gasped Hope incredulously.

'His aim was a little off,' responded Gabriel ruefully. 'Clearly throwing people out of windows is not something my cousin does every day.'

Hope opened her mouth to speak again, but Nicholas held up his hand to forestall her. After throwing an apologetic smile her way, he turned back to the Viscount.

'But the French didn't simply walk into Cadiz. Marshal Victor's troops surround the island still, but they have not been able to take it. Major General Graham abides there yet and has by all accounts transformed the fortifications of the city.'

Gabriel grinned savagely. 'If you will allow me to continue, your grace, I have much yet to tell you.' He waited until Nicholas nodded, a touch impatiently.

'As I said, my cousin's aim was most definitely off. As he pushed me from the window, he stupidly did not wait to check whether I'd hit the ground. I actually fell onto a ledge two floors down and fainted. When

I came to, it was dark. I managed to drag myself to the window where I was observed by a priest. He did not ask any questions, merely took me in and saved my life.

'I don't remember much of the days that followed. I was incredibly fortunate that the monsignor had a knowledge of healing - rivalling even that of yours, Malcolm.' He turned to the valet who raised his eyebrows in mock disbelief.

'By the time I had recovered enough to speak, we were well into January. I had no idea where the *Seahorse* was or indeed what had happened. The monsignor quickly apprised me that the French had already bypassed Cadiz and were marching onto Seville.' Gabriel shook his head wearily and looked around at his mesmerised audience. The only sound in the room was the fire crackling in the grate and Freddy's soft snoring in front of it. The Duke did not interrupt again, merely leaned forward and refilled the Viscount's glass.

Gabriel took a sip of the amber liquid before continuing.

'I didn't know how much to tell the priest. The man was kindness itself, but I had no idea whether Henry was still in the city. I was afraid to ask if the *Seahorse* was still at anchor - I did not know until this evening whether the bastard had actually returned home. According to the monsignor, Napoleon's troops were entirely preoccupied with subduing Seville, but clearly it was only a matter of time before they turned their attention back to Cadiz. The Andalusian capital had all but fallen, and as I'm sure you are well aware, your grace, once they had taken Cadiz, the French would finally have succeeded in their long-awaited subjugation of Andalusia.'

Nicholas glanced at Adam at this assessment, and both men nodded in agreement.

'No further Spanish reinforcements had arrived in Cadiz while I was insensible. The city was entirely unprotected with what was left of the Spanish army marching south in a desperate attempt to save Seville. I finally left the city under cover of darkness. Although the monsignor did not know what had befallen me, he was persuaded that I needed to leave in secret, and he arranged for a small fishing boat to take me across the Rio Santi Petri to the mainland.'

Gabriel shrugged and took another sip of his brandy. 'From there I made my way towards Seville, hoping to intercept the Spanish armies marching south. At the very least I felt duty bound to warn someone in authority that Cadiz was entirely unprotected. We were now into the last days of January, but as I found to my cost, only the Army of Extremadura under the Duke of Albuquerque had actually succeeded in reaching Andalusia before Seville finally fell. I wasted days trying to catch up with them, and by the time I was granted an audience with his grace, his troops were only twenty miles from Seville.

'As luck would have it, the Duke had that morning received new orders to move his army on to Córdoba. I remember it was the twenty-fifth of January. His grace was incensed knowing that it would be an entire waste of his time as Córdoba had been taken by the French that very same day. I impressed upon the Duke that Cadiz was entirely defenceless and would almost certainly fall to the French without even a shot being fired. Should such a calamity transpire, then the war would be all but over. I had no proof on me. Nothing to authenticate my claim that Cadiz would be forced to simply open its gates to Napoleon's army when it finally turned its attention away from Seville. I don't know what persuaded him about my sincerity, but he made a fateful decision.'

'It was your information that convinced Albuquerque to ignore his orders and retreat to Cadiz?' questioned Nicholas incredulously.

Gabriel shrugged. 'I doubt my words were his only consideration. He was well aware of the wretched state of the Spanish army and no doubt conceived it very possible that Cadiz had been left completely undefended, but whatever made up his mind, the Duke marched twelve thousand men into Cadiz on the third of February. Two days before the French army arrived.'

'Did you return to Cadiz?' asked Hope breathlessly.

'I did not,' responded the Viscount. 'I realised I needed to return to England as soon as possible.' Gabriel looked around the room and spread his hands in surrender.

'And there you have it. My story in its entirety. My closest family went to great lengths to put an end to me, and I'm certain that should my uncle or cousin get wind of my survival, they will not hesitate to try again. Indeed, they now have no choice. But I cannot simply walk in and accuse the Admiral of parricide. My uncle has more connections than one can shake a stick at, while I have few friends and am generally considered an eccentric recluse with a relatively unimportant title.

'But now, I have no idea who I can trust. My uncle could well spin a tale convincing everyone that I am addled and simply have me locked away.' Gabriel paused and turned to the Duke. 'But you have been like a brother to me Nick, and not only that, you're the most honourable man I know. That's why I decided this tale would be for your ears only.' The last was said drily as he shook his head in exasperation.

There was a small silence, then Adam asked, 'How the deuce did you finally get home?' Admiration was clearly evident in his voice.

'It took me months to make my way to the east coast, and I finally managed to secure passage aboard a merchant ship by selling the last of my trinkets. Naturally, I dared tell no one of my real identity, though by then, I don't think anyone would have believed me if I'd declared myself.'

'But someone must suspect you still live?' argued Hope. 'Else why did those men chase after the carriage? And why did they question whether it belonged to Nicholas?'

'It would appear that we are not the only ones who believe the news of your demise may have been a trifle premature,' Nicholas commented wryly.

'Your reputation as a man of honour is well known,' observed Gabriel, 'as is our connection, so...'

'So, if you happened to miraculously rise from the dead,' the Reverend chimed in, 'it's reasonable to assume you would head for Blackmore.'

'What are we to do now?' Temperance pressed.

'Tonight, we do nothing,' responded the Duke wearily. 'It's late, it's Christmas Day and it's my belief we are all entirely done in. The varmints who harried the coach did not believe it mine so are no further forward in confirming whether Gabriel is either alive or in the Country. While we suspect them to be working for either the Admiral or Henry Atwood, we currently have no proof of that. Tomorrow, after a good night's sleep, we will reconvene and decide our strategy.'

Gabriel looked around helplessly at the nodding heads around the room. He had sought one man's help but had ended up with an entire clan. He shook his head. Truly he was weary unto death and wanted nothing more than to seek oblivion between some clean sheets. His efforts to convince Nicholas that it was sheer folly to involve his entire family in such treachery, would have to wait until the morrow.

And in truth, he had a sinking feeling that the choice had been entirely taken out of his hands.

∞∞∞

Hope lay in her bed and tried to sleep, but her mind had entirely different ideas. Her siblings had always considered her the boring sister, with little imagination or bottle, but mayhap they wouldn't think her quite such a dullard now, lying in her bed fantasising about a man she knew nothing about and had only met twenty-four hours earlier. It was exactly the kind of daydreaming her siblings might have indulged in, but Hope had believed herself above such foolishness.

She thought back to the sequence of events since Gabriel Atwood staggered into the church the night before. Even at first glance, there had been something about him. As thin and bedraggled as he was, he had a presence that had set her heart racing. His piercing grey eyes that were so guarded, clearly down to the suffering he'd endured at the hands of his family, no less.

But that didn't mean he was in any way a suitable focus for her girlish fancies. Undoubtedly, his story had tugged at her heartstrings she decided, turning over and plumping her pillow up viciously. That was the only reason for her preoccupation.

Nevertheless, she spent the next hour planning her attire for the morrow which, as her wardrobe was paltry at best, would normally involve mere minutes.

∞∞∞

'I canna begin to imagine what the laddie's been through these last months,' growled Malcom once the ladies had retired. 'I hardly recognised him when he walked through the door.'

Nicholas leant back against his chair, fingers steepled as he pondered the matter. 'Gabriel has indeed been wronged most sorely by those he thought family,' he agreed heavily. 'In truth, I would like nothing more than to announce to the world that the rightful Viscount Northwood has returned, thus rubbing Benjamin and Henry Atwood's noses well and truly in the dirt. But we must tread carefully, or Gabriel's life may yet be forfeit.'

Adam nodded in agreement. 'I believe his immediate safety is assured,' the Earl added. 'As long as he remains out of sight within these grounds and his tormentors do not get wind of his return.'

'You'd give the laddie a roof then?' questioned Malcolm.

'I would not see the man with nowhere to go,' Adam responded easily.

'The question is, how are we going to put a deuced rub in the way of their plans?' The Reverend had been quiet thus far. It was late, and in truth, the other men thought he had fallen asleep. His question was weary in the extreme, reminding Nicholas that his wife's irascible father was no spring chicken.

The Duke stood up. 'We are all tired,' he announced, 'and staying up until the early hours will not achieve anything. Besides, Roan will be arriving with Faith in a few hours, and I would certainly value his input. But for now, I think we would all benefit from a good night's sleep.' He finished the last of his brandy before adding grimly. 'Not to mention the fact that rushing into such smoky business without due caution may well get us all killed.'

∞∞∞∞

Rear Admiral Benjamin Atwood stared into the dying embers of the fire. By his estimate it was approaching midnight on Christmas Day. Caroline had long since sought her bed.

Aside from the ticking of the grandfather clock in the corner and the faint pop of the dwindling flames, the room was silent. There were a paltry half a dozen candles scattered around the room that did very little to dispel the shadows, and nothing at all to disperse the darkness that coiled itself around his heart.

He looked around the room that had been his sanctuary for over thirty years. As the sixth Viscount Northwood he could have established himself in glorious comfort at Northwood Court instead of freezing in the now shabby confines of his marital home.

But really that was it. Rutledge Manor was home. In the way that Northwood Court would never be. *Could* never be. Not in the circumstances. Henry was welcome to it. Atwood closed his eyes in sudden anguished realisation. What did it matter? His son had taken everything else he possessed.

Fighting the urge to cry out, the Admiral staggered to his feet and reached for the decanter of brandy. Fiend seize it, he felt as though he was in his cups, but nothing could be further from the truth. Gritting his teeth, he picked up the decanter, his whole arm trembling with exertion.

Finally, after spilling a generous amount onto the small table, he managed to fill his glass before promptly collapsing back into his chair, causing another measure to slosh onto his waistcoat. Fighting back a sob, Benjamin put the glass to his lips and allowed the fiery liquid to chase away the lump of self-pity as it burned its way down his throat. Then he wearily leaned his head against the back of the chair, just as the clock chimed midnight.

'Merry Christmas,' he muttered. The silence answered him back. God's teeth, if his peers could see him now, they would hardly recognise him, especially since he hadn't been to London in months.

How the bloody hell had it come to this?

He was dying.

Naturally, he hadn't seen a doctor. He was well aware of what ailed him - had known for nearly fifteen years. Ever since that cursed whore in Belgium.

He thought back to the first time he saw her. Madam Marie Bouchard. That was the name she used. Fed him a complete Banbury story about her dead husband. He should have seen right through her lies, but his cock hadn't been interested in anything but her voluptuous curves. He shook his head. The truth was he'd been determined to give a good prigging to the first prime article who crossed his path once he'd gotten across the Channel, and by the time Madam bloody Bouchard showed her true colours, it was too late. And to think he'd wanted to make her his mistress. Set her up in a house in London. He gave a hoarse chuckle which turned into a cough.

Fortunately for him, though not so much for Marie, before he had chance to make her an offer, a former recipient of her … machinations, who clearly did not have such a forgiving nature, decided to blow her brains out before turning the gun on himself.

Benjamin Atwood glanced down at his hands, the dark red blotches just visible in the flickering candlelight.

Following that ill-judged affair and Napoleon's delusions of grandeur, he spent the ensuing years away at sea, and after he was finally promoted and able to return to England, it hadn't been too difficult to avoid any intimacies with his wife. For his part, he'd only ever performed his duty anyway.

Unlike...

No. He would not. She was dead. Years ago now. The Admiral squeezed his eyes shut and forced back the memories. That path would lead him to madness quicker than the French pox.

Of course, he'd not exactly enjoyed spending the following years almost entirely celibate, but he couldn't risk infecting the mother of his child with bloody syphilis. His Naval career would have been finished. Caroline's father would have seen to that.

And the occasional doxies he'd tupped since? Well seeing as it was one of their ilk who gave him the pox in the first place, he could argue that they deserved it.

He gave a weary sigh. Might even have gotten away with that piss poor excuse at the pearly gates, but he wouldn't get away with cold blooded murder.

Not even if he hadn't been the one to pull the trigger.

And whatever plaudits he'd received in the past meant nothing in the face of that.

CHAPTER 8

The next morning, the grounds of Ravenstone resembled something out of a fairy tale. Everywhere was white over, and the snow sparkled and shone as the sun rose into the clearest of blue skies. Naturally, the younger Shacklefords could hardly wait until after breakfast before charging outside to throw snowballs and build snowmen. Their shrieks and screams under the watchful eye of a couple of stable hands provided a cheery backdrop to the more leisurely breakfast enjoyed by the adults in the party.

The problems of last night were not broached as everybody helped themselves to the delightful repast laid on the sideboard by the Earl's housekeeper Mrs Donnell. Indeed, the tone was determinedly light-hearted, and if it was a trifle forced, well Gabriel at least was glad of it.

For the first time in months, the Viscount felt able to truly relax. Having unburdened himself the night before, he'd slept like the dead, and the awareness that he was no longer alone lifted his spirits more than he thought possible.

Seating himself at the table, he eyed his new acquaintances with interest. Most especially Hope. The sun shining in through the large breakfast room window turned her red hair into molten copper. She was dressed simply, certainly not in the same league as her two older sisters whose attire reflected their husbands' status. But her dress, though simple, complemented her colouring and clung to her ample curves in a most distracting fashion. She had elected to tie her hair back with a simple ribbon, but the addition of a Christmas rose pinned behind her ear gave her ensemble a cheerful festive air. Gabriel wanted nothing more than to remove the flower, pull out the ribbon, and shove his hands into the resulting auburn waterfall.

'I have to say Lord Northwood, you're looking decidedly spoony. Did you happen to contract malaria during your time on the continent?'

Brought back to earth with a bump, Gabriel turned to regard Reverend Shackleford's wife as she enthusiastically seated herself next to him, all the while eying him with an almost eager expression. 'I was most fortunate, madam, not to have suffered from such a horrifying malady,' he responded politely.

'What about cholera?'

'Err … no, I was indeed fortunate not to have acquired cholera either.'

'Yellow fever? Dengue?' Gabriel shook his head mutely.

'Well, it's certain you haven't developed Leprosy,' she accused with a sniff, glaring reproachfully at his rudely healthy fingers, almost causing the Viscount to put down his toast on the off chance a digit might be about to drop off.

'Agnes, how is your gout this morning?' interjected Miss Beaumont. Clearly, deciding her reticent breakfast companion's enduring health was not worth her continued interest, Mrs Shackleford happily turned away and engaged his dinner companion from the night before with an enthusiastic account of her latest ailments. Gabriel flashed Miss Beaumont a grateful look from behind the elderly matron's head, and her lips twitched in response. Clearly, the lady had the patience of a saint.

He looked back over at Hope and found her eyes twinkling back at him in amusement as she attempted to cover her mirth with her hand. He was ridiculously glad to see that despite her down-to-earth attitude, she obviously did have a sense of humour. Raising his eyebrows at her, he wondered why it was so important to him.

'Tell me, Lord Northwood, we know nothing of you outside of your recent exploits, mayhap you would be kind enough to favour us with some anecdotes from your earlier, and one hopes, less hazardous adventures.' The speaker this time was the Duchess of Blackmore. Her warm smile took any implied criticism out of her request.

Before Gabriel could come up with something suitable however, her husband gave a shout of laughter. 'I'm not sure accounts of Gabe's younger days are entirely suitable for either tender ears, or indeed the breakfast table,' he chuckled.

Against his will, Gabriel's lips twitched. 'I am entirely certain that I must have at least some interesting anecdotes to tell that would be acceptable to the gentle company present,' he drawled.

'Oh, we are most certainly not interested in how you fell out of a tree at five, my lord,' Temperance interrupted mischievously. 'I am entirely certain you have far more interesting things to share. Are you married perchance?'

'My love, your penchant for slinging mud simply to see where it sticks does not appear to have abated since you've become a wife.' Adam's reproof was mild, and he was clearly trying not to laugh.

'Poof, *my love*,' his wife responded with a wave of her hand. 'If you'd wanted a boring life, you should not have married me.'

'Indeed,' grinned Adam, 'I tell myself that daily.'

'I pray for you both every night,' added the Reverend, only half joking. After all, he'd lived with his two eldest daughters far longer than their husbands.

Gabriel stared at the laughing couples nonplussed. *Ton* marriages in his experience were nothing like this. By all accounts, his own parents' certainly wasn't.

'How are you feeling, Percy?' asked Hope hurriedly. She did not wish Gabriel to know of her own contributions to the unruly antics of her siblings.

The curate looked up, startled, unused to being included in such banter. 'I ... I am feeling perfectly well, my lady, thank you for asking.'

'I am no lady,' scoffed Hope, 'as well you know, Percy.'

'Nor are any of us,' added Grace. 'It's simply the exalted company we keep.' She winked at her husband as she spoke.

The Duke shook his head ruefully. 'Truly, there is no hope for any of us poor gullible males,' he sighed.

'Are you entirely sure that your brain has not developed a swelling?' Everyone looked over at the earnest face of Agnes Shackleford. 'I have recently purchased a most interesting ointment from the apothecary...'

'...Who undoubtedly got it from the pedlar,' interrupted the Reverend.

His wife gave him a glacial stare, then sniffed and turned back to Percy who was now regarding the matron with palpable alarm.

'Pray do not worry yourself further, Percy,' she enthused. 'I shall ensure to have some placed in your bedchamber for your use before you retire. Be sure to rub the ointment all over your forehead and leave it overnight. Any swelling will be instantly subdued.'

'Either that or you'll have a deuced apoplexy,' growled the Reverend. He turned back to his wife, who was now turning an interesting shade of purple and winced, changing his tone completely - much to the smothered amusement of the rest of the table. 'My dove,' he cajoled, 'I cannot risk either my dearest love or my oldest friend to such a potentially ... *powerful* ... concoction without first using it on my own person…' He paused as Temperance snorted inelegantly and favoured his daughter with an indignant glare before continuing. 'At least allow me to ensure your safety first, my love.'

Agnes sniffed, slightly mollified, and her husband breathed an audible sigh of relief.

Coughing to stop himself from laughing out loud, Nicholas deemed it pertinent to change the subject. 'Gabriel, with any luck, Hope's twin sister Faith will be arriving before dark along with her husband, Roan Carew. He was in the Navy for many years, and before resigning his commission, was the Commanding Officer of the *Albatross*. Mayhap you know him?'

Gabriel raised his eyebrows. 'I certainly know *of* him - anyone with even the remotest naval connections has heard of the *Lucky Albatross* and her Captain. Truly Nicholas, I hope you won't think me ill mannered, but you certainly have the most err … *fascinating* family.'

'No offence taken,' chuckled the Duke. 'If you'd described my future wife's family to me beforehand, I'd have believed you spouting some Canterbury tale.' His wife laughed and punched his arm good-naturedly. 'Indeed,' she offered impishly, 'it is amazing how fortunate you were, is it not?'

'Truly the work of the Almighty,' added the Reverend, his eyes piously heavenward.

'As I was saying,' interrupted Nicholas drily, 'I would very much like to have Roan's contribution into the err … problem of Gabriel's murderous family…' He paused and nodded his understanding towards Gabriel. 'So, with your permission Gabe, we will put the whole affair on hold until Faith and Roan arrive.'

Gabriel gritted his teeth. It did not sit well at all to be doing nothing, but what choice did he have? He could understand the Duke's request to wait. Roan Carew's successes as Captain of the *Albatross* certainly indicated a man whose counsel was worth seeking. At length, he nodded. Indeed, he could see no other recourse.

Nicholas nodded back sympathetically. Clearly, he recognised and understood Gabriel's need to take action. 'So, given that we are currently at a loose end while we await the arrival of Roan,' the Duke went on, 'I believe there is no reason at all why we cannot spend some time enjoying such a beautiful day.'

'It *is* Boxing Day, after all,' added Temperance, 'and the servants will shortly be leaving us to fend for ourselves until this evening. I suggest we take our cold repast down to the lake.'

'It will definitely be cold,' commented Adam with a mock shudder.

'We have blankets, and I'm sure we can find a sheltered spot without too much snow,' exclaimed Grace.

'Surely, it will be too cold for little Peter?' worried Hope with a slight frown.

'Nonsense,' Nicholas replied. 'It will put some colour in his cheeks.'

'And I'm persuaded that Briony might also benefit from some fresh air,' added Grace referring to their son's nanny.

'Freddy too could undoubtedly do with the exercise,' declared Temperance looking over at the foxhound's decidedly round stomach as he snoozed in front of the fire.

'That's decided then,' announced Adam, rising from his chair. 'I do hope you will consider joining us,' he added to Gabriel. 'I know you have been through so much, and this waiting must be most tedious for you, but in my opinion, there's no sense in sitting around Friday faced dwelling on a problem. When Roan gets here, we will work on the solution together.'

He waved his hand to encompass the whole table, and unaccountably, Gabriel felt a lump come into his throat. 'You've been very generous, Lord Ravenstone,' he responded huskily.

'Adam, please,' the Earl responded with a grin. 'Nick's strange predilection for informality has rubbed off on all of us, I'm afraid.'

'I do think there is one thing we must deal with before we brave the snow,' interrupted Temperance, drawing all eyes to her. She smiled warmly towards Gabriel before continuing with her customary forthrightness, 'Am I right in believing that you are currently wearing the only clothes you actually have?'

'Aye, and they're my deuced castoffs,' retorted the Reverend gruffly before Gabriel had chance to answer.

'I must beg your indulgence,' returned Gabriel ruefully. 'You've presumed correctly. The only attire I have is the one I'm standing up in.'

'Then we must put that to rights immediately,' answered Grace. 'I'm sure both Nicholas and Adam have a surfeit of clothes that are unfortunately too tight for them to get into.' She gave a sly glance towards the Duke before raising her eyes towards Temperance.

'Of a certainty,' agreed her sister, standing up to take her husband's arm. 'We will attend to your depleted wardrobe immediately Gabriel, after which, we will go out and attempt to make merry while the light remains. With luck, Faith and Roan will be with us before it gets dark.'

'I'm afraid I will not be joining you,' shuddered Agnes rising and gathering her shawl around her shoulders. 'The cold plays havoc with my bunions. I will request a small repast to take with me into the sitting room where I'm certain I shall be more than cosy.'

'Would you like some reading material to accompany you?' asked Temperance solicitously.

The Reverend gave a muffled grunt. 'She'll be snoring on the chaise longue within half an hour.'

'And it's no more than you deserve, my dove,' he added hurriedly at his wife's narrowed glare.

Within the hour Gabriel had been furnished with a whole new wardrobe despite his protestations, and the party were warmly wrapped up and making their way down the snow-covered paths towards a small lake.

The younger Shacklefords were already rosy cheeked and proclaiming themselves starving, so Hope and Gabriel found themselves embroiled in more than one snowball fight as the older members of the party sought to divert their younger siblings' attention from their stomachs. Freddy naturally chased after snowballs and anything else that took his fancy.

As they got closer to their destination however, the children skipped off in front towards the frozen lake, and after instructing them not to venture out onto the ice, Hope found herself walking alone with the Viscount. It was the first time they'd been alone since the morning before in the vicarage kitchen, and unlike that occasion, Hope now found herself inexplicably tongue tied. So much had happened in such a short space of time, it seemed perfectly ridiculous to now be indulging in small talk as though they'd just met in someone's drawing room.

Gabriel, for his part, couldn't remember the last time he'd been in close proximity to an attractive woman. The occasional dalliance he'd indulged in before Spain seemed a lifetime ago, and though his trip to Cadiz had only been the last of many uncertain trips abroad, some at sea during his time in the Royal Navy and others as an envoy for Admiral Atwood, he'd never been forced to survive alone on only his wits for such a long duration. He recognised that the experience had changed him forever.

After being forced to retire from the Navy, he'd found himself at a loss. He was nothing like his father, preferring life away from the excesses of the capital. Though initially he'd believed that throwing himself into the running of Northwood would be enough to occupy him, it had failed to quench his aspiration to leave his mark on the world - to do something that might make a difference.

The Viscount became aware that his companion was speaking. 'A penny for your thoughts?' Hope was saying softly.

Gabriel looked down into the luminous hazel eyes of his companion and drew in his breath. God she was lovely. The cold had rendered her cheeks and lips a dark pink, and tawny curls framed her face where her hair had escaped its pins. Against the backdrop of white, she looked almost exotic. As her face slowly suffused with colour, he realised he'd been staring at her impolitely for nearly half a minute. What the hell was wrong with him? He was behaving like a complete dolt. He coughed self-consciously. 'Forgive my deplorable manners, Miss Shackleford,' he finally murmured. 'In truth, I was thinking you a rare vision, especially for one who has been without such a feast to the eyes for longer than he can remember.'

Hope's colour deepened at the intensity in Gabriel's scrutiny, and she had no idea what to say in return. She felt like a gauche country chit just out of the school room, though she'd been the one teaching her younger siblings for nigh on two years.

Abruptly, she looked down, feeling like a complete fool. She did not know how to flirt. This was the first time she'd even held a conversation with a man. Did he believe her worldly like her older sisters? That she could indulge in witty banter at the drop of a hat? If so, he was about to be sorely disappointed.

'I… I am sure they are waiting on us,' she stammered in the end, though she could clearly see that the rest of the party were not even looking their way. With a quick curtsy, she picked up her skirts and fled towards safety, forcing back sudden tears of humiliation.

∞∞∞∞

The sun was shining through the dining room window as Benjamin Atwood attended his wife Caroline at breakfast. They might have been sitting at the same table, but that was the extent of their intimacy. Neither spoke, but simply got on with the business of breaking their fast.

Caroline was not aware of his affliction. The Admiral had managed to get through Christmas Day without resorting to his bed. He'd half expected Henry to turn up, but he should have known better. And now it was Boxing Day, and there had been no word from his son and heir.

His son and heir. He didn't know whether to laugh or cry. But then what he really wanted to do was smash everything within reaching distance. He smiled and nodded politely at his wife, his inner turmoil completely hidden, as she asked him if he wished for more tea.

Sipping at the lukewarm liquid, he thought back to when it all went so badly wrong. Oh, not the onset of his disease, he'd controlled that well enough for years. Even reaching the pinnacle of his career whilst secretly hiding his shame.

And it wasn't even when his son took up gambling, depleting his doting mother's modest inheritance to fund his habit.

No, it was when Henry sought to put a deuced hole in his cousin. The *correct* Viscount Northwood. The idiot had not only missed but cheated. It had cost his father practically everything he had to hush the sordid incident up. The favours he'd had to pull in to buy Henry a commission and install him in his own bloody ship. Atwood felt the sweat blossom on his brow at the thought of how much he'd actually owed prior to Gabriel's death.

Gabriel may have died at Henry's hands, but he'd been the one who'd murdered the Viscount, just as surely as if he'd pulled the trigger.

And the worst of it?

He'd always loved Gabriel. In truth, much more than he ever had Henry.

CHAPTER 9

*H*ope huddled down inside her warm blanket and watched the rest of the party cavort in the snow. Or rather her eyes may have been on their antics, but her mind was busy reprimanding herself for her gaucheness when conversing with Viscount Northwood. There was no getting away from it, she'd acted like a complete pea goose. She glanced over at Grace and Temperance who were arguing animatedly with Felicity. Their faces were flushed from a combination of cold and laughter. The fact of the matter was, she was never going to possess the boisterous confidence of her older siblings. Even Faith, as close as she and Hope were, would always possess far more wit than she.

And it wasn't just about self-confidence. Her only experience of men were her sisters' husbands, which meant she had absolutely no idea how to converse socially with a member of the opposite sex, whether noble, commoner or indeed, possessed of two heads.

In short, she was matter of fact, kind to a fault, unfailingly polite and dull as dishwater.

What man would countenance that list of attributes, especially in a penniless vicar's daughter? Hope frowned. Surely, she had more positive qualities?

For instance, no one could deny that she'd saved her sisters from a sound thrashing on numerous occasions, and it could be argued that her actions had deterred those thugs on Christmas Day. In truth, she had surprised herself by her quick thinking. Mayhap her opportunity to shine had not yet appeared.

Unexpected shrieks interrupted her musings, and she focused on Patience who was currently being sat on by Chastity who was busy tucking snow down her collar. Involuntarily, she smiled. Despite her frustration with her eccentric family, she could not deny that the feeling of belonging was a wondrous thing. What did it matter if she remained unwed? She had her family around her, and despite ofttimes longing for solitude, she knew that her older sisters would never see her destitute or alone.

'It's Faith and Roan,' shouted Prudence suddenly pointing at a distant carriage making its way up the manicured drive towards the house.

Immediately, the picnic-type atmosphere fled as Nicholas wasted no time in climbing to his feet while the ladies packed away their cold collation. Hope watched anxiously as the Duke nodded to the Viscount.

Their light-hearted sojourn was over.

∞∞∞∞

The whole party arrived just as Faith and Roan were alighting from their carriage. 'Zooks, I think my rear end is about to fall off,' complained Faith as she climbed down with a groan. Then glancing around, her eyes lit up as she spied her twin. Seconds later they were hugging, the laughter interspersed with some tears. 'Truly, I have missed you,' Faith murmured vehemently.

'What, is married life not suiting you after all?' asked Hope mischievously. Faith chuckled and tucked her arm into her sister's. 'Married life is wonderful,' she enthused with a wink, 'but I cannot deny I've missed your no-nonsense counsel.' Before Hope could respond, she glanced round and whispered, 'Who is the handsome gentleman currently being introduced to my husband? Is he perchance a possible suitor for my practical, sensible twin?'

Against her will, Hope's cheeks reddened, causing Faith to laugh delightedly.

'I don't know about you lot, but I'm entirely done with frolicking around in the deuced cold. If I stay outside much longer, I will no longer be able to vouch for my extremities.' The Reverend's grumble cut short their conversation, and hurriedly, the party made their way inside.

The staff had returned from visiting their families, and there was a roaring fire in the entrance hall where Adam's butler waited with a tray of hot chocolate.

'Jamieson, you really are a treasure,' commented Temperance wrapping her icy hands around the steaming cup.

'Could you show Mr and Mrs Carew to their room?' Adam requested of the hovering footman. Then he turned to the rest of the party.

'I think now would be a good time for everyone to freshen up before we reconvene in the drawing room … in an hour?'

Faith frowned and looked over at her husband. She felt as though she was being summarily dismissed which wasn't the usual way of things at Ravenstone. She opened her mouth to protest that she did not need to freshen up but caught the sudden tension and closed it again. What was going on? Clearly, something had happened. She glanced over at Hope in time to catch her sister looking towards the newcomer.

Whatever was happening, it undoubtedly had something to do with the handsome stranger.

By the time the party reunited in the drawing room, the candles had been lit, and a cheerful fire burned in the hearth. The younger siblings had been ushered for an early supper in the nursery, much to their disgust - all except Patience, who at sixteen had decided she was old enough to listen in.

It was full dark by the time Roan and Faith had been apprised of the events of the last few days, and though Gabriel had recognised the wisdom of seeking the former sea captain's counsel, he was nevertheless grateful to see no censure in the man's regard, but a compassion that caused a lump in his throat.

'Naturally, we must seek to reinstate the Viscount's Seat, but more importantly, our aim must be to ensure his continued well-being.' Roan nodded at the Duke's words.

'You have my sympathy, Northwood,' was all he commented with a slight bend of his head. 'Truly, I know how it feels to be entirely alone in the world with no one to aid you.' He turned to Nicholas. 'Henry Atwood is known to me, though only vaguely. There were rumours that his father paid a considerable amount of money to ensure his son's command, but it wasn't common knowledge, and no one really questioned it. Of course, Admiral Atwood is extremely well respected in naval circles and has more connections than most. So why would he seek the death of his only nephew? Mayhap he covets the North-wood title, but it seems a little extreme to go to such lengths to secure it.'

'My thoughts exactly,' responded Gabriel. 'My cousin has always detested me, but I put it down to family rivalry. If as you say, my uncle paid a substantial sum to further Henry's career, we can also assume at least some of that was to cover up the scandal of our duel. If it became known that my cousin cheated, he would be barred from everywhere that mattered to him. In truth, the opinions of his peers have always been more important to him than to me.' He frowned. 'My uncle's reputation too, would have been ruined had Henry's stupidity become common knowledge.'

'So, his determination to see you joining Davy Jones' locker could be either that he fears you will not keep his son's indiscretions a secret or he needs the blunt,' stated the Reverend matter-of-factly.

'Last I heard, the Admiral's share of prize money was enough to see him well into his dotage,' commented Roan, 'so it's possible this is more about the title.' He frowned. 'Unless he had expenditures we know nothing about.

'Did your uncle ever indicate a desire for your title?' he asked Gabriel.

'Not to my knowledge,' answered the Viscount. 'I believed him close to my father, and he was always a dedicated military man. Of course, there were whispers that Benjamin Atwood would have been a better choice for Northwood, and in all honesty, I can't disagree, given that my father's main concern was always the next wager.' He shook his head ruefully. 'Atwood never seemed to pay any attention to the rumours - simply laughed them off.'

'Did the Admiral have anything to do with you joining the Navy?' asked Adam with interest.

'Everything,' answered Gabriel simply. 'He was the one I looked up to as I was growing up. Without his influence, I would likely have spent my formative years drinking and gambling along with my peers.'

'Was he even then hoping you might not live to inherit?' the Earl continued.

Gabriel frowned. 'It's possible, I suppose, but I always believed him very fond of me. In truth when I was younger, I spent more time with my uncle than did his own son.'

'Forgive me, gentlemen, but all this speculation is getting us nowhere,' intervened Nicholas. 'The truth remains that Gabriel's cousin tried to murder him in cold blood. Although he declared it was at the behest of his father, we have only his word for that. The whys and where-fores are not our main concern. Our main concern is to ensure

Gabriel's continued safety, and to do that, we must bring the miscreants to justice.'

'Naturally, we must also seek to restore his title,' added Grace, her anger at what had happened to the Viscount palpable.

'Once your cousin at least knows you live, he will endeavour to put an end to you permanently,' commented Roan. 'He has to or else he stands to lose everything. He will no doubt be aware that his attempt on your life in Cadiz would be difficult to prove, but at the very least, he will not wish to have his name blacklisted through rumours or indeed lose his claim on Northwood.'

'I still believe it important we get to the bottom of why,' interrupted Temperance. 'If money was the prime motivator and we can prove it, then it adds weight to our cause.'

Adam nodded slowly before speaking directly to Nicholas. 'I believe I'm the best person to do some digging.' He held up his hand to forestall the Duke's protest. 'They will be watching you Nick, and we cannot say the same about me. There will be no undue interest in my movements, should I decide to spend some time up in the Village on business.'

'You do not have the same military connections,' argued Nicholas, clearly reluctant to let anyone else put themselves in danger.

'But I do,' offered Roan. 'My connections may not be as illustrious as yours, Nick, but I'm persuaded you can quietly furnish me with notes of introduction to those people you trust? It's logical, after all, that I would seek to invest my prize money. It may even get me straight to the horse's mouth.'

Although Faith did not argue, her expression spoke of her unhappiness at the idea of her husband putting himself at risk.

However, before anyone else could speak, Gabriel burst out, 'Fiend seize it, I cannot allow any of you to risk yourselves for me, you have done more than any sane person could ever have asked. I'm a deuced stranger to most of you.' His frustration and anguish were palpable.

'We could not, in all conscience, abandon you this late in the game, Gabriel, especially as we are now on first name terms,' responded Adam drily.

'Nothing this family loves better than a mystery to solve,' exclaimed the Reverend.

'Mayhap you are referring to yourself on this occasion, Father,' countered Faith, eyebrows raised.

Reverend Shackleford coughed uncomfortably before waving his hand airily and saying, 'Oh I am undoubtedly far too old to go cavorting round the countryside in search of suspected murderers.'

'Well, it didn't stop you last time,' responded Faith tartly.

Reverend Shackleford sat back against his chair and regarded his daughter guiltily. After a lengthy pause, he said, 'You may rest assured, Faith dear, that I have indeed learned the valuable lesson the Almighty sought to teach me in Torquay.'

'Well at least you're not the instigator of this one, Father, and that makes a welcome change,' commented Grace, ignoring her parent's indignant glower.

'What about Gabriel's safety in the meantime?' asked Hope, speaking for the first time. 'Clearly, his relatives will seek to put an end to him before the world knows he has returned.'

'That's what we're banking on,' responded Nicholas. 'Somehow, we must draw them out into doing something reckless. Once that happens, we'll have them.'

'But what if we don't give them the opportunity to act?' responded Hope, 'But simply proclaim to the world that the former viscount has returned? Once it's out in the open, will that not be sufficient to forestall any further murderous impulses they may have?'

'That brings us back to money,' shrugged Roan. 'If Admiral and/or Henry Atwood are cleaned out, they could well be desperate enough. That's aside from their fear that the truth could well come out, and naturally, they would assume Gabriel will not leave unfinished business. Again, consider the scandal.' He shook his head. 'In my opinion, it's a risk we dare not take, unless we can first uncover enough damning evidence of their duplicity.'

'But I will willingly take that chance rather than put any of you in further jeopardy,' protested Gabriel hotly.

'If you hadn't thought they'd be putting you to bed with a deuced shovel as soon as you showed your face,' growled the Reverend, 'you wouldn't have sought out Nicholas in the first place.'

'The Devil take it,' interrupted a small, exasperated voice, 'it seems transparently obvious that this Henry fellow is entirely dicked in the nob. So, I say enough prittle-prattle. How are we going to throw a rub in the way of the bastard's plans?'

There was a deafening silence as everyone in the room looked over at Patience who was glaring back rebelliously.

'In all honesty,' commented Felicity Beaumont a few seconds later, 'I couldn't have put it better myself.'

∞∞∞∞

Henry Atwood was in his cups. Not that that in itself was particularly unusual, but usually he wasn't quite so jug bitten before eleven o'clock in the morning. But then he supposed, it was Christmas.

He was sprawled on the chaise longue, perfectly situated to observe the beautiful view from the drawing room at Northwood Court. It had been snowing, and the scene resembled that of a fairy tale.

Henry saw nothing of it. He was eying the nearly empty bottle of port and debating whether to ring for his new butler now or when he'd finally downed the dregs. For down them he would and most assuredly another bottle on top of the two he'd already consumed. There was something strangely satisfying in depleting the decent stuff in his old man's wine cellar.

The problem was, no matter how much he denied it to himself, he still thought of it as Gabriel's. And he knew his father did. That was why the old skinflint couldn't bear to step foot in Northwood Court.

Damn Gabriel Atwood.

Henry looked around the room blearily. He shouldn't even be here. His father was supposed to have taken charge. Swept in and become the Viscount everybody wanted while his only son and heir resigned his commission and concentrated on enjoying the carnal delights of London.

His father had promised him he wouldn't have to stay in the bloody Navy. It was only temporary until people forgot. But here he was, still Captain bloody Atwood while Viscount *bloody* Northwood languished in his tattered, tired old manor. Nobody had seen him in months.

And to top it all, Henry couldn't rid himself of the notion that Gabriel wasn't really dead. That despite being thrown from the top of a bell tower, his cousin had somehow survived.

Unable to shake the feeling, he'd had someone watching Blackmore. That was where the bastard would go if he managed to crawl back to England. He'd even had his men chase down a bloody carriage from Blackmore on Christmas morning in case it turned out to be his *dead* cousin.

Clearly, the whole thing was turning him addled. Somehow, he had to get a grip. He emptied the bottle of port into his glass and rang for the butler. Tomorrow. Tomorrow he would take charge.

CHAPTER 10

*L*uckily, the snow did not linger for the promised weeks, and a mere three days later, Roan was on his way to London accompanied by a determined Faith.

'We can tell everyone that we are seeking a house in town,' she'd commented when her husband protested. 'It is a perfectly feasible excuse for me to be there.' To Roan's frustration, the rest of the family believed it a worthy idea, and Adam offered the use of his town house for them to stay in. In fairness, the former sea captain did not put up much of a fight having been down this road with his extended, not to mention single-minded, family before.

It was decided that the rest of the party would continue with their previous plans to return home but with an additional coachman. As he climbed on top of the box, Gabriel was mainly grateful that this time he was wearing woollen undergarments.

The only alteration to their previous intent was to return to Blackmore in a single day, though the Reverend grumbled that he'd been looking forward, on this occasion, to the prospect of not having an arse like a pancake by the time he got to his destination.

Once at Blackmore, they would endeavour to hide their unexpected guest. Pear Tree Cottage on the Duke's estate was decided upon as the ideal location. Aside from its obviously negative memories for Grace, it was far enough away from both the village and the house to avoid any gossip or undue interest from either villagers or outsiders.

From there, the intention was to wait a few days while life ostensibly returned to some semblance of normality before planning their next move. A move that would depend entirely on whether Roan uncovered enough or indeed *any* damning evidence against either the Admiral or Henry Atwood.

Fortunately, the journey home to Blackmore, though tedious, passed uneventfully without any added excitement, much to the younger Shacklefords' disappointment as they spent the whole journey watching eagerly for the sudden appearance of a knight of the road.

Installing the rightful Viscount Northwood into his temporary abode also went without observation.

As the Reverend commented piously on his first night back in the vicarage, 'Things always work out for the righteous.'

Percy didn't trust himself to comment.

∞∞∞∞

In the three days since they'd smuggled him into Pear Tree Cottage, Hope had not managed to find an excuse to visit Gabriel Atwood.

That wasn't to say she hadn't tried, but in truth, her time was entirely taken up with looking after her siblings. Although their father had recently instructed Patience to assume a share of the responsibility, the sixteen-year-old preferred to spend her days roaming the countryside dressed as a boy.

The rest of the family had long since given up trying to put a stop to it, mostly because Patience had proven herself a consummate lock picker. Where she had obtained such an unladylike skill was entirely debatable since Patience had persistently refused to divulge the name of her tutor. Between that dubious talent and the fact that she could also climb like a monkey, it was virtually impossible to ensure she remained anywhere she didn't want to be.

And besides, in their father's view, Temperance had already plumbed the depths of depravity (or etiquette anyhow) with her actions a couple of years earlier, and according to his wife's periodicals, she was now all the crack.

Or it might also be, as Hope privately believed, that he'd simply surrendered to the inevitable.

But today, she was resolute. The last evening, she had tracked Patience down and made her sister promise to take over the classroom on the morrow. Naturally, the agreement had not been elicited without cost, but Hope tried not to dwell too much on exactly what kind of favour Patience might choose to ask for at an unspecified time in the future.

Obviously, Hope refused to ask herself the question of *why* she wished to see the Viscount again so desperately. Indeed, it was entirely unlike her to be quite so vehement about anything, so accustomed was she to fading into the background. But somehow, the thought of his piercing grey eyes and crooked smile did something to her insides. It was an experience she'd never had before.

Their last private conversation had been a disaster, but if she did nothing else in her entire life, Hope was determined that she would not have him leave with the impression she was simply totty-headed.

Although she was assured that Gabriel was being provisioned extremely well from the Duke's household, nevertheless, as soon as she was dressed, she headed into the vicarage kitchen to see if Mrs Tomlinson had done any baking. Luckily, the room was empty aside from Freddy in his customary place by the fire, but the first thing she spied was a bread-and-butter pudding on the sideboard which had clearly been made for tonight's supper. Shuddering, she wondered what excuse she could come up with to avoid eating any. Mrs Tomlinson's bread and butter pudding was legendary in its awfulness. Indeed, if it hadn't been produced for consumption, it could feasibly be used to block up incoming drafts.

She didn't think she would win the Viscount's heart by presenting him with that... Her train of thoughts skidded to a halt. What the deuce was she thinking? Win his heart? Was she addled or just plain stupid?

She sat down at the kitchen table and put her head in her hands. Clearly, she really was totty-headed if she believed there was even the smallest chance that Gabriel Atwood would be interested in her. Oh, she filled out her clothes well enough - a little too well if she was honest, but her hair was an unfashionable red and she was reliably informed by the boys in the village that no man would willingly put his baubles anywhere near a redhead 'lest'n she cut 'em off.'

In truth, Hope was not entirely sure what a man's *baubles* were or why any woman would want to cut them off, but the upshot of the matter was that clearly women with red hair were simply not popular.

There was absolutely no point in her making a complete cake of herself.

With a sigh, Hope lifted her head and regarded the sleeping foxhound with something approaching envy. If only life were that simple. Climbing to her feet, she decided to go and fetch her book instead. Reading would take her mind off her foolishness, and at least she could make the most of Patience's rare visit to the schoolroom.

Just as she was about to leave, the door to the yard was flung open. It was Jimmy, the Duke of Blackmore's unofficial messenger, and he looked frantic.

At twelve, the rascal was beginning to fill out a bit, showing promise of the handsome man he might become if he could but desist in his inclination to cut a wheedle at every opportunity. If not, Hope very much feared he may well find himself on the wrong end of the morning drop. Why Nicholas trusted him so much, she had no idea.

But now the boy was looking at her with an expression she hadn't seen on him before.

Self-reproach.

'If'n yer pardon, Miss Shackleford, is the Revren about?'

Hope frowned. 'I don't think so, Jimmy, he usually does his parish rounds in the morning. Is something wrong?'

The young rogue stood irresolute for a moment, clearly fighting an internal battle. Then abruptly, he blurted out, 'It's 'is grace's lodger - the one in the cottage. I think he might be dead.'

CHAPTER 11

*I*t took Hope a few seconds to realise Jimmy was actually referring to Gabriel, and as soon as she did, her heart plummeted. 'What? How?' she stuttered feeling sick.

'I dunno miss. Looked to 'ave 'it 'is 'ead. There was blood everywhere.' The boy looked about to burst into tears, making him look suddenly much younger. All his bluster had gone, and he just looked scared.

'I can't tell 'is grace, 'e'll never trust me again. It was my bloody job to keep an eye on the bastard.'

'Language, Jimmy,' Hope said automatically while her mind was frantically thinking what to do. Had his enemies found him and left him for dead? There was no time to look for her father, or anyone else for that matter. She would have to go.

'Tell Seth to hitch Lucifer to the cart,' she said, before running into the pantry to gather anything she could that might help. As she was tossing items into her basket, she wondered hysterically if some of Mrs Tomlinson's bread and butter pudding might be useful in plugging a head wound.

Five minutes later, she was throwing on her cloak and running out into the yard. Luckily, Seth, their one and only stable hand, had taken one look at Jimmy's face and refrained from arguing with the lad's request. Jimmy was already seated on the slatted bench along the front of the cart. Hurriedly climbing up beside him, Hope took the reins, and seconds later they thundered out into the lane.

Unlike her sisters, Hope was actually more at home with horses. Or mayhap that was a slight exaggeration. The truth was she could get their single horse, Lucifer, to do what most of the rest of her sisters couldn't. Her father had always said it was because she looked like her mother who was evidently the only human the evil-tempered beast had ever remotely tolerated. That's not to say she would ever dare to actually climb on his back.

Still, it meant that she was able to wield the reins confidently enough to at least get the horse to go in the direction she wished. It also helped that Lucifer hadn't properly stretched his legs since before the Christmas holidays. Indeed, the wind was fairly whipping past them as they careered up the road, and if Jimmy had been fearful before, a quick glance showed her he was now absolutely petrified.

All thoughts of a romantic nature had long since fled as Hope concentrated on getting them to their destination as quickly as possible. She did not allow herself to even entertain the possibility that the Viscount might be dead. Surely, the Almighty would not have put him through so many trials only to have him die just at the point where safety finally seemed within reach.

Luckily, the route to the cottage did not take them through the village. Although it was likely she'd find her father somewhere about, their breakneck speed would also attract undue attention, and to Hope's knowledge, the Reverend's doctoring skills were no better than his sermon writing. Clearly, Malcolm was the one they needed, and she intended to drop Jimmy off at the bottom of the drive leading to the Duke's estate so the boy could fetch Nicholas's valet as quickly as possible. As she careened to a halt outside the imposing entrance, she told Jimmy in no uncertain terms that if he did not appear with Malcolm within the hour, she would string him up herself.

'Do not even think of scarpering,' she shouted as the boy climbed down.

'Keep yer 'air on miss,' he grumbled, relief at surviving the journey clearly making him cocky. 'I'm 'ere, not in bloody Torquay.'

'And don't swear,' she yelled behind her as the still frisky Lucifer launched himself forward.

A mere fifteen minutes later, the horse was galloping down the track that led to Pear Tree Cottage, the cart bouncing along behind him. Torn between exhilaration and sheer terror, Hope pulled hard on the reins as they approached the small building and for a few heart-stopping seconds didn't think Lucifer was going to slow down, but just as she began to think she might have to jump, he finally came to a trembling stop.

For a few moments, she simply sat there stunned, then recollecting why she was there, she quickly jumped down, grabbed her basket and hurried into the house. 'I'll make it up to you, Lucy,' she shouted as she pushed open the door. An equine snort was the only answer she received.

The interior of the cottage was dim, and she had to pause for a moment to get her bearings. 'Lord Northwood?' she called. 'Gabriel?' There was no answer. Heart clattering, she took a step into what looked to be a sitting room.

There on the floor, she could see the shape of a man. He was unmoving. With a small cry, she placed her basket on the ground and knelt beside the prone figure. Jimmy had been right, there did seem to be a copious amount of blood on the floor. Swallowing a sob, she bent forward and hovered her hand over his mouth to see if he was breathing.

She was unable to stop the small moan when she couldn't feel any air escaping from his mouth, but just as she was about to begin massaging his chest, a method she'd read about being used on people suffering from an apoplexy, his mouth opened and emitted a soft snore.

And that wasn't all that emanated from his now parted lips. The stench of alcohol was enough to fell even the most hardened drinker. Coughing and spluttering, she leaned back.

Her relief to find him alive was now warring with vexation. She glanced around and finally noticed two *empty* bottles of brandy. Zooks, had he drunk them both? She looked back down at the comatose figure on the floor. While he was evidently still alive, she still had no way of knowing how bad his head injury was. Clearly, he'd fallen whilst in his cups and hit his head on something. She knew little about head wounds but was naturally aware they could be extremely serious.

She bent down again and moved his head to the side exposing a sticky mass of red on the side of his head. With all the blood, there was no way of knowing how bad it was. Getting to her feet, she ran into the small kitchen and breathed a sigh of relief to find some water, still barely warm hanging over the embers of the fire.

Taking the kettle back into the sitting room, she extracted a small rag from her basket and dipped it in the tepid liquid. Then she set about cleaning the affected area. After five minutes of careful dabbing, she sat back on her heels, relief making her giddy. The exposed injury looked to be little more than a flesh wound, albeit a nasty one. Mayhap it would need some stitches, but she could safely leave that to Malcolm when he finally arrived.

The question remained, what should she do next? She certainly couldn't get him upstairs to his bed, and it wouldn't be seemly for her to do so anyway. She frowned. In truth, of course, she shouldn't even be here with him now, which in retrospect was something she'd never even considered earlier in her determination to see him again. She looked down at his slumbering face. He was hardly likely to ravish her in his current state. She tried to ignore the strange tingling sensation that travelled from her throat right down to her legs at the thought. What the deuce was wrong with her? She was getting as bad as Temperance.

A pillow. That's what she could do. Make him more comfortable by placing a pillow underneath his head. Climbing to her feet, she picked up a cushion from the fireside chair and turned back to her patient, only to find him staring at her bemusedly.

'Wha…' he mumbled, trying to lift his head.

'Stop,' she yelled, only to flinch as he put his hand up to his head with a groan. 'Sorry,' she continued in a much softer tone, kneeling beside him again. 'Please don't try to move. I think you fell and hit the back of your head.' She held up the pillow as he continued to stare at her blankly. 'I'm going to place this pillow underneath your head,' she continued after a few seconds, wondering if the accident could possibly have left him slightly addled.

Carefully, she leaned over him and lifted his head towards her, the movement necessitating his face being briefly buried in her bosom. Unable to stop her face from flaming, even though he couldn't see it, she shoved the pillow underneath him and dropped his head hurriedly.

A muffled oath accompanied the sound of his head falling back against the pillow, and she winced, immediately contrite. 'Are you alright?' she questioned.

'Currently, I cannot feel my body at all, while my head feels as though it's likely to burst,' he mumbled lifting his hands to probe where it hurt the most.

'Don't touch it,' she shouted instinctively.

'God's teeth, has anyone ever informed you that your voice is some-what loud, Miss Shackleford?' he grumbled faintly.

'Indeed, Lord Northwood, but had you not imbibed so liberally rendering you entirely foxed, you would not have fallen and hit your head, and subsequently, I would not have had to shout.'

His eyes opened again, and he looked up at her groggily.

'Foxed you say?' He shook his head and winced. 'I cannot remember beyond this afternoon, but that does not mean I am disguised. It could just be the bang on the head. I'm sure you must be mistaken, madam.' He struggled to rise before giving up and falling back against the cushion with another groan.

'Are you accusing me of shamming it?' Hope responded indignantly, getting to her feet and fetching the two empty bottles of brandy. 'If so sir, I suggest you take note of these.' She waved the bottles over his head. 'I certainly did not drink them, and I suspect there is nobody else here who had the opportunity either.'

The Viscount narrowed his eyes as he stared up at the dancing bottles above his head. Fiend seize it, had he drunk two bloody bottles of brandy? He remembered sitting next to the fire earlier feeling unaccountably low and deciding that since the sun must assuredly be over the yardarm somewhere in the world, a drink would be in order - but then, nothing.

'I could not possibly have drunk both of them since this afternoon,' he muttered.

'This afternoon? Lord Northwood, it is now morning and by my esti-mation you have been lying on this floor for most of the night.'

Momentarily incredulous, Gabriel wondered if he cared but decided he didn't. He closed his eyes again, the effort of focusing on the waving bottles turning his stomach unpleasantly. Briefly, he wondered if he feigned slumber, would she simply leave him be and go away? The answer came a second later.

'Mayhap you would feel better if you were seated,' she suggested, her voice thankfully losing its waspish tone.

He opened his eyes again, and this time stared directly up at the curvaceous female figure above him, noticing for the first time her dishevelled state. Her hair was half tumbling from the confines of its pins, curling almost wantonly around her face. Her cheeks were flushed, and a fine sheen of sweat dotted her brow.

She looked as though she'd just been bedded.

Immediately, images of their bodies naked and entwined sprang into his mind. He could almost exactly picture her face, lips parted, her skin pearlized with moisture as she writhed beneath him. His cock became instantly hard. *Damn.* He swore internally, coming completely to his senses.

He realised at the same instant that there did not appear to be anyone with her. No chaperone.

'Did anyone accompany you here, Miss Shackleford?' he asked hoarsely, almost dreading the answer.

'Err … no,' she responded, her rising colour indicating she knew exactly what he was insinuating.

He groaned again, this time for different reasons. 'You need to leave immediately,' he rasped, trying again to rise.

'I most certainly will not,' she snapped, her voice instinctively going up a decibel causing him to squeeze his eyes shut and collapse back against the pillow.

'Sorry,' she mumbled. 'It's just that … well, Jimmy came to me for help, and I thought … well he thought … you were dead … so I sent him to fetch Malcolm, and I came here immediately.'

'Alone,' he interspersed wearily.

'Yes, *alone*,' she retorted. 'Should I have waited to find a suitable chaperone? I thought you *dead.*' She bellowed the last word with no apology, feeling inexplicably close to tears.

She thought he was going to argue further, but instead, he sighed. 'I need to get off this floor,' he muttered. 'I am loath to ask more of you, Miss Shackleford, since you have most assuredly gone above and beyond with regards to my welfare, but would you be so kind as to help me get up?'

'I'm not sure that would be the best thing for your head,' Hope argued in a complete about turn from her earlier suggestion.

'If others arrive and find me lying on the floor in a state of undress, it will not be the best thing for your reputation,' he returned through gritted teeth.

For the first time Hope's attention was drawn to his attire. Or lack of it. He was clad in only the flimsiest of britches which were currently unfastened, together with an untucked muslin shirt, the material so fine, it was virtually transparent. He wore no cravat, and the shirt was undone almost to his waist revealing a sculpted chest sprinkled with a smattering of black hair that trailed down to the hard planes of his stomach - and beyond...

This time her face flamed. So fiery was her colour, it rivalled that of her hair. He quirked a mocking brow at her belated realisation and held up his hand. 'If you could but assist me into a sitting position, I am sure from there I will be able to complete the process without further help.'

Not trusting herself to speak, Hope simply stepped forward and took his hand. It was hot to the touch, and she willed her heart to slow its ridiculous beating.

'On three - pull' he mumbled. 'One, two, three...' She yanked backwards as hard as she could. Unfortunately, his grasp was much stronger than hers and even as he managed to rise into a sitting position, she could feel herself overbalance. Feeling her grip waver, Gabriel immediately let go, but it was too late, with a small shriek, she fell forward, only managing to twist to the side at the last second so that she fell into his lap.

CHAPTER 12

*A*s her hands grasped his shoulders to steady herself, Hope's first thought was that it was not just his hand that was hot, then all thought fled as she turned her head and stared into his eyes.

She had never had a man stare at her with desire before. Indeed, had wondered whether she could ever inspire any man to feel anything remotely akin to passion. Looking into Gabriel's eyes, she doubted no more. His pupils were huge, and the grey surrounding them, the colour of a stormy sea. They devoured her with such longing in their depths that she caught her breath, her heart pumping wildly.

Without thinking, she shifted position, unconsciously seeking to get closer to his heated flesh. Her move was purely instinctive, and it was Gabriel's turn to catch his breath. Then, eyes glittering, he gave a muttered oath, pulled her towards him and covered her mouth with his.

His lips slanted across hers with all the hunger of a drowning man, and with a low whimper Hope yielded to his desperation, her lips parting beneath the pressure of his. Lost in a sea of sensation, she did not protest when his hand sought out her breast, his fingers expertly teasing its peak. Instead, she moaned against his mouth and strained towards him as a restless need shot down from her breast to her core. Feverishly, she curled her fingers into the hair at the nape of his neck, until … suddenly, shockingly he tore his mouth away and pushed her from him.

'We have to stop,' he ground out, his voice hoarse.

Panting, Hope shook her head blindly and pressed herself back towards him. The small, sane part of her knew he was right, but her whole body tingled from his touch. She felt more alive than she had ever been, and dear God, she did not want these feelings to end. Ever.

'Hope,' he groaned as she lifted her mouth once more to his, 'if you do not pull away now, I may be unable to help myself.' She knew he was telling the truth. She could feel the evidence of his desire in between her legs, but instead of pulling away, she shifted impatiently, causing him to throw his head back and dig his hands further into her shoulders. Panting, he closed his eyes. 'I have not touched a woman in over a year,' he continued between gritted teeth. 'You need to remove yourself *now*.'

His words penetrated her consciousness like a dash of cold water.

He had been without a woman for a year.

That was why he wanted her. That was why he'd kissed her.

Not because he found her irresistible, but because she was there.

Feeling suddenly sick, she scrambled ungainly to her feet and rushed into the kitchen. Dear God, what had she done? Hastily, she restored her clothing, smoothing down her skirt with almost violent swipes. Then she put her hand to her hair. Damn, it was almost out of its pins, and she was certain that many of those missing would be scattered on the floor around the Viscount. Fighting the urge to cry, she gathered the mass and tied it back with some string. If it was only Malcolm who arrived to help, mayhap he wouldn't notice.

But then, if she left now, mayhap she would be well on the way to the vicarage before the valet even arrived. The sudden sound of voices outside put an end to her agonising. Looking through the window, she spied Malcolm dismounting from his horse, the small anxious face of Jimmy standing waiting.

Too late to run now. Hope bit her lip, then squared her shoulders, telling herself to get a deuced backbone. She'd gotten herself into this hobble, so it was up to her to get herself out of it.

She marched back into the sitting room just as Malcolm entered through the front door. To her relief, Gabriel was now sitting in the fireside chair, both his breeches and his shirt buttoned up. She had time to notice the sheen of sweat on his forehead and the uncommon paleness of his face. If he hadn't been kissing her senseless not five minutes earlier, she would have believed him a corpse, so waxlike was his pallor.

'What bloody japes have ye been up to laddie?' asked Malcolm as he strode in. He barely cast a glance in her direction for which Hope was profoundly grateful.

'As you can see, I sustained a nasty blow to the head,' Gabriel answered faintly turning his head to the side to expose the wound.

'Indeed, you have and no doubt the two empty bottles of brandy have nought to do wi' it I suppose.' He bent forward as he spoke, and Gabriel gritted his teeth at the Scotsman's probing.

'It'll need stitching laddie, the sooner the better.' He straightened up and turned to Jimmy who was hovering in the doorway. 'Fetch some water from the well and set it over the fire.'

'It needs more firewood,' interrupted Hope. 'The fire is almost out.'

Malcolm turned to look at her for the first time, and she held her breath, expecting to see disapproval in his gaze. Instead, she saw kindness and gratitude.

'Thank ye kindly for your aid, Miss Shackleford,' he said gently, 'without your quick thinking, I suspect Lord Northwood here would be in a considerably worse state.' Hope fought the urge to laugh. She doubted that very much.

'But,' he went on, 'Jimmy and I have things in hand now. You are free to go.' She opened her mouth to object, though unsure why, but the concern in his eyes stopped her. He recognised what a precarious position she was in. She nodded stiffly, not trusting herself to say anything else without bursting into tears. Pulling on her cloak, she busied herself collecting her things.

'Jimmy, gather some firewood,' Malcolm was saying 'and build up both fires. Lord Northwood is cold to the touch and would undoubtedly benefit from the heat.'

He had definitely been hot enough earlier she thought a trifle hysterically.

Finally, picking up her basket, she bid the valet a quiet good day, but he didn't answer, taken up as he was with his patient. She spared a glance for Gabriel, but the Viscount's eyes were closed. She told herself it was for the best and headed out into the cold sunshine.

Lucifer was busy munching on some dandelions and eyed her irritably as she climbed back onto the cart. 'It's no good looking at me like that,' Hope commented, taking hold of the reins. 'We have to go, but I promise to give you something much nicer when we get home.'

Minutes later they were trotting back along the track towards the lane. Hope tried her best to avoid tormenting herself with the undeniable fact that she'd made a complete mull of the whole business, or indeed dwelling on the myriad of unexpected feelings Gabriel's kiss had provoked. Instead, she focused on the anxiety in Malcolm's eyes.

She didn't know whether to laugh or cry. Never in a thousand years could she have imagined herself in this position. What had she even been thinking when she determined to visit with an unmarried man?

Did the look Malcolm had given her mean she was now branded a fallen woman?

And if she was, would it matter? After all, given the past performances of other members of her family, what was one more?

∞∞∞∞

It had to be said that despite the Reverend's earlier protestations, he was indeed finding it challenging to go about his daily business while such an intriguing dilemma hung over their heads, and the day he was too old to investigate such havey-cavey business was the day they might as well pack him off for tea and toast with the Almighty.

In the meantime, it was deuced hard to get back into focusing on the upcoming Sunday sermon, which on this occasion predictably included ominous warnings for those indulging in murder, robbery and dishonesty with a side dose of kidnapping. The Reverend shook his head. If *that* didn't tell any listening perpetrators they'd been rumbled, he didn't know what would.

Sighing, he tucked the address back into his bible. He still had three days to tone the sermon down a little, put a little light at the end of the tunnel, so to speak. He glanced down at his fob watch. It was nearing four. At this time of year, The Red Lion would be busy with Blackmore locals who lived their lives with the rising and setting of the sun. What wasn't gossiped about at the Lion, wasn't worth knowing. Mayhap he could persuade Percy to accompany him there for a swift tankard of ale before supper.

Entirely for a spot of information gathering obviously.

Calling Freddy, he set off towards the church to fetch Percy who would undoubtedly be polishing the alter candlesticks at this time of day and pondered on the pretext he would use to persuade his curate to accompany him.

Truly, it was nonsensical how deuced difficult it was becoming to prise Percy away from his duties. Even on a good day, the pretext had to be extremely compelling. Simply ordering the curate to accompany him didn't work at all. Not if he didn't want to suffer the repercussions in the following week's sermon.

Still, at the very least, Percy served as his conscience, for which the Reverend was grateful - most of the time.

Unfortunately, it had to be said, it also had a tendency to make the curate deucedly chuckleheaded when it came to taking matters into their own hands.

On this occasion, Reverend Shackleford felt he'd come up with an excellent ruse that would make it extremely difficult for Percy to refuse. And what's more, it wasn't a complete Banbury story either which was certainly a plus in the whole *thou shalt not lie* bit of the bible.

'Are you there, Percy?' he yelled as he opened the door to the vestry. Freddy immediately slipped past his master to throw himself eagerly on the small man who was predictably on his hands and knees with a rag in one hand and a sconce in the other.

'Can I help you, Sir?' the curate asked eying the Reverend warily.

'I was thinking more about helping you, Percy lad,' was the cheerful response.

Regrettably, Augustus Shackleford's jovial demeanour did not appear to impart an answering spark of good humour as Percy sat back on his heels and regarded his superior dubiously. Sighing, the Reverend ploughed on. 'You've been on your hands and knees long enough, Percy, and now a spot of fresh air is definitely called for. Get your coat.'

'Where are we going?' was the curate's mistrustful response. The Reverend coughed and took a deep breath. 'We've got two hours before supper,' he beamed, 'so I thought a bit of a stroll was in order. Enjoy the beauty of our surroundings. Take in God's majesty and all that.'

'It's dark,' commented Percy flatly.

The Reverend ground his teeth in frustration. It was no good, he was going to have to put his hand in his pocket. 'I would very much like to buy you a tankard of ale, Percy lad,' he managed finally, 'for going beyond the call of duty … services rendered … and whatnot.'

His curate regarded him silently, and for a moment, Reverend Shackleford thought he'd overdone it. Then Percy gave a diffident smile and climbed to his feet.

'I'd like that, Sir, and … thank you.'

'That's the ticket,' responded the Reverend. 'Hurry up and put your coat on, it's cold enough to fart snowflakes out there.'

Rubbing his hands together to keep warm, he waited impatiently for Percy to return the candlestick to the alter and tidy up the vestry before donning his coat.

Naturally, Reverend Shackleford didn't mention his real purpose was to seek out information at the pub, being firmly of the opinion that it wouldn't add anything to the conversation.

∞∞∞

Hope did not simply hand Lucifer over to Seth when she returned home, but decided the horse warranted a little more tender attention due to his earlier heroics. The fact that he attempted to bite her throughout the whole of his grooming, in no way diminished her affection for the bad-tempered animal. In fact, the whole process was strangely calming aside from the occasions she wasn't quick enough to avoid his teeth.

In truth, she was also putting off going inside in the event her father had already been informed of her earlier precipitous departure and wished to know exactly what the deuce had had her galloping down the lane like the devil himself was after her.

Accordingly, she loitered in the stables for a couple of hours while Seth took advantage of the respite. All too soon however, the sun began to set, and she could no longer put off going inside. It would be dark shortly, and candles in the stable were forbidden unless there was an emergency. Sighing, she finally filled Lucifer's grain trough and gave the horse his promised apple. Then risking a swift kick, she gave him a quick pat on his rump and made her way out of the stable.

To her relief, the house was quiet, which when she thought about it, was actually a bit suspicious. There was no sign of Freddy, which meant her father was very likely out. Probably at the Red Lion if she were to guess.

While she was naturally happy about his absence, if the Reverend was going to hear about her activities anywhere, it would be at the inn. And Hope very much doubted they would get any more palatable with embellishment.

Sighing, she poked her head into the sitting room and spied her step-mother snoring softly on her favourite chaise longue. At least someone was where they were expected to be. Nodding satisfactorily to herself, she quietly closed the door and turned to go up the stairs, wondering whether she needed to send out a search party for her siblings. Mayhap if they'd been up to something, it would take precedence over her own indiscretions.

Almost optimistic that her sisters had indulged in something outrageous, Hope made her way upstairs to the small schoolroom. Pushing open the door, she was surprised to note that the room looked exactly as it had when she'd left it yesterday afternoon. Frowning, Hope stepped inside. While she hadn't expected Patience to conduct anything as demanding as an actual lesson, she had thought her sister would at least have run through the motions.

Perturbed, Hope stepped over to the window and stared outside into the darkness.

CHAPTER 13

$\mathcal{P}$redictably, the Red Lion was extremely busy. To Percy's surprise, the Reverend eschewed his favourite spot in the corner and headed instead towards the melee around the small bar.

'Evenin' Revren,' came a chorus of gruff voices, accompanied by the removal of a myriad of head gear out of respect for Blackmore's revered spiritual mentor.

'Saw summat funny earlier today, beggin yer pardon, Revren,' offered a lone voice once the greetings had died down, 'an' was thinkin' you might be wantin' to know about it.'

The Reverend beamed at the speaker as his and Percy's tankards of ale were slid across the bar. This was more like it. The Lion was guaranteed to uncover any gossip, juicy or otherwise, the very moment it transpired.

'Pray enlighten me, Bernard, I am your servant and all ears.' Reverend Shackleford requested, taking a sip of his ale.

'Well, it went like this. First off, I was out in the turnip field and spied your 'Ope driving that cart o' yours down the lane like all the bloody demons o' 'ell were after 'er.'

The Reverend frowned. *What the deuce was Hope doing gallivanting round the countryside on her own?* It was completely out of character. The one daughter he could trust to be where she should be was Hope. And even if he didn't know her whereabouts immediately, he only had to wait for her to open her mouth, and her location was usually quickly determined.

'Now, if'n that weren't the strangest thing, she had that rogue Jimmy Fowler seated up next to 'er.' Bernard paused and chuckled, secure in the knowledge that all around him were hanging on his every word. 'Poor lad looked to be about to cast up 'is account. Either that or cack 'iself.' There was a chorus of snickers as each man pictured the unfortunate boy's obvious terror.

'Is that it?' Reverend Shackleford interrupted the laughter, filled with the first stirrings of disquiet. His pint was not going down in quite the manner he'd hoped.

'Nay, I wish it were, Revren,' Bernard answered sobering up. 'Not an 'our later, your Patience walks along with three o' your youngens tagging behind 'er, just like the bloody pied piper.' He paused again but this time no one laughed, sensing he was coming to the nitty-gritty of the story.

'I asked 'er where she was goin',' Bernard continued. 'Beggin' yer pardon, Revren, but I wanted to make sure the littleun were alright.' Augustus Shackleford nodded tersely. Everyone in the village knew that Anthony, at nearly eight, followed his sisters everywhere, even to the deuced privy.

'Well,' Bernard went on, now lowering his voice conspiratorially, 'Patience tol' me they was perfectly well an' under no account was I to tell anybody I'd seen 'em.'

The man stared around him earnestly at the accusing stares of his audience. Everyone knew you never snitched … well not unless it was profitable to do so, of course.

'Crook me elbow an' wish it never comes straight,' he added to those staring at him reproachfully, 'I would o' kep' it to meself, but afore they carried on, the little lad admitted they was lookin' fer Prudence cos she'd gone to see the man who 'ad 'is 'ouse nicked.' He paused for effect, looking around at his rapt audience before continuing.

'Now I've asked around, and no one knows of any cull 'erabouts who's 'ad 'is house filched from under 'im, so I thought it best bring the whole bloody - begging yer pardon - the whole bag o' moonshine to you, yer Revrenship.'

'Did he say anything else?' the Reverend asked hoarsely.

'No sir, that 'e did not. 'Is big sister tol' the boy to stubble it and ushered 'im along quick like.'

Reverend Shackleford took a reflexive swallow of his pint while his mind endeavoured to process what he'd just been told. It was perfectly normal for his offspring to be out and about kicking up a lark during the day, but they usually turned up well before dusk lest they miss out on supper. He thought back to the vicarage as he'd left. He couldn't deny it had been ominously quiet. So, chances were, they were still out looking for Viscount Northwood. He felt a sick feeling right down in the pit of his stomach. It was left to Percy to voice the fear that was tightening his gut.

'If they make it as far as the cottage, Sir,' whispered the curate, 'one or all of them could easily have fallen in Wistman's pool in the dark.'

∞∞∞∞

Gabriel didn't think he'd ever been so relieved to be left alone. Leaning his throbbing head back against the chair, he reflected that

Malcolm was entirely too astute for his own good. It was a trait he'd forgotten the Scotsman had.

All the time he'd been stitching the wound, Malcolm had remained silent, seemingly concentrating on the task at hand, but once the injury was sealed, the look he'd given Gabriel had spoken volumes. It may have been Gabriel's imagination, of course, since even without Malcolm's unspoken censure, the Viscount felt like the biggest cad alive.

What gentleman takes advantage of a chit just out of the schoolroom? Certainly not one with even a scrap of honour. And even worse, Gabriel couldn't get the picture out of his mind.

Hope Shackleford, face flushed, lips swollen and rosy from his kisses, her hair almost entirely free and cascading over her shoulders.

It was the most erotic thing he'd ever seen, and even with the pain of his wound and the inevitable headache that went with it, he was rock hard at the mere thought.

Gabriel didn't know whether to be glad or sorry that Malcolm had not asked the question directly. That said, he was under no illusion that the Scotsman would pass on today's events to the Duke, and the inevitable demand would eventually be voiced.

How the bloody hell was he going to answer? Restless, he ran his hand through his hair, wincing as his fingers accidentally probed the wound. He felt hot and wondered if he might be running a slight fever. Malcolm had made sure that both fires were built up enough to last the night and he'd left some bread and cheese in the kitchen for Gabriel's supper.

The valet had however removed the remaining bottle of brandy after callously pouring a good third of it into his stitches. The injury smarted even now, and Gabriel suspected he smelled like a blasted brewery.

He groaned out loud. Fiend seize it, what the bloody hell was he going to do? He was in no position to take a wife. To his surprise, the thought of marrying Hope Shackleford did not come with the aversion he might have expected. Marriage was something he'd never really given much thought to, and he avoided the *ton* marriage mart like the plague, finding the whole circus distasteful in the extreme.

Naturally, he knew he would be expected to get leg shackled eventually, if only to produce an heir, but in the meantime, even in the wilds of Hampshire, there had never been a shortage of convenient females willing to warm his bed at night should he feel the need. It wasn't as if the Northwood coffers were empty, so given that he was only three years over thirty, he'd believed he had plenty of time.

Which would have been quite true if he'd not been possessed of such murderous relatives.

But then, even if Nicholas demanded Gabriel make an honest woman of his sister-in-law, he was unlikely to do so as long as there was the possibility she might end up the world's swiftest widow, or mayhap even put to bed with a shovel alongside her husband. At the very least, Gabriel guessed his friend would bide his time.

The truth was that at this point in time, Gabriel Atwood, Viscount Northwood was not a very good catch.

Sighing, Gabriel dragged himself to his feet, intending to avail himself of the bread and cheese. It was almost dark outside, and for tonight at least, he believed himself safe from Nick's wrath. Picking up a candle, he stopped and closed his eyes, feeling a sudden wave of dizziness. When he opened them again, he thought he was hallucinating. Three white faces stood staring at him in panic.

'What the deu…?' he began, only to be interrupted hysterically.

'It was all dark.'

'We didn't see it.'

'He fell in.'

'He can't swim.'

'She can't hold him up for much longer.'

'He's going to drown.'

'Then he'll haunt the pool, and we won't be able to go swimming there anymore.'

'Stop,' thundered Gabriel feeling as though his head was about to explode. He regarded the three sobbing children in front of him and belatedly recognised them as Shacklefords.

'Please, you need to help,' whispered the tallest.

Gabriel snapped out of his stupor, and ignoring the protesting throb in his head, strode quickly over to a lantern placed near the porch, lighting it with the candle he was holding. Once the flame had taken, he turned back to the terrified children. 'Stay here,' he ordered the two who looked to be the youngest. Then he turned to the taller girl. 'Can you take me there?' he asked. She nodded without speaking and darted outside into the gloom.

'Wait,' he shouted in exasperation as he followed her out. 'It'll do no deuced good if you fall in there too. Take my hand.' For a second, he thought she was simply going to run, then she stopped and held out her hand. Grasping it tightly, Gabriel took a deep breath and told her to lead on.

∞∞∞

Reverend Shackleford immediately dispatched one of those listening to the vicarage to see if the children had returned home. He told himself there was no sense in sending out a search party if the culprits were sitting in his kitchen. Unfortunately, the man returned all too soon with the bad news. Not only had the children failed to return, but now Agnes was having a possible apoplexy. 'Thunder an' turf,' he muttered, at a sudden loss as to what to do next.

'We need to send word to the Duke,' stammered Percy.

'By the time he gets there, if they're in some kind of deuced scrape, it'll be far too late.' Augustus Shackleford felt an unaccustomed stab of dread. 'We'll have to go, Percy,' he decided to the small man who was busy wringing his hands.

'Has anyone got a horse?' he shouted to the bar in general. It was a forlorn hope, the Reverend realised. Horses were generally only owned by people of means, but he thought there were mayhap one or two proud owners of a nag and even a cart dotted around the village.

'Old Miller saved that bone setter from the knacker's yard.'

'It'll take 'em the rest o' the bloody night to get to the pool on that old screw.'

Reverend Shackleford fought the uncommon urge to swear. Percy looked as though he was about to collapse.

'Father.' Hope's loud voice unexpectedly cut across the pub.

'What the deuce are you doing here?' the Reverend asked, forcing his way through the avid onlookers.

'I have Lucifer outside,' she continued breathlessly much to the excitement of bystanders. Everyone knew that the effort to get the Shackleford nag to do anything at all would at the very least be entertaining. And if the Reverend was intending to ride, well he'd definitely need a direct ear to the man upstairs…

'I can't ride that deuced animal,' spluttered Augustus Shackleford, who was clearly of the same opinion.

'Don't be ridiculous, Father,' Hope scoffed over her shoulder as she turned to go back outside. 'I have the cart.'

The rest of the pub pushed and shoved their way through the door behind them, determined not to miss a second.

Without pausing, Hope climbed up onto the waiting cart before turning back to her father and Percy who were now looking at her as if she possessed two heads.

'What are you waiting for?' she yelled, gesturing urgently as Lucifer pawed the ground snorting.

'Tare an' hounds, Hope my girl,' the Reverend puffed approvingly as he clambered up onto the bench beside her, 'a chip off the old block you are and no mistake.'

Once he was seated, he leaned down and shouted to Percy who was just about to climb up, 'Take Freddy back to the vicarage, Percy lad and get Agnes her salts. With a bit of luck, she'll have swooned by now.'

There was a wave of shudders and winces throughout the crowd with most of the onlookers muttering that the curate had definitely got the short end of the stick, but before Percy himself could argue, a villager quickly handed up an extra lantern to her father, just as Hope cracked the reins and the cart clattered off down the road, lamps bobbing wildly.

For the second time that day, Hope found herself hightailing it towards Pear Tree Cottage, but on this occasion, she had an audience which had now swelled to include most of the village.

And three men who hung back under the eaves apart while silently observing the proceedings. Not only were the strangers possessed of horses, but they wasted no time before slipping away to fetch them.

CHAPTER 14

*H*ope had been just about to retire to her room when the commotion began. Hearing her stepmother's hysterics, she quickly ran downstairs in time to see one of the villagers standing awkwardly in the doorway, wringing his hat whilst Agnes shrieked, 'Anthony,' at the top of her voice.

'What's happened?' Hope spoke directly to the stranger on the doorstep, recognising she would get no sense out of her stepmother who was now tottering around the hallway with a kerchief to her head.

'The Revren wanted to know if the chilern have come 'ome.' Hope felt a sick feeling in the pit of her stomach.

'No, they have not,' she responded briskly. 'Does my father have any idea as to where they could be?'

The man shook his head, clearly anxious to be gone. 'Ol' Bernard reckoned he seen 'em 'eading down Green Lane. Littleun said they was looking fer Prudence.'

'Prudence was missing?' Hope faltered.

'Reckoned she was lookin' fer some cull who'd 'ad 'is house nicked.'

Hope felt a sick feeling deep in the pit of her stomach. Her siblings were lost while heading to Pear Tree Cottage. Suddenly, she knew what she had to do.

'Go back to my father and inform him the children have not returned home,' she ordered. The villager hastily doffed his cap and took to his heels. Slamming the door, she turned back to look for her stepmother. There was no sign of her in the hall, and hurrying into the parlour, she found her collapsed onto the chaise longue wailing.

Reasoning there was no time to waste, and in truth Agnes was unlikely to put aside her histrionics any time soon, Hope shouted for Lily, their maid of all work, and as soon as the girl appeared, instructed her to prepare her mistress some tea. Then grabbing her cloak, she put a taper to a lantern and hurried outside to the stables.

Leaving the lamp safely outside the stable door, she waited for her eyes to become used to the gloom. Fortunately, it was a clear night, so with the moon behind her, it only took seconds to make out Lucifer in his stall. Putting on his tack was difficult in the semi darkness, but to her surprise the stallion remained still without trying to take a chunk out of her. Even more astonishing, he not only trotted willingly out into the yard, but allowed her to tether him to the cart. Shaking her head in disbelief, she quickly fetched another lamp to hang on the far side of the cart before climbing up. Picking up the reins, she reasoned that mayhap the horse was enjoying the adventure. Clearly, it was the most excitement he'd had in years.

Once out of Blackmore village, Hope slowed the cart down a little to lessen the risk of losing their lamps and finding themselves mired in a ditch somewhere.

'We cannot take the cart off the road, Father,' she said, 'so if you think the goose wits are anywhere in the vicinity of Wistman's pool, we'll have to look for them on foot.'

'I'll give 'em deuced goose wits,' muttered the Reverend peering ahead into the dark. 'If Anthony so much as wets his big toe, Agnes is likely to string me up herself.' His curt words belied the concern Hope realised he was feeling. For all their father's generally ill-tempered bluster, Hope knew that he cared about them. All of them.

'Gabriel will be able to help us,' she declared with much more confidence than she was feeling 'His head is likely to be much better since being stitched.'

'Gabriel is it now?' the Reverend commented brusquely, 'And what stitches are these?'

Hope felt as if her heart had dropped down to her knees. *Botheration.* Out of the corner of her eye, she could see her father regarding her, frowning, but she stared determinedly straight ahead. Truly, to be a good liar, one had to have an excellent memory…

∞∞∞∞

The next five minutes were the longest in Gabriel's life. He hadn't even felt this kind of fear when he lay dying in Cadiz. He even found himself praying that the girl knew where she was going - surely this was taking too bloody long. Then all of a sudden, the light reflected on something shiny.

Water.

He let go of the girl's hand and told her to remain where she was, then he ran the rest of the way waving his lantern about wildly in an effort to see something - anything.

There.

A small figure lay flat amongst the reeds. 'HERE!' The scream was filled with panic and Gabriel knew he only had seconds. Holding the lantern high, he raced towards the sobbing girl and threw himself down beside her. The head of the youngest Shackleford was only just out of the water, and the boy had clearly lost consciousness. Holding the lantern with one hand, Gabriel reached down and grabbed the boy's collar with the other. Then with a heave, he managed to lift the boy's upper body clear of the water. Quick-wittedly, the girl beside him got onto her knees and leaning forward, grabbed hold of the child's breeches. Together they finally managed to yank the boy out of the frozen pool.

'Did he swallow any water?' Gabriel barked at the shocked figure next to him.

'I ... no, I don't think so.'

'We need to get him warm as soon as possible. Take this.' He held out the lantern, and Patience Shackleford took it without arguing, which her father would have said was a first. 'Hold it high, so I can see the way back,' the Viscount grunted, taking hold of Anthony's limp body and lifting the boy to his chest.

Carefully, Gabriel made his way back to where the younger girl still stood wringing her hands. The time it took them to get back to the cottage this time seemed endless, and several times the Viscount stumbled on the uneven ground. By the time they spied the welcome lights of the small building, both girls were sobbing openly, and Gabriel felt as if his whole body was on fire.

The smallest two he'd left inside the cottage were crowded anxiously in the doorway, and he had to yell at them to get out of the way. Wordlessly, they stepped aside, and without pause, Gabriel laid the boy close to the fire.

'Go upstairs to the bedroom and fetch blankets and pillows,' he ordered anyone who was listening, then quickly began removing the child's wet clothing. To Gabriel's overwhelming relief, as he peeled off the boy's wet jacket, Anthony finally opened his eyes and started to cry. A loud clatter told him the girls were returning with the blankets, and he grabbed hold of one, then the other and wrapped the boy inside. 'You're safe now,' he murmured, placing a pillow under the boy's head.

Fortunately, Anthony's tears dried up after only a few minutes, and after looking around for a few seconds, he stared up at Gabriel and asked if there was anything to eat.

The Viscount shook his head in disbelief. Truly children were the most resilient creatures on earth.

Then, climbing to his feet, he went to share out his meagre supper.

∞∞∞∞

It seemed to take forever to reach Pear Tree Cottage, and Hope felt almost lightheaded with a combination of anxiety and weariness by the time she spied its lights.

She'd managed to deflect her father's questions about the Viscount's head wound by declaring that Jimmy Fowler had told her about Lord Northwood's accident. She'd held her breath in the silence that had followed her explanation, giving her enough time to reflect that mayhap she had more of her older sisters in her than she'd allowed herself to believe.

Swallowing, Hope concentrated on keeping Lucifer on the path towards the cottage. The closer they came, the more her fears for her siblings rose to the forefront of her mind. If Gabriel proved in no condition to help them, she and her father would simply have to search without him. Any discomfiture she felt about her earlier indiscretion had entirely paled in the face of the possibility that members of her family were in trouble.

In the event, Lucifer actually came to an abrupt stop right outside the gate to the cottage without her even having to pull on the reins. 'Tare an' hounds,' her father muttered as he hurriedly began to climb down. 'What the deuce have you done with the beast?' Hope shook her head, as nonplussed as he, then all other considerations fled as the door to the cottage was flung open.

'Father!' Two voices shouted almost in unison. To Hope's overwhelming relief, it was the twins, Charity and Chastity.

'What the deuce have you rascals been up to?' Reverend Shackleford bellowed stomping down the path towards them. 'Where the devil is Patience? Is Anthony safe? What about Pru? Are they with you?'

'We're all perfectly fine, Father, but Lord Northwood isn't. He hit his head on the fireplace.'

'Zounds, not again,' Hope muttered as she hurried over to the comatose Viscount lying next to the fire. He'd been covered with blankets and Patience was hovering over him sniffling. Anthony and Prudence were staring wide eyed at his feet.

'What happened?' Hope demanded.

'I think he became dizzy,' Patience stammered.

'Is he dead?' asked Prudence bluntly.

'No, he's not dead,' snapped Hope bending down. Staring at his sweat slick face, she recognised he was running a fever.

'What the deuce has been going on?' the Reverend quizzed, feeling as though he was losing his grip on reality. 'Was he taking liberties?' he demanded of Patience. 'Is that why you clocked him on the head?'

Patience frowned. 'Don't be ridiculous, Father, of course he wasn't taking liberties. For goodness' sake, at the very least, he had four witnesses. What do you think he is, bacon brained?'

'I thought you said Jimmy proclaimed him perfectly well, so what the devil happened?' he demanded to Hope.

'I think this is mayhap another knock on his head,' Hope responded, unable to keep the anxiety out of her voice.

'Thunder an' turf, how many deuced times has he bashed himself now? Any more bumps and he'll be rivalling Percy.' The Reverend shook his head. 'What if these knocks have sent him addled? Or at the very least befogged? If he wakes up thinking he's Julius Caesar, we could all be in the basket and no mistake.'

'What on earth are you talking about, Father?' Hope snapped, before turning back to Patience who was regarding the comatose man anxiously.

'What happened?'

'He saved Anthony from drowning,' piped up Prudence, 'which is very good 'cos I don't fancy swimming in a pool with his dead body floating next to me.' Both Patience and Hope stared incredulously at their sister.

'He wouldn't be floating,' scoffed Chastity, 'he'd be down in the weeds waiting to grab unknowing swimmers. And when they looked down into the water, they'd see his white face staring up at them while he planned their doom.'

'What's a doom?' questioned Prudence.

'*A horrible death*,' intoned Charity, doing her best doom-laden impression.

'I don't want to be down in the weeds,' wailed Anthony, 'there's nothing to eat down there.'

'Well, you'd get plenty of greens,' argued Prudence.

'What a deuced bag of moonshine,' thundered the Reverend abruptly proving to everyone just where Hope had got her loud voice from. 'Truly, I'm tempted to think you all dicked in the nob.'

'Don't be absurd, Father,' Hope stated, interrupting his tirade. 'It's simply children's imagination.'

'That's not what Willie Thatcher said,' responded Prudence matter-of-factly. 'He said…'

Before she could say exactly what it was that Willie Thatcher had alleged, she was interrupted by a loud groan. As one, they all turned to look at the Viscount who was struggling to rise. 'What the devil is all that bloody noise?' he muttered.

'Please, my lord, you must not move,' Hope murmured, pressing him back toward his makeshift bed. 'You have sustained another blow to the head.'

'And are you here to offer me further succour perchance?' responded Gabriel thickly, lifting his hand to run it through her hair. Hope froze as his fingers began pulling out the pins securing her tresses.

'Unhand her, sir,' snapped the Reverend stepping into Gabriel's view for the first time, 'lest you wish to find yourself on the end of my cutlass.'

''Tell me you didn't bring that old thing with you, Father.' Patience shook her head. 'We don't want you skewering yourself again.'

'I'll have you know I've taught many a varmint a useful lesson using that very same weapon,' was the Reverend's defensive retort.

'Like the time you nearly chopped Percy's finger off,' interrupted Chastity.

'And almost impaled the Abbot,' added Charity.

'And very nearly…'

'Enough,' shouted Augustus Shackleford and turned back to Gabriel who was staring at them all entirely bewildered.

'Lord Northwood, my daughter reliably informs me that you have developed a fever from your recent endeavours. It is that and only that which prevents me from calling you out.' He ignored the derogatory snorts behind him.

'To that end, we will remove you to your bed, there to await the arrival of Malcolm. Again.'

He looked down at Hope who was still on her knees next to the Viscount. 'You and Patience take his feet, and I'll take his shoulders. And have a care not to bang his head on the deuced bannister. He hardly needs another clout on his noddle.' Hope nodded, not daring to say anything that might make matters worse.

'You may rest assured that I am perfectly capable of taking myself to bed,' declared Gabriel stiffly from the floor. To illustrate his complete capability, he climbed to his feet and promptly wobbled dangerously towards the stone mantel.

'Tare an' deuced hounds,' muttered the Reverend. 'Here, my lord, give me your arm.' Slowly they tottered towards the narrow stairs at the back of the sitting room.

Ten minutes later, Augustus Shackleford returned looking concerned. 'How is he?' asked Patience anxiously.

The Reverend sighed and frowned, collapsing gratefully into the fireside chair. 'He appears slightly delirious if his mumblings were anything to go by.'

'Well, we cannot leave him alone,' Hope declared. 'After all, he is in this state because he helped to rescue Anthony.'

'And he stopped Anthony turning into a ghoul,' added Prudence, admiration clear in her voice.

'A what? questioned the Reverend.

'Willie Thatcher says that's what happens when you drown.'

'Fustian nonsense,' snapped Patience, 'and nobody's died.'

'Not yet,' answered Prudence darkly.

'For pity's sake Pru, will you stop with such ghastly imaginings.' Hope rounded on her sister in exasperation, then shaking her head, she turned to the Reverend. 'Father, it is clear he cannot be left. One of us must remain until we get word to Malcolm. We owe Lord Northwood that at the very least.'

Augustus Shackleford sighed, but before he could speak, Hope continued, 'I will remain to watch over his lordship while you see these five mischiefs safely home. Once there you can dispatch Seth to Blackmore to request Malcolm's urgent assistance.'

When the Reverend looked about to argue, Hope finally lost her patience. 'For goodness' sake Father, the state he's in, Lord Northwood couldn't ravish a piece of wet lettuce. My virtue is entirely safe.'

Augustus Shackleford frowned, clearly not impressed with the analogy, but when he opened his mouth to protest, he couldn't actually find anything to argue with. In truth, he was done to a cow's thumb and suspected that should he remain behind to watch over the Viscount, he would be neither use nor ornament. Indeed, he would more than likely be asleep on the bed beside the patient.

Abruptly, he nodded and climbing tiredly to his feet, waved the five younger Shacklefords towards the door. 'Come along you horrible bunch, you've kicked up enough of a lark for one night.'

'I should stay with Hope,' Patience protested, clearly feeling guilty for her part in the proceedings.

'For once, my girl, you'll remain right where I can see you,' the Reverend responded flatly, clearly leaving his wayward daughter no wriggle room. Then taking hold of her shoulder, he marched her towards the front door. Just as he was about to pull it open, Hope spoke again.

'Once the Viscount is recovered, we must look to getting him moved,' she declared vehemently. 'As of this evening, the whole village knows we are harbouring *someone*, even if they don't know exactly who or what he is. And after his performance on Christmas eve, it will be only too easy for Gabriel's enemies to put two and two together.'

The Reverend stared back at his daughter thoughtfully for a second, then giving a quick nod, he turned round to usher the children out. Within minutes, the noise of their departure had faded to a distant clopping of hooves, and Hope was finally alone.

Sighing, she collapsed into the chair and stared into the now dying flames in the fireplace. She should feed the fire before it got too low, but sudden exhaustion took hold of her, and for a few minutes, she simply sat, relishing the silence.

An unexpected noise aroused her from her stupor. Had her father returned? Mayhap Lucifer had cast a shoe. Wearily, she climbed to her feet and went towards the door. She was just about to shout, when she saw the knob begin to turn slowly. Heart in her mouth, she froze, staring as the latch clicked and the door carefully pushed open. Moments later, she stood face to face with a man she didn't recognise. He faltered, seemingly as surprised to see her as she was him, and they stared at each other for what seemed like endless seconds.

Then finally spying the pistol in his hand, she gasped, turned on her heel and ran towards the stairs.

She got as far as the bottom step before a large hand grabbed hold of her hair and yanked her backwards. There was a loud crack before blackness descended and she knew no more.

CHAPTER 15

*R*everend Shackleford found it hard to believe it was still early evening when he finally guided the horse and cart into the yard next to the vicarage. He wasted no time yelling for Seth who was likely somewhere about. At least the Reverend hoped so. He knew it was the stable lad's wont to go for a swift tankard at the Lion before heading to his bed above the stable, but hopefully, the lad had not yet finished his supper.

Fortunately, Seth was still in the kitchen and clearly acquainted with recent events, came running out quickly. Behind him was Mrs Tomlinson and Lily and lastly a very reluctant Freddy.

The front door however remained closed, the loud wailing coming from the other side of it clearly masking any noise coming from outside.

With a wince, the Reverend handed the reins to Seth, expounded the events at the cottage and gave him his instructions. Then he steered his now very subdued offspring towards the ominously closed front door.

'Mayhap we should go straight to bed, Father,' offered Chastity, clearly anxious to avoid their stepmother.

'Without any supper?' responded Charity with a frown.

'I'll starve and die a skeleton if I don't get anything to eat,' complained Prudence.

'I want my supper,' wailed Anthony.

'Fiend seize it,' muttered Patience bringing up the rear, out of her father's earshot obviously.

Just as they reached the entrance, the door was flung open, and a wild-eyed Percy appeared. Indeed, he looked as though he was about to make a run for it.

'What the deuce are you doing, Percy?' demanded the Reverend. 'Did you give Agnes her salts?'

'Don't you give me that bag of moonshine, Percy Noon,' came a screech behind him, causing the Reverend to swallow nervously, his earlier pint curdling ominously in his stomach.

'You tell me where my son is right now, or you'll wish you'd never been born.'

Percy groaned and without speaking, tossed the bottle of salts at the Reverend and disappeared out into the night.

'Thunder an' turf,' muttered Augustus Shackleford. He stared longingly after the fleeing curate, wondering for a second if he should take a leaf out of Percy's book.

But hiding in the deuced vestry wasn't going to get him out of the basket. His wife could carry on her Friday face for months if required.

Squaring his shoulders, he thrust the youngest four siblings through the door in front of him, much in the manner of a battering ram, then he coughed and called, 'Dearest, I've brought him home. Anthony is here.'

'Anthony,' screamed his mother, picking up her skirts and running towards her pride and joy. Indeed, the Reverend had never actually seen her move at such a pace and couldn't help wondering if she'd actually be able to stop. Just in case, he steered his offspring to one side.

Unfortunately, the recipient of her attention chose that moment to burst into tears and tell his mother he'd nearly drowned and been turned into some porridge.

'Ghoul,' muttered Prudence, 'not gruel.'

'Oh, my darling boy,' wept Agnes, who not only succeeded in stopping before she crashed into the front door, but actually managed to get down on her knees. If the Reverend hadn't been so concerned about how she was going to get back up again, he would have been quite impressed. He did think briefly about slipping quietly away while she fussed, but unfortunately after barely a minute of enduring her smothering, Anthony decided enough was enough, and fought his way clear of her tearful embrace, with the announcement that he was now ready for his supper.

Deciding the gallantry was clearly the way to go given that the alternative was to leave her by the front door for the rest of the evening, Augustus Shackleford stepped forward and held out his hand. 'Dearest, let me help you to your feet,' he murmured solicitously.

'Don't you dearest me, Augustus Shackleford,' his wife snapped, nevertheless grasping his proffered arm. 'If anything had happened to my darling boy, you'd have been meeting your maker minus your demned head.'

After that, there didn't seem to be anything else to say, and fortunately, Lily chose that moment to announce that dinner was served.

∞∞∞∞

Hope's first thought as she drifted back to consciousness was that she finally realised how Lord Northwood must have been feeling. Indeed, she couldn't help wondering if her head was about to fall off. Her second thought was that she felt sick, and with that, her eyes flew open, and she promptly cast up her account all over the breeches of whoever was seated behind her. For seated she was. On a horse.

'Blast and bugger your eyes,' swore a voice crudely as a pair of hands shoved her forward towards the horse's neck. With the realisation that the beast on which she sat was actually moving, Hope threw up again, now consumed with a white-hot fear. Instinctively, she began to struggle against the hands that held her, all the while looking around her wildly.

'Give me a bloody hand, will yer,' a voice ground out behind her, yanking the horse to an abrupt stop. 'If the bitch flashes 'er 'ash agin, I'll toss 'er on 'er bloody 'ead.'

Hope's vision finally cleared, and through the darkness she could just make out two more horses picking their way along the path to the right and behind. As they got closer, she recognised the man riding the first horse as the swarthy stranger from the cottage. He was holding a lead rein tethered to the horse behind.

On which, a clearly insensible Gabriel slumped forward, his body strapped to the saddle and his arms tied around the horse's neck.

Hope did her best to stifle a moan.

'Why the bloody 'ell don't we just kill 'er?' her captor was saying. 'She can't cry rope if she's pushing up bloody daisies.'

His companion drew to a halt and handed over a soiled rag. 'John said to keep 'er alive 'cos it gives us a bit o' summat extra to bargain wi' if 'is nibs tries anything.'

'Sounds a bit bloody smoky to me. Thought John was all fer cutting up a wheedle with the murderin' bastard.

'He might not be agin a bit o' toad eating, but he ain't willing to risk the mornin' drop fer nobody, and I ain't either.'

'But we don't even know if we've got the right bloody cove,' Hope's captor argued, dabbing half-heartedly at the dark patches of vomit liberally decorating his breeches.

The other man gave a snort. 'No worries on that score. We've got the right one. They look like two bloody peas in a pod. John only 'ad to take one look at 'im afore he was hightailing it back to 'is nibs to pass on the good news.' He grimaced in distaste at his companion's soiled clothes.

'Alright for you, ain't it,' Hope's captor snarled, throwing the soiled rag back at his companion. 'If old Tam hadn't 'ave fell off 'is nag and broke his bloody neck on Christmas Day, you'd be 'aving Atwood kissin' the back o' your bloody neck. As it is, you ain't got to share.'

'T'ain't my fault you're the skinny runt,' was all his companion sniggered, before clicking his heels against his horse's flank to set the beast moving again.

Hope fought against despair as the hours wore on. She had no idea of the identity of their abductors, but she was almost certain who was behind it. Did that mean they were being taken to Gabriel's old home in Hampshire? If so, they clearly had a long way to go, and despite the lack of moonlight, their kidnappers showed no sign of stopping which gave weight to her belief. They were travelling across unfamiliar countryside, and since coming round, she hadn't seen so much as a rundown cottage. To top it all, she couldn't rid herself of the fear that Gabriel was already dead.

She could see no sign of life in his shadowy form, and thinking back to his sweat-soaked face back at the cottage, she was very much afraid that he may have succumbed to his fever. What would become of her if the journey proved too much for the Viscount's weakened body?

Her thoughts went round and round in between repeated dozes - as soon as her throbbing head lolled forward, she would wake with a start, and the lurid thoughts began again. As the night wore on, despite being covered in a filthy blanket, the cold slowly began to creep into her bones until her teeth were chattering helplessly, and her body was racked by shivers.

Abruptly, just when she thought she couldn't go on any longer, the shadowy figure in front spoke. 'There's a shed up a ways. Used it before. I could do wi' takin' a piss an' the 'orses need to rest a spell. Good a place as any to stop.'

She felt rather than heard her captor's agreement, and five minutes later, she was lifted off the horse and dumped unceremoniously onto the ground. As the feeling began to come back into her legs, she first felt a tingling, then shooting pains which caused her to groan out loud. As soon as she could get her legs to bear her weight, she staggered over to Gabriel who was lying unmoving on his back.

Crouching down she put her face close to his. Was he still alive? It was almost impossible to tell in the near darkness. Fighting back a sob, she laid her hand against his forehead. Still warm, but no longer boiling hot. It seemed the cold might have done some good after all.

'He needs some shelter,' she blurted to the shadowy figures who to her revulsion were making no effort to conceal their ablutions.

'Best get him in the 'ut then,' was the careless response. Squeezing her eyes shut for a moment and fighting the urge to scream, Hope got to her feet and went to pull open the door to the abandoned building. The interior was completely black, and to her horror, she could hear the faint squeaking of rats. She looked back at her captors who were even now refastening their breeches. Disgusted, she looked away as a sudden sick fear swept through her body. If they decided to violate her, she would be unable to stop them. Panting to keep the panic away, she went back to the Viscount. Clearly, he was in no state to stop the louts from doing whatever they wished, but nevertheless, she gained comfort from his presence.

Taking a deep breath, she slipped her hands underneath his shoulders and began dragging him towards the shelter. He must have regained consciousness at least in part, as he mumbled something and pushed his heels into the ground, instinctively aiding her.

Minutes later, they were out of sight inside the shack, and Hope collapsed, wheezing. Looking down at Gabriel beside her, she was relieved to see his eyes were open.

'What happened?' he rasped. Hope gave a half laugh, half sob as she shoved her hair away from her face with dirty fingers. Where the devil to start? Then she shook her head. Now was not the time. He needed to rest. And so did she, if they were to stand any chance of escaping with their lives.

Shrugging off the blanket, she laid it over the both of them and huddled into Gabriel's still warm body. She felt him move slightly, and suddenly an arm slipped underneath her head to pull her closer. For a moment, she resisted, then with a weary sigh, relaxed and allowed her head to rest against his chest. Her head still hurt, but the pain had finally faded to a dull ache, and despite her fear of the despicable curs who'd abducted them, she found herself quickly falling asleep.

∞∞∞

On listening to Seth's garbled account of what had transpired at the Red Lion and after, Malcolm immediately went to inform Nicholas.

The Duke was playing with his son in the small drawing room watched over by his wife who was laughing at the little boy's antics. The scene was idyllic, and the valet was beyond reluctant to destroy his master's hard-won peace, wondering if he was overreacting.

His grace's reaction to the brief retelling of the stable hand's story, however, gave Malcolm the conviction that he was doing the right thing in bringing the tale to the Duke's ear.

'Do you think there was a chance the conversation at the Lion was overheard by someone unsavoury?' Nicholas asked, handing Peter over to his nanny.

'Aye, the pub was crowded, so if some blackguard was watching Blackmore, we canna discount the possibility.'

Nicholas sighed and told the Scotsman to instruct the head groomsman to ready two horses. Then he looked over at Grace. 'My love, while I have a great deal of fondness for your family, it has to be said that their meddling does, on occasion, cause slight frustration.'

His wife snorted. '*Slight* frustration? Darling, you are being remarkably restrained. In retrospect, it would possibly have been better if we'd installed Lord Northwood somewhere in deuced Scotland.'

Climbing to his feet, Nicholas chuckled. 'It may yet prove to be the best way forward.'

'I will inform Mrs Tenner to hold back dinner until you return.' Grace lifted her face up for his kiss then watched as he strode swiftly to the door. Underneath her light-hearted banter, her heart thudded uneasily. She could only hope the sick feeling in the pit of her stomach was the result of the fish she'd eaten at lunch.

A mere half an hour later, Nicholas and Malcolm were dismounting outside Pear Tree Cottage after riding their horses through the gate and right up to the front door. Leaving their mounts loose to nibble at the sparce greenery, they knocked and shouted Hope's name but received only silence. Taking a deep breath, the Duke pushed open the door, and they both went inside.

It did not take long to ascertain the downstairs at least was deserted. Swearing, the valet quickly climbed the stairs, only to return seconds later with the news that the bedroom too was empty. 'There are signs that the Viscount was dragged from his bed,'

Malcolm declared grimly. 'Do we have any idea what happened to Hope?'

Nicholas shook his head, glancing around the room. 'It's clear she was here when whoever it was entered the cottage as her cloak is pooled on the floor.' Malcolm nodded. 'It looks as if the lass was wearing it when the bastards came in. Mayhap she dropped it in her panic.'

'Or perhaps they removed it for her,' bit out Nicholas unable to keep his anger at bay any longer. 'Did she run? And if so, where to?' He strode towards the staircase, and on the bottom step he spied a hairpin. Bending down to pick it up, he held it to the candlelight. 'It certainly belonged to a woman. Naturally, we can't prove it was Hope's, but it's possible that she intended to run up the stairs to Lord Northwood.'

'She didn'a get there,' commented Malcolm through gritted teeth. Bending down he retrieved a small clump of copper-coloured hair. 'I think she tried to reach Gabriel, but the wretches used her hair to drag her back down the stairs.'

'We need to look outside,' Nicholas growled and striding quickly back to the front door, he retrieved their lanterns and stepped outside. 'I'll head to the left, while you search to the right,' he ordered handing one of the lamps to his valet.

Minutes later, to the relief of both men, they had found nothing. Certainly nothing to suggest Hope had been murdered or left for dead.

'The time span between Augustus leaving and us arriving is at most two hours,' declared the Duke. 'I doubt the kidnappers would have had time to kill and bury a body, not if they believed themselves likely to get caught.' He watched as Malcolm held up his lamp and walked towards the gate, studying the ground intently.

'There are too many prints here on the path to give us any clue,' the valet mused, as he opened the gate. Once outside the cottage garden he wandered backwards and forwards, finally bending down to examine the earth.

'What do you see?' he demanded as Nicholas came through the gate to join him. There was a pause as the Duke studied the ground. 'Horses,' he murmured, 'and more than one.'

'Aye. They were tethered to the fence here,' guessed the Scotsman. 'Those tracks further away belong to the Reverend's horse and cart, but these do not. I estimate there were four mounts.' He looked over at Nicholas. 'My guess is they took both of them. They would not have left Hope here to perchance identify them, that way they'd be sure to swing if caught.'

Nicholas nodded in agreement and looked out into the darkness.

'They cannot have been on the road for more than a couple of hours at the most,' he predicted. 'They are travelling in the dark so will be forced to take extra care lest they cripple one or more of their mounts. We could catch them easily.'

'But we dinna have any idea which way they are headed,' groaned Malcolm. 'We canna go wandering around in the pitch black ourselves for the same reasons. And any tracks they leave will be nigh on impossible to discern without daylight.'

Nicholas ran his hand through his hair in frustration. His valet was right. It would be the height of foolishness to chase after such dangerous ruffians in the middle of the night. He forced back his fury at the delay and the underlying fear that waiting might cost Hope and Gabriel their lives. Then he had a sudden thought.

'As you say, we are not certain where they are headed, but we can guess. If they are taking Gabriel to his cousin, it will either be North-wood Court or his father's manor which I think is close to Portsmouth. Once there, Atwood will be able to do as he wishes.'

'So why haven't the bastards killed him already then?' demanded Malcolm.

'Mayhap they are not sure they have the right man,' speculated Nicholas, 'or perhaps they do not wish to add murder to their crimes. After all, it's likely they acted quickly once they found out Northwood was still alive. I don't think they waited for instructions from their employer.'

'You think they are acting on their own?' queried Malcolm with a frown.

'I think it likely they've been instructed to report back any smoky business, but mayhap they believe they will receive a much better pay day if they return with the Viscount himself.'

The valet nodded thoughtfully, following the Duke back through the gate into the garden. After blowing out the remaining candles inside the cottage and shutting the front door, Nicholas whistled to his mount. 'We'll get on the road at first light,' he decided, swiftly mounting his horse then waiting impatiently for Malcolm to do the same.

'We can no longer wait on any evidence Roan might uncover incriminating Admiral Atwood,' he threw back over his shoulder, as he guided his mount back through the gate. 'The enemy has now brought the game to us Malcolm, and we have no choice but to play it through to the end.

CHAPTER 16

$\mathcal{H}$ope was woken a few hours later by furtive movement inside the hut. For a few brief seconds she lay there disorientated, until her memories flooded back and instinctively, she tried to move, only to be gripped forcefully by the arm around her shoulder. 'Hold still,' murmured the Viscount against her hair. His voice was the barest whisper, but she did as he asked, feigning sleep as their captors evidently readied themselves to sleep.

'I wouldn't mind givin' the bitch a good prigging afore we 'and 'er over.' Hope swallowed a moan at the obscene comment and Gabriel's arm tightened.

'Well, ye'd need to have a good bloody dunking aforeand, stinking o' puke like ye do,' his companion sniggered. 'I think I'll wait an' buy me a nice meaty piece who knows just 'ow to give a good quiffin. Scrawny chit like 'er won't last through one tuppin'.'

There was more movement as the men obviously tried to get comfortable. 'Ere, give me a bit more o' that blanket,' came a sleepy complaint after a few minutes, but his only answer was a loud snore.

About half an hour later, Gabriel finally moved, carefully inching his arm from underneath Hope's shoulder. A low hiss as he flexed his fingers told her how much pain he'd been in. 'How are you feeling?' she whispered lifting her head, trying to see his face.

The Viscount put his finger to his lips and glanced back at their sleeping abductors. Then he lifted his head and whispered directly in her ear. 'Turn over onto your right side,' he requested. 'I will follow suit. It's the simplest way for us to talk without being overheard.'

Heart slamming against her ribs, Hope did as he asked, and immediately Gabriel turned over and pressed the front of his body against the back of hers. The intimacy of the action had her stifling a gasp, especially when his left arm curled around her middle. 'Turn your head slightly towards me,' he mouthed against her ear. Again, she did as he bade and was rewarded by the softest of kisses against her ear lobe. Indeed, she thought mayhap she'd imagined it until he placed another one, even softer above her ear. 'Forgive me for dragging you into this mess,' he breathed with a sigh.

'I think they are working for your cousin,' Hope whispered back half hoping he would kiss her again. What the devil was wrong with her, thinking about kissing at a time like this?

'How are we going to get away,' she continued trying to ignore the feeling of his mouth so close to her ear.

Gabriel heard her speak but was finding it increasingly difficult to concentrate on her words. What the bloody hell had possessed him to suggest they move into this position? And what kind of goat was he that he was actually dwelling on the shape of her in his arms? But no matter how tempting an armful she was, he didn't believe himself capable of getting up off the floor unaided, let alone anything further.

Sighing, he closed his eyes and let his head rest against the hard ground. He could still smell the underlying lavender scent of her hair. 'I do not think I am recovered enough to effect an escape,' he murmured to the back of her head. 'I fear if I attempt any heroics, I will get us both killed.' He felt her nod and hated himself for putting her in such an untenable situation. She had only him for protection, and in all honesty, in his current weakness, he suspected he might be worse than useless.

That said, he would die before he allowed either of the bastards to lay a hand on her person.

They lay in silence for a few moments, and gradually, he became aware that her body was shaking, and with a sinking heart realised she was crying though trying very hard to stifle it.

'Please don't weep,' he whispered huskily, raising his head to murmur directly in her ear again. 'I will not allow any harm to come to you, I swear. My guess is they are taking us to Northwood Court. The journey there is at least two or three days, and I will bide my time and gather my strength. As soon as I am well enough, we will escape from these varmints.' Unable to help himself, he pressed another light kiss on the top of her ear.

Again, he felt her nod, and slowly, her silent sniffles began to lessen, until eventually, her breathing deepened, and he realised she was asleep.

Gabriel tightened his arm around her. Never had he experienced such an array of emotions for a woman. He felt humbled that she so willingly put her trust in him, fiercely protective as though she belonged only to him and desperately afraid he would let her down.

He didn't know when it had happened, but Hope Shackleford had succeeded in getting under his skin in a manner no other female had ever done, and he was achingly aware that when the time came, he would find it almost unbearable to let her go. But let her go he must if they were to stand even the remotest chance of a future together.

For himself, Gabriel knew he had to see this through. He could no longer hide like a coward away from Henry Atwood. Whatever happened, he was determined to see an end to it.

∞∞∞

The Duke of Blackmore was reluctant to send word to Reverend Shackleford concerning the kidnapping of his daughter, mostly because the clergyman could not be trusted not to set off at half cock with some wild idea of rescuing Hope and subsequently getting everybody killed. The fact that the Reverend had succeeded in the past where others had failed, did not sway him in the least. Augustus Shackleford was entirely a loose cannon, and on this occasion, Nicholas was determined he would remain out of it.

That said, his grace did not, in all conscience, feel as though he could simply lie to a man of the cloth, a conundrum he expressed to Grace when he grimly apprised her of what he and Malcolm believed had happened.

They were seated in the Duke's study along with the valet and the remains of their dinner which Mrs Tenner had delivered on a tray. Despite her concern for her sister, Grace did not express the same reluctance to tell her father a plumper. 'You are perfectly correct, Nicholas,' she declared, 'we simply cannot risk my father taking matters in his own hands.'

With that, she wrote a short note assuring the Reverend that Hope was, in fact, in good health and would be home very soon. 'It's not a complete Banbury story,' she argued when her husband read it dubiously. 'We are indeed optimistic that Hope remains in good health and will be reunited with her family directly.'

Nicholas knew his wife's bullish stance was entirely to cover up her internal fear that something dreadful had happened to her sister, that they would never see Hope again. Thus, he reluctantly agreed to send the note, and ten minutes later a grumbling Jimmy was called upon and despatched to deliver it.

Aside from the three of them, no one knew of Gabriel and Hope's abduction. 'At first light, I will send word to Roan,' the Duke decided.

'I do not know whether there is anything he can do, and indeed, by the time he receives the news, Hope and Viscount Northwood...' he paused and ran his hand through his hair despairingly.

'...they may well have already been rescued, I agree,' interrupted Grace determinedly, forcing back her tears. Nicholas laid his hand comfortingly over his wife's as Malcolm spoke.

'I recommend we request Roan's assistance as soon as he is able,' the Scotsman suggested sombrely. 'The laddie's known to be good in a fight, and growing up on the streets has given him an edge that softies like yerself may not have.' Nicholas snorted at his valet's assessment of his prowess but agreed, nonetheless. 'If our messenger rides continuously, only stopping to change horses, he could be in London in as little as twenty-four hours,' the Duke concluded. 'In fact...' he stopped and got to his feet. 'As much as I am loath to do so, I believe a calamity such as this warrants getting someone out of their bed. If our man leaves within the hour, mayhap he will reach Town before the end of tomorrow.'

'It's a tall order and no mistake,' grimaced Malcolm, 'but I think it worth a try. You'll need to select your best horseman.'

Nicholas nodded and went to his desk. Then paused. 'I'll send word to Ravenstone also,' he announced. 'Adam is no dandy, and I am certain he will offer his aid. Indeed, there's a chance he could reach Northwood Court before we do.' He sat down and picked up his quill.

'I'll ask both of them to meet us on the east side of Gabriel's Estate. The grounds are extensive I believe and should provide ample coverage.' He paused with a brief scowl. 'God help us though if we've presumed the wrong destination.'

∞∞∞∞

There was no doubt in Augustus Shackleford's mind that something smoky was afoot. Grace's letter was tantamount to a screaming admission that something was amiss, and reading it, he couldn't help but think his children actually believed him beef witted...

After dinner, he'd taken himself off to his study. Indeed, he was fagged to death after all the excitement and had decided that ringing a peal over Hope's head as soon as she returned would not do his liver any good, so the lecture would simply have to wait until the morrow. Instead, he decided a stiff brandy would be just the thing to get himself in order. Percy was naturally nowhere to be seen. The curate had not appeared for dinner, and the Reverend had instructed Lily to take some bread and cheese over to the vestry before she retired.

Freddy was snoring by the fire, now in much better spirits after a large helping of Mrs Tomlinson's bread and butter pudding, and all in all, Reverend Shackleford had believed the commotion over and done with.

Truly, he should have known better.

Around nine o'clock, the doorbell rang. Frowning, the Reverend heaved himself to his feet, stepping over Freddy as he headed to the door. The foxhound didn't even twitch. 'Some guard dog you are,' he muttered to himself. Ten minutes later, after despatching the Duke's messenger with a flea in the impertinent little varmint's ear, he was back seated by the fire and his previous serenity had entirely disappeared up the chimney.

'Thunder an' turf,' he muttered to himself. Something had happened to Hope, he could feel it in his water. Grace could deliver him all the faradiddles she liked; Augustus Shackleford knew his offspring.

In truth, though they might all vehemently deny it, his children all thought like he did. Act first, think later. He hated to admit it, but that was why they were in this deuced hobble in the first place.

Sighing, he looked down at the letter again. Clearly, he should leave the problem to Nicholas. He was entirely certain the Duke had everything under control.

Well, mayhap not *entirely*. But it was *most likely* his grace knew exactly what to do.

Well, mayhap not *exactly* what to do.

Devil take it, this called for another brandy.

∞∞∞

At first light, Gabriel was woken to a hard kick in his back. 'Time to get moving.' Wincing at the sudden flare of pain in his ribs, the Viscount eased away from Hope who was still sleeping. Closing his eyes, he gritted his teeth and pushed himself up to a sitting position. He still felt wretchedly unsteady but realised the thudding in his head was gone. Glancing over at his companion, he wished with all his heart that he could let her sleep, but he knew if he didn't wake her, their kidnappers would. Before he could touch her however, Hope stirred, brought to waking with the sudden loss of Gabriel's body heat.

Suddenly terrified he'd left her, she came wide awake and sat up with a gasp, only to groan as every muscle in her body protested against the abrupt movement.

Gabriel put out his hand to touch her shoulder reassuringly. 'It seems we are to continue our journey. If you wish to see to your needs, I will stand watch to ensure our captors cannot observe.'

Confound it, now he'd mentioned it, Hope realised her bladder was uncomfortably full. If she tried to hold it much longer, she would simply end up embarrassing herself.

'May I have your word that you will not *observe* either sir?' she commented tartly, climbing to her feet with a grimace.

The Viscount raised his eyebrows. 'Whatever you think of me, Miss Shackleford, I am first and foremost a gentleman, and as such, I would not dream of witnessing your personal activities.' His voice was stiff, and it took a great deal of effort to reject the ungentlemanly thoughts of Hope baring her legs. Not to mention the distinctly ungentlemanly position they had slept in for the last few hours. Coughing to cover his awkwardness, Gabriel climbed painfully to his feet, swallowing a groan as he did so. God's teeth he felt as weak as a kitten. Taking a deep breath, he indicated that Hope should remain behind him and stepped outside the shed.

'Both the lady and I wish to attend to our needs,' he commented coldly. 'We will be but a moment.'

In the cold light of day, their captors truly looked a slovenly pair. Clearly, neither had seen a bucket of water in a very long time, and the clothes they wore were threadbare at best. It was easy to see why they had taken such risks. Undoubtedly, neither had sixpence to scratch with. As he guided his companion around to the back of the shed, he wondered whether they were from the village and asked Hope as much while he stood with his back to her.

'I do not think so,' she murmured. Her words were breathless and accompanied by a rustle of skirts that had Gabriel's imagination running overtime. Gritting his teeth, he stared resolutely ahead.

'I don't think I've seen them before at any rate. And don't forget, we were accosted on the way to Ravenstone.' She hesitated, and Gabriel imagined her frowning. 'The faces of the men who waylaid our carriage were covered apart from their leader, and neither of these two gallows birds is he.'

Another rustle of her skirts interrupted her speculation. 'In any event,' she continued eventually, 'it's my belief your cousin has long suspected you alive.' There was another pause, then, 'You may turn round now, I am finished.'

Her face was flaming as he twisted round, but the sudden insistence in his own bladder, put a halt to further carnal thoughts. 'If you would be so kind as to turn around,' he commented drily when she remained simply staring at him.

'Oh,' she gasped, her face now the colour of a ripe tomato. Then, squeezing her eyes shut in an entirely superfluous gesture, she hurriedly faced the opposite direction.

'Bloody hell, how long does it take a nob to 'ave a piss,' shouted one of their kidnappers crudely. 'If yer not back 'ere in five seconds, I'll come round there and fetch yer.'

Swallowing his anger with effort, Gabriel swiftly fastened up his breeches. Now was not the time for a confrontation, but how he longed to plant the bastard a facer he'd never forget.

Ten minutes later, they were back on the path. Gabriel was no longer secured to his saddle, but his hands were tied together behind his back which made riding extremely difficult. Even then their kidnappers clearly believed him capable of escaping his bonds and warned him that one wrong movement on his part would see his companion's throat cut. Their conviction in his ability to escape might have been flattering if not for the desperate look Hope cast him, her face white with fear. That and the fact that he was actually incapable of even moving his fingers.

Grinding his teeth, he glared at their captors backs as the horses broke into a slow canter and promised himself that he'd see the bastards cropped before this was all over.

CHAPTER 17

*R*everend Shackleford was entirely convinced he'd not closed his eyes once during the night, and by first light he was dragging a bewildered Freddy out of his warm bed and tethering Lucifer yet again to the cart. To say the stallion was not happy was an understatement and by the time he was climbing onto the seat, the Reverend was not absolutely sure if he still possessed ten fingers. Clicking the reins, he gritted his teeth when the horse refused to move. Clearly, Lucifer's unexpected compliance the day before had been down to Hope's presence.

Uncharacteristically, Augustus Shackleford felt a lump come into his throat at the thought of what could have happened to her and felt a renewed determination to get the truth out of Grace. He had no doubt that Nicholas would already be abroad so the Duchess would be unable to hide behind her husband's coattails.

In the meantime, he had to somehow persuade the stallion to deuced well move. Sighing, he climbed down and went to fetch a bag of apples.

An hour later the Reverend was red faced, sweating and had run out of apples. In fact, the devilish beast had eaten so much fruit, he very much feared that Seth would be mucking out the stable hourly for the next week. That's if he actually delivered the bad-tempered beast back to his stable. At this point in time, Reverend Shackleford was entirely tempted to hand him over to the knacker's yard instead. He glanced enviously back at Freddy who had long since given up running beside the cart and was now curled up in a ball, snoring.

Fortunately for Lucifer, though the stallion was blissfully unaware of his close call, Blackmore's gates appeared round the corner and given that the sun, such as it was, was well and truly up, the Reverend trusted that Grace would be unable to come up with an excuse not to see him. Certainly not on such short notice anyway.

Tying the horse to a convenient bush at the bottom of the steps, Augustus Shackleford was determined to waste no more time and puffed and panted his way up to the front door as quickly as he was able.

However, it was another half an hour before Grace arrived in the small drawing room where the Duke's butler Huntley had placed him and more reluctantly, Freddy, who'd refused to remain outside in the cart. By the time the Duchess arrived, the Reverend was in no mood to be courteous. Clambering to his feet, he began the conversation with, 'And don't think you're going to wheedle your way out of this one my girl. I am entirely certain your note was a complete Banbury story, and it simply won't do.' Then drawing himself up, he puffed out his chest and bellowed, 'Indeed, I *insist* you enlighten me this very second as to what the devil has happened to your deuced sister.'

'Oh, for goodness' sake, stubble it father,' was Grace's mild retort, entirely taking the wind out of his sails. 'Of course, I knew you wouldn't fall for such a plumper. I've been expecting you since dawn.'

∞∞∞∞

They rode with only brief stops for most of the day. During that time, Gabriel had no opportunity to speak with Hope, and on the few occasions he was freed to take care of his needs, she remained firmly in the grip of one or the other of their abductors. They had been thrown a hard chunk of stale bread to break their fast, together with a few sips of brackish water, but that had been hours ago, and Gabriel was very concerned as he regarded Hope's drawn weary face. She wasn't accustomed to hardship such as this. He was undoubtedly faring better due to his misadventures in Spain.

As dusk began to fall, to his relief, their captors finally decided to stop for the night. This time however, there was no hut in which to shelter, and Hope's pinched face and persistent shivering spoke of someone nearing the end of their endurance. Somehow, he had to get her away from these bloody miscreants.

Seated on the ground, he looked around him. At first, he thought it unfamiliar, but the more he studied the land, the more convinced he became that they were near to Northwood Court. If he was correct, there was a village just over the hill, back the way they'd come. It would take a mere pair of hours to walk there. He glanced over at a silent Hope, seated across the clearing. She was staring dully at the ground. Did she have the stamina for such a hike? Mayhap after a few hours sleep. He decided to take a chance.

'As you can see gentlemen, my companion is suffering severely from the cold. If you would allow her to sit next to me, our proximity will engender some warmth into her body.' He gritted his teeth at the expected lewd response and wasn't disappointed.

'I got more 'n you'll ever 'ave to warm the bitch's bones,' leered one, while the other chuckled and spoke directly to Hope. 'Come an' cuddle up wi us darlin', we'll keep yer nice and cosy.'

'If you wish to use her as extra bargaining power with my cousin,' Gabriel countered icily, 'you would do well to ensure she does not contract a fever. A dead hostage is no use at all and may well land you in deeper hot water.' He paused for a second before adding, 'As will rape.'

Gabriel knew he was taking a risk by baiting them so, but he had to convince them to allow Hope to share his body heat. He recognised she was on the verge of collapse. 'My hands are tied behind my back, for pity's sake,' he bit out when they failed to move. 'You can tie us both to that deuced tree if you wish, but if you do not allow her to share my warmth, I believe she will die this night.' Hope looked up at the word die, and for a second, the indifference in her expression sent chills shooting down his body.

Fortunately, a few seconds later, one of them shrugged, and going over to Hope pulled her roughly to her feet. He tied her hands in front of her, then all but dragged her over to where Gabriel was seated. 'Any 'avey cavey business, and I'll bloody finish her meself,' he snapped, throwing her to the ground. Almost instinctively, Hope shifted towards the Viscount, seeking the meagre warmth of his body. A few seconds later, the second rogue came over and threw some more bread at them. It was so hard, the pieces bounced off Gabriel's chest and landed in the mud at his feet. 'Don't eat it all at once,' their captor sniggered.

Biting back a scathing response, Gabriel leaned towards Hope who hadn't shown any reaction to their paltry meal. 'Can you reach it?' he asked gently nodding towards the now filthy hunks of bread. At the sound of his voice, she looked over at him. 'We both need to eat, Miss Shackleford. It's hardly the finest fare, but at this stage anything in our bellies is better than nothing.'

She regarded the bread silently for a second, then bent forward and gathered up both pieces in her cupped hands. Turning back to Gabriel, she held out her hands to him. 'Dinner is served, my lord,' she whispered drily, 'and I think, given the circumstances, you may now call me Hope.'

At her words, Gabriel felt a surge of relief so strong, he almost groaned. Indeed, when it was followed by an even stronger upwelling of affection, he had to stifle an almost desperate need to lean forward and kiss her.

'Hope,' he amended, unable to contain an almost boyish grin. She was going to be alright. He had feared her too far into the megrims to pull herself back, but he should have realised she was made of sterner stuff.

'Food for the gods,' he murmured wryly, biting into the dry crust she held to his mouth and chewing determinedly.

'Provided they're not very hungry,' responded Hope, half-heartedly taking a bite of her own piece.

For the next few minutes, they concentrated on getting the stale bread down. Hope alternated between feeding the Viscount and herself, much to the ongoing amusement of their kidnappers who watched them sniggering.

'Pay them no heed,' Hope murmured when the Viscount's fury seemed to be getting the better of him. 'They are looking to goad you into doing something foolish. You must know that, my lord.'

'I do,' he replied ruefully, 'and Gabriel please.

Hope smiled at him. It was such a small thing, but her face seemed to light up, and his heart thudded hard inside his chest. It was the strangest feeling and one he was entirely unfamiliar with. For the first time, he knew what it meant to be in love. Because he could no longer fool himself that his feelings for Hope Shackleford were anything less. The thought of losing her filled him with an agony that was beyond physical. Her safety had become paramount. Somehow, he would help her escape from this hellish mess, and then he would free himself from his murderous uncle and cousin once and for all.

Somehow.

∞∞∞∞

'I'm actually surprised you waited until this morning, Father,' was Grace's matter-of-fact comment as the Reverend remained staring at her nonplussed. 'I had half expected to see you last night, but then I'm relieved you waited until after Nicholas had left. We'd have had the devil's own time convincing my husband to allow us to spy on Admiral Atwood's house.' She bent down to fuss the foxhound who was capering delightedly around her feet.

'I'm not surprised,' Reverend Shackleford snorted in response, 'I've never heard such a bottle-headed idea.'

'Nicholas and Malcolm are headed to Northwood Court,' Grace explained impatiently. 'They have quite rightly sent messages to Adam and Roan requesting they meet them there.'

'Why the deuce have they gone to Northwood Court?' interrupted the Reverend wondering what the devil his daughter was prattling on about.

Grace sighed. 'Truly, Father, it appears you have lost your edge. You most certainly used to be much quicker than this.' She stood to ring the bell, and for the first time, the Reverend noted she was dressed in travelling clothes. Turning back to her father she continued, 'Lord Northwood and Hope have been kidnapped by at least two hell hounds. We believe they were privy to the conversation in the Red Lion and most likely followed you and Hope when you went to Pear Tree Cottage.'

'Thunder an' turf,' groaned the Reverend. 'Then this whole deuced debacle is my fault.'

Grace shook her head in disagreement, but before she had chance to speak, the door of the drawing room opened. 'Please ready my carriage and ensure the Reverend's horse and conveyance are taken care of, Huntley. My father and I may possibly be travelling overnight and will require a cold repast and some warm blankets to take with us… Oh, and please also ensure that the two coachmen are armed and dressed warmly.' If the butler thought his mistress's request strange, he did not show it, but instead simply nodded his head and withdrew.

'It is no one's fault, Father. Your anxiety for your offspring was perfectly understandable, even commendable.' She paused and much to her father's indignation, added, 'In truth, it was also surprising.' Then ignoring the Reverend's sputtered outrage, she pulled on her gloves before continuing. 'These men were watching, and if you had not enlightened them, I am assured they would have discovered the whereabouts of Lord Northwood another way.

'Anyway, I digress. Nicholas believes that Henry Atwood is behind their abduction and their kidnappers are even now conveying the hostages to Northwood Court. Most likely Hope was simply in the wrong place at the wrong time so was dragged along as extra surety.' Her voice wobbled, and she swallowed, taking a deep breath to force back the onset of tears.

'I am inclined to agree with his assessment. Nevertheless, there is an outside chance that their destination is Rutledge Manor, the residence of Gabriel's uncle.' Back in control, she paused again, this time to ensure her father had not entirely lost the thread of the conversation. His expression of outrage reassured her.

'You and I, Father will make our way to the Admiral's home in an effort to cover the back door so to speak. If we leave within the hour, with the protection of the carriage, we can travel through the night and conceivably arrive early tomorrow morning.'

For a few seconds Reverend Shackleford was actually speechless. Truly, Grace was his daughter, more than he'd ever thought possible. He almost felt like crying. Then a sudden thought occurred to him.

'What about Percy?' he demanded.

'I have already sent a note to the vicarage informing Agnes that you'll be away from home for the next day or so and requesting Percy's attendance outside the Red Lion,' she answered, opening the door.

'Won't that inform everyone what we are doing?' protested the Reverend following her out into the hallway with Freddy at his heels.

'Naturally,' Grace retorted, 'but then, the likelihood of us departing from Blackmore stealthily are slim to none, so we may as well take advantage of the local scuttlebutt. Who knows what useful on-dits the villagers might provide to send us on our way?'

∞∞∞

Gabriel Atwood wasn't dead. Henry Atwood had always known it, and so had his father. But now they had proof. One of the men he'd had watching Blackmore had only today arrived with the news that his bastard cousin had been found holed up in some kind of hovel on Nicholas Sinclair's estate. Henry felt no elation that he'd been correct in his disbelief of Gabriel's demise, nor his assumption that the former Viscount would seek out the Duke of Blackmore. Indeed, the whole bloody business had just become infinitely more complicated.

If Gabriel was allowed to make his accusations, it would ultimately come down to his word against his cousin's. Henry had covered his tracks well with his father's help, and he doubted that Gabriel would be able to actually *prove* any allegations of parricide, even with the help of an influential member of the *ton*.

But neither Henry nor his father would ever recover from the scandal. At the very best, he would be relegated to the penniless cousin and shipped back off to sea. And the worst? His father would be stripped of his rank, and his son thrown out of the Royal Navy. Both would be considered pariahs, almost assuredly blackballed from every drawing room and club in London.

Henry Atwood's life would be over. As would Admiral Atwood's, though in truth he was unsure whether his father actually gave a rat's arse, intent as the idiot was in drinking himself into an early grave.

'*Blister it,*' he muttered to himself, feeling an imaginary noose tightening around his neck. The truth was, he'd been brought to Point Non-Plus. Gabriel Atwood had to die, and quickly. And when he finally put an end to his troublesome cousin, Henry had to ensure the bastard was buried in the deepest pit he could dig. Preferably before the Duke of Blackmore got wind of the fact that the former Viscount was no longer in hiding on his Estate.

CHAPTER 18

*G*abriel spent the whole night trying to come up with some kind of plan to effect Hope's escape. Sleep had been almost impossible anyway given that his hands remained tied behind his back. He'd been unable to even turn over, and his only consolation was the delightful feel of Hope huddled up in front of him. If he hadn't been so deuced uncomfortable, the feel of her bottom pressed intimately against him would have had much more of an effect on certain areas of his anatomy.

He could of course have asked her to lie behind him and surreptitiously untie his hands once their captors finally fell asleep. Unfortunately, the bastards were much more cautious now they were nearing their destination, and they took watches, with one of them remaining awake throughout the night. Clearly, they were not going to risk losing their prisoners at this late stage.

In the predawn darkness, Gabriel finally accepted that Hope would be forced to accompany them to Northwood Court. He had no illusions that Henry would show any mercy to his annoyingly very much alive cousin - after all, there had been none in Cadiz, and now the stakes were even higher - but the thought of what might become of Hope brought him out in a cold sweat.

He had no idea whether Henry had been apprised of an additional captive, and in truth it was a moot point. Whether he already knew they'd dragged Hope along or had that surprise to come, there was no way Henry would allow her to live, and despite their kidnappers' certainty of a large reward, Gabriel very much feared the thugs would be put to bed with a deuced mattock alongside their hostages.

The Viscount gnawed on his cracked lips, deep in thought despite the agonising pain of his arms. Mayhap he would be able to convince their abductors they were likely to receive far more blunt by ransoming their prisoners to the Duke of Blackmore? He had no notion of Nicholas's opinion concerning the payment of ransom money, but he was certain his grace would do everything in his power to ensure the safe return of his sister-in-law at least.

Did their captors even know that Hope Shackleford was a relative of the Duke's? Gabriel felt the first sliver of optimism. There was no reason for them to be aware of such a fact. As far as he could ascertain, they were not locals and had merely been watching and listening for information about Gabriel Atwood. Most likely Henry had given them as little information as possible. He suddenly started. For that matter, was his cousin even aware of the connection?

What a dolt. Gabriel struggled into a sitting position, causing Hope to whimper in her sleep and burrow further into his warmth. Unfortunately, his movement also caught the attention of their captor on watch. Undoubtedly the man had just been about to doze off.

Neither spoke, and the Viscount was quick to break eye contact. The last thing he needed was an altercation right now. The kidnapper sneered as Gabriel turned away, likely believing he had his prisoner cowed.

Hope stirred beside him, raising her head to regard him drowsily. After a couple of seconds, she groaned and shuffled herself into a sitting position. 'Is something wrong?' she murmured, trying to bring some feeling back into her locked fingers. Gabriel shook his head in the gloom, all the while staring over at their captors. The one keeping watch was clearly dozing again, but the Viscount had no doubt he would wake quickly enough if they tried to run.

Gabriel looked down at the indistinct features of his companion. Her usually vibrant hair was matted and dirty, and she had smudges across her cheeks. Her eyes were wide with worry and concern. For him.

Gabriel wanted nothing more than to take her into his arms and kiss her until the fear melted away. Instead, he bent his head and rested his forehead against hers. She did not shrink back, but simply sighed, and after a second, lifted her face, gently seeking his lips with hers. 'Thank you,' she murmured, 'for giving me the courage to carry on.'

'You would not be in this mess if it wasn't for me,' he responded, his voice low and filled with anguish.

Hope shook her head. 'My father will have informed Nicholas by now. The Duke will come for us, I am certain.'

Gabriel stilled. 'Your father knew you were in the cottage with me?' he questioned with a frown.

'Naturally,' she responded puzzled. 'He intended to call for Malcolm once he'd taken my siblings back to the vicarage.'

Gabriel frowned again, vague shadows and voices drifting into his mind. 'What siblings?' he whispered.

Hope leaned back and stared up at him silently. Then she suddenly understood. 'You don't remember rescuing Anthony do you,' she murmured.

'I...' Gabriel paused and frowned. Hazy memories of screaming and shouting and then carrying someone ... a boy, he'd been carrying a boy.

Hope placed her tied hands onto his arm. 'Gabriel, you rescued my brother from Wistman's pool. It caused the onset of an ague. My father and I had come to the cottage looking for him and my four sisters but when we arrived, we found you collapsed. I remained to watch over you while my father took all five of them home before going on to Blackmore to request Malcolm's aid.'

Gabriel shook his head and blinked. The last thing he could remember clearly was thinking how much his head hurt and whether he would be able to stomach any supper. He had supposed her simply there to watch over him and given no further thought as to whether she'd been alone. Which now he considered it, was patently ridiculous. It had been dark for pity's sake. Slowly, the memories began to come back, hazy and disjointed.

Glancing over at their captors who were beginning to stir, Gabriel looked down at Hope's concerned face. 'So, you're saying your father was planning to inform Nick of my fever?' he whispered urgently.

Hope nodded. 'And bring Malcolm back to the cottage.' She paused before adding softly, 'We were very concerned for you.'

Gabriel closed his eyes as sudden relief swamped him. Nicholas was *already* fully aware of their abduction.

Henry did not know of the connection between the Duke of Blackmore and the Shackleford family. He only knew of the former friendship between Gabriel Atwood and Nicholas Sinclair. His cousin would not be anticipating the Duke's intervention - certainly not immediately. But due to Hope's involvement, Gabriel had no doubt that Nicholas was even now putting plans in motion for a rescue.

Henry had overplayed his hand. All Gabriel had to do was keep himself and Hope alive until the Duke and the rest of the cavalry arrived.

∞∞∞∞

Nicholas and Malcolm rode hard until the light began to wane. They'd chosen to travel on a well-used thoroughfare linking Devon to Hampshire which encompassed an abundance of inns in which to shelter for the night. Consequently, they'd been able to continue until the light was almost gone before finally seeking accommodation. Although the Duke chafed at the idea of stopping for the night, Malcolm had persuaded him that it would do neither Gabriel nor Hope any good if their potential rescuers arrived at Northwood Court entirely done to a cow's thumb, or indeed with their horses pushed beyond endurance. Eventually, Nicholas had grudgingly acquiesced though he made it clear he intended to be back on the road by dawn the following day.

∞∞∞

The journey to Rutledge Manor felt as though it took forever. At least for Grace and her father. Percy slept like … well … like Grace imagined a warthog might. Freddy didn't help matters by twitching and grumbling in his doggy dreams. By the time they passed into Hampshire, both Grace and the Reverend were ready to throw the snoring curate out of the carriage.

There had been no opportunity to refine any kind of plan between them, and in the time it took them to reach their destination, the Duchess and Reverend Shackleford had surreptitiously come up with entirely dissimilar strategies.

Grace fully intended to march in through the front door and announce to the world (or at least the Admiral's wife) exactly what havey-cavey business her husband and son had been indulging in.

Reverend Shackleford on the other hand, to whom skulking was unfortunately becoming second nature, naturally assumed they would be taking a more clandestine approach - much as he and Percy had when they'd investigated Redstone House in Torquay. Freddy was simply concerned about breakfast.

Grace requested the carriage pause in a concealed clearing just outside of the modest gates to Admiral Atwood's home while they broke their fast and endeavoured to wake Percy. Once he'd finished eating, the Reverend took Freddy outside, ostensibly to see to the foxhound's needs, and Grace swiftly took the opportunity to speak with the curate alone.

'You are fully acquainted with my father's penchant for dramatic entrances, Percy,' she observed briskly, 'and I would ask that, on this occasion, you do your best to curb his more excessive inclinations. He will undoubtedly suggest I remain in the carriage whilst he scopes out the lay of the land so to speak.' She paused and sighed, feeling her heart sink as she watched her father making his enthusiastic way back to their carriage. 'I will naturally wait until you are both out of sight,' she went on hurriedly, 'then I will instruct the coachman to continue. Once inside the manor, it is my intention to bring the whole smoky business out into the open. I cannot believe the Admiral's wife is fully cognisant of her husband's treachery. If Hope and Gabriel are imprisoned in Rutledge Manor, I will simply demand to know.' She paused, then coughed and added, 'Naturally, I cannot guarantee that my err … approach will go *entirely* to plan and would ask that you and my father simply remain close by but out of sight *just in case…*'

Percy stared at her nonplussed. While he would entirely agree that the Reverend's haphazard approach to any and all hobbles they found themselves in was not always the most sensible, on this occasion, he was of the opinion that her grace's strategy was every bit as irrational. 'Shouldn't we at least wait unt…'

He was interrupted as the carriage door was thrown open to admit the Reverend's excited face, and Percy couldn't help wondering what the deuce he was doing here with two individuals he very much feared were entirely dicked in the nob…

∞∞∞∞

By dawn, they were back on the horses and on the move. An hour or so later, Gabriel recognised the landscape surrounding his ancestral home. Neither he nor Hope had been given anything more to eat, and looking over at Hope, slumping in the saddle, held up only by the ruffian seated behind her, the Viscount could only pray that what little honour Henry retained as a gentleman would persuade him to provide them both with a last meal before undoubtedly dispatching them to provide fertilizer to Northwood Court's spectacular show of roses.

And if courtesy didn't do the trick, then mayhap curiosity over Gabriel's apparent rise from the dead would get the better of his cousin.

Truly, the Viscount doubted he had the strength to put up much of a fight should Henry simply decide to do his worst without question.

Fortunately, their captors had freed his hands from behind his back, tying his wrists instead to the pommel of his saddle. He assumed they'd done so not out of concern for his well-being, but to draw less attention from any chance observers. The pain in his hands and arms had at first been excruciating, and it was all Gabriel could do not to cry out in agony. Within an hour though, the shooting pains had faded to a dull ache, and he was again able to flex his fingers. Indeed, he had spent the whole time repeating that simple movement, recognising that being able to use his fingers might be the difference between life and death.

The weather was bitterly cold with the wind whipping across the Hampshire Downs. He could barely see Hope's face, huddled as she was in her filthy blanket. Despite her earlier fortitude, he knew she was reaching the end of her strength, and the urge to kill either or both of their kidnappers became ever stronger as they approached his former home.

Then, suddenly, the gates to Northwood Court appeared, and despite his desperate fear, Gabriel felt a sense of homecoming that brought a lump to his throat. Truly, he'd been far too long away, and despite the less than idyllic circumstances, he realised he was still glad to be back.

Hope, on the other hand, barely noticed when they passed through the gates into the manicured grounds of Gabriel's ancestral home. She was instead concentrating what little remained of her energy into simply remaining in the saddle. In truth, she was a little ashamed of her lack of stamina. Gabriel had received far worse treatment than she but had born it with an impassive fortitude that even to her dulled senses had screamed of future vengeance. She could only assume her captors were thick skinned as well as greedy, but despite her dread, the Viscount's strength instilled in her the utmost faith that he would somehow extricate them both from their current predicament.

She had no idea how, and right this very second, her secondary focus, aside from the prospect of falling off, was to get something - anything - to eat. Truly her stomach believed her throat had already been cut.

She became aware that the nag she was riding had finally come to a stop. Lifting her head wearily, she couldn't contain her surprised gasp at the delightful façade of Northwood Court. While not as magnificent as Nicholas's family pile or indeed as grand as Adam's, Gabriel's home spoke of just that. A home. The honey-coloured brick oozed warmth, even in such inclement weather. However, before she had chance to gauge Gabriel's reaction to his homecoming, she was unceremoniously pulled off her horse and dumped onto her feet, causing her legs to buckle helplessly beneath her.

A dirty hand gripped her arm as she stumbled, stopping her from ending up in a heap on the ground. She was about to pull away when she realised the hand belonged to Gabriel. The Viscount made no effort to hide his concern as he studied her features, and while she knew she must look dreadful, the worry in his gaze nevertheless warmed her, and with a sudden shock, she realised this man really cared about her. Before he could say anything, however, he was abruptly shoved towards the steps.

In a daze, she allowed herself to be dragged up the staircase to the front portico and just as they reached the top, the elegant front door was pulled open from inside. Standing there regarding them with contempt and something else Hope couldn't quite define was Henry Atwood. She had no trouble recognising him. The likeness between the two cousins was remarkable. The only difference she reflected was in their eyes.

Gabriel's eyes were warm and compassionate while his cousin's regarded her much as he would an insect. She realised with a nauseous chill, that Henry Atwood's eyes were quite simply dead.

CHAPTER 19

'*R*ight Percy, now we've left Grace safe and sound in the carriage, we can get on with the plan.'

The curate sighed, wondering whether he should wait to find out what the plan actually was before throwing a rub in the way of it, or flatly refuse to take part in *whatever* scheme the Reverend had in mind before he even voiced it. Of course, there was a third option which was to cry rope on the Duchess, but somehow, doing so seemed a bit lily-livered, especially as he was actually very fond of Grace. On the other hand, throwing a rub in the way of her intention, though it would undoubtedly incite her ire, might be the responsible thing to do given that he privately considered it an entire bag of moonshine.

In truth, whatever he decided, he was in the suds.

'Tare an' hounds, are you even listening, Percy?' The Reverend's irritated voice intruded upon his musings, and the curate looked up. 'Sorry, Sir,' he answered after a moment, 'I admit I was thinking about her grace. Mayhap leaving her in the carriage was in retrospect a trifle bird-witted...' Reverend Shackleford scowled, and Percy faltered to a stop.

'Percy Noon, my affection for you endures through thick and thin,' his superior announced with an expression that clearly said he wondered why. 'That said, during our last undertaking, I had thought you finally getting a little pluck to your backbone.' He paused and sighed dramatically before continuing, 'but recent events have shown you remain every bit as chuckleheaded. If I am truly asking too much of you, you may wait in the carriage with Grace.'

When he'd finished, Reverend Shackleford regarded his curate with the heroic despondency of a man cut to the quick. When Percy simply stared back at him mutely, he clearly took the curate's silence as shamefaced acknowledgement of his shortcomings, and patting the small man on the shoulder, nodded sympathetically. 'The Almighty works through us all in his own inimitable way,' Augustus Shackleford went on in his most soothing tone, 'but every now and again, it's up to us as his earthly servants to give him a nudge in the right direction.' He smiled at Percy encouragingly.

'Right then,' he declared with another supportive whack when Percy still didn't answer, 'let's get on with it, shall we? Come along, Freddy, we're going this way…'

∞∞∞∞

Grace gave a relieved sigh once her father and Percy were out of sight, then rapping on the roof of the carriage, she indicated her wish to continue up the drive towards the main house. Her heart was beating nineteen to the dozen, and she had to constantly remind herself that she was the Duchess of Blackmore and as such, far above these varmints who sought to put an end to someone she called a friend.

When they finally came to a stop outside the front door, Grace took a deep breath as one of the coachmen leapt down to open the carriage door. Climbing down, she smiled gratefully at each of them, recognising they must both be fagged to death. Then mindful of the fact that they undoubtedly had families to consider, she gave them instructions to withdraw to a less prominent location to wait.

As the carriage rumbled away, she stared up at the silent façade, then squaring her shoulders, she lifted her skirts and made her apprehensive way to the front door. She was fully aware of the irregularity of her visit and had no intention of dissembling once in Mrs Atwood's company. She was hopeful that the woman's husband would not be present, at least at first. Although if Hope and Gabriel were imprisoned somewhere in the house, she had no doubt he would be in residence. Grace was also perfectly aware of the precariousness of her strategy, but she believed it a necessary gamble on the off chance that the Viscount and her sister had indeed been delivered to Rutledge Manor.

And lastly, despite the rapid thudding of her heart, she did not believe Admiral Atwood would dare harm a person of her standing. Before she could turn tail and run, Grace took another deep breath and pulled on the brass bell hanging next to the door. The noise clanged deep inside the house, and she bit her lip, waiting anxiously.

∞∞∞

'Truly cousin, you are becoming most tiresome. One would hope that this time when I put an end to you, you will at least do me the courtesy of remaining *dead*.' The last was said with a venom that reenforced Gabriel's belief that Henry would show no mercy, and the way his cousin was even now eying Hope made him pull at his bonds in frustrated anger.

'Henry,' he responded through gritted teeth, hoping to drag his cousin's attention away from his companion. 'You, on the other hand, are becoming tediously monotonous. Only a man with no imagination would consider cold blooded murder to be the answer to all his problems.'

Henry's eyes swung back to the Viscount and even from here, Gabriel could see them glistening with angry malice. Mayhap it was reckless to push the snake so, especially when both he and Hope were securely restrained, but he knew that now more than ever, he needed to somehow keep his cousin on the back foot.

'You would be surprised at the extent of my imagination,' was all Henry answered, clearly refusing to be drawn. His eyes turned back to Hope. 'So, is this your trollop?' he drawled stepping closer to Hope, eying her with interest. 'I must admit I was not expecting *two* captives.' He raised his eyebrows and stared over at his henchmen.

'She was there, me lord. We couldn't just leave the doxy behind,' he answered with a shrug. 'We coulda killed 'er right there, o' course, but thought you might want to ask 'er a few questions first.'

Ignoring the kidnapper's less than respectful tone, Henry nodded thoughtfully. 'So, who is she?' he demanded instead.

'Don't rightly know. She turned up at the pub and went hightailing it with the local bloody vicar to the cottage where this bastard was in hiding. By the time we found their trail and managed to get there, there was just 'er and Atwood. Summat had 'appened though, cos his 'ighness was in bed, out of it, sweating like a bloody pig.'

'So John informed me,' their employer murmured eying both men impassively.

'We dint 'ave time to do 'er, *and* dump the bleedin' body,' added his companion, 'so we brought 'er wi' us.'

'And you think she's just some village doxy who was there to offer my cousin a quick prigging. Shame he wasn't in any fit state to enjoy her.' Henry sniggered and turned to look over at Gabriel. 'Come to think of it cousin, you are a tad sickly looking. Mayhap it won't be necessary to shoot you after all.' He stepped forward and grabbed hold of Hope's chin. 'Zooks, you really are hellishly dirty,' he muttered, stepping away hurriedly. 'It seems my dear cousin has had to lower his sights.' He wiped his hand in distaste on his breeches, then seemingly weary of tormenting his captives, abruptly turned on his heel and ordered the two henchmen to bring the hostages inside.

As they were unceremoniously pushed through the door, Gabriel looked around to see if there were any witnesses, but the large entrance hall appeared deserted.

'If you're hoping to see any of your servants, you will be disappointed,' Henry threw over his shoulder as he led the way to the back of the house. 'Heavers and Reynolds, the doddery old fools, were turned out months ago. I prefer to use servants of my own choosing, so don't think to find any allies, cousin.' He stopped at the entrance to a small room which had evidently been used as a small study. Gabriel's heart sank as he realised where Henry was taking them.

Pushing open the door, he headed to a panelled wall. Pressing … something, Hope heard a click and blinked as the panel opened to reveal a dark narrow staircase leading down. 'Remember when we were trapped down here overnight?' commented Henry jovially as he started down the shadowy stairs.

'You mean when you locked me in,' responded Gabriel through gritted teeth.

'Oh yes, that was it,' chuckled his cousin. 'I seem to remember you having peed yourself when your father finally freed you. Gave you a thrashing to punish your cowardice, didn't he?'

'I seem to remember you receiving a similar beating from your own father,' Gabriel ground out as his cousin reached the bottom of the stairs.

'True,' Henry conceded. 'It was more than worth it though.' With another chortle, he threw open the door and stepped to one side, waiting.

Hope shrank back as she was hauled down the stairs towards the yawning blackness. 'I'll bloody throw you down if you don't move,' she was warned.

'Hope, it's alright, I'm here.' Gabriel kept his voice low and soothing, when what he really wanted to do was kill all three men with his bare hands.

'I'm here,' sneered Henry from the bottom of the stairs. 'Not for much longer, cousin. It's merely my curiosity keeping you alive for the moment.'

Gabriel felt a small jolt of satisfaction as he was shoved through the door into complete blackness. He was right, Henry could not help himself. He had to find out just how his cousin had survived in Cadiz. The Viscount bit back a groan as he was thrown to the floor but struggled immediately to his feet to catch Hope as she was forced in after him.

'We need a light,' Gabriel bit out as his cousin started to close the door. 'And some food,' he yelled, trying to keep the desperation out of his voice. The encroaching darkness paused, then, after a few seconds, the light grew again as Henry reopened the door and placed a lantern on the floor.

'Wouldn't want your little *lady* to be scared of the dark like you,' he mocked, stepping backwards and pulling the door closed behind him.

'Food,' bellowed Gabriel again just as the door slammed shut. He heard some laughter on the other side, followed by receding footsteps. '*Bastard*,' he swore violently, entirely forgetting Hope's presence for a moment. He hated the desperation in his last entreaty.

A small sniffle brought him back to his senses, and muttering another oath, this time under his breath, he went to pick up the lantern. The burning candle inside was relatively new and Gabriel estimated it might last them for two or three hours. Taking the light back to Hope, he seated himself next to her crumpled form and after placing the lamp on the floor, simply took her in his arms.

'Forgive me' he murmured, feathering soft kisses over her forehead.

Burrowing into his warmth, Hope was silent for a moment. Then, 'for which bit?' she murmured with a half sob, half laugh.

Gabriel placed his finger under her chin and tipped her head to look up at him. Henry was right, she was dirty - they both were. Her hair was mussed and tangled around her face … and she stared at him with complete trust and belief. As her dark gaze clung to his, in Gabriel's eyes she had never looked more beautiful.

'For my language,' he breathed, 'for getting you into this deuced mess … and for this.' He stopped speaking and bent his head, taking her mouth in a gentle kiss. In answer, Hope's fingers slid upwards around his neck, her lips opening against his. With her unexpected acquiescence Gabriel's kiss deepened, taking on a desperate edge that suddenly turned into an all-consuming melding of mouths that forgot everything except need. Hope gave a small whimper as she rose up onto her knees, pressing herself against him, seeking that same elusive … something. Groaning, all coherent thought gone, Gabriel instinctively sought to position her where he needed her most and sliding his hands down her back, pulled her bottom towards him, crushing her softness against his already hard cock.

Heedless of the cold damp floor, Gabriel fell backwards, taking her unresisting body with him. She fell onto him with a small oomph, briefly breaking their kiss, and staring down into his starkly handsome countenance stole away what little breath she had as her heart continued to pump wildly, erratically.

'Hope,' he groaned as she lowered her mouth back to his. 'Hush,' was all she breathed as she planted her hands on either side of his shoulders and bent her head until their lips came back together, searching, demanding, giving. She felt his hand slip between them, pulling at her bodice. The sudden blast of cold air on her bare breasts made her gasp for a second until his hand cupped the exposed globe, his fingers unerringly finding its peak and rubbing his thumb back and forth across the already stiffened bud. Sensation shot straight down between her legs, and with a small moan, Hope pressed herself into the hardness at the junction of her thighs, instinctively knowing that it was there … right there that she needed to be. His fingers continued their relentless rubbing backwards and forwards across the sensitive nub, even as his mouth continued to plunder hers, and helplessly, she ground that most sensitive part of her onto the unfamiliar hardness between her legs, gasping as he raised his hips to push against her.

But it wasn't enough. Hope knew there had to be more than this. Tearing her lips away from his, she rose up until she was straddling him. His eyes stared up at her, almost glittering with desire as he lifted his hands, both of them this time, to once again cup her breasts with their shadowed peaks, now fully on view to his heated gaze. Panting, Hope arched her back offering them to his hands and oh so skilful fingers. Reaching behind her, she fumbled at his breeches, and abruptly Gabriel stilled below her.

Almost mindless with desire, Hope paused and looked back down at him, at the harsh tautness of his features. 'We have to stop,' he ground out, panting with effort.

Hope stared down at him, realising his words were taking every ounce of strength he possessed. Licking her lips, she deliberately resumed her investigation of his britches, finally finding the buttons holding them closed. Gazing down at him, she slowly undid each of the buttons and slipped her hand inside. Without breaking eye contact, she took hold of his thick shaft and watched as he sucked in his breath and groaned.

'Show me what to do,' she whispered, slipping his cock free of his britches.

'Hope, we cannot,' he bit out, even as he instinctively lifted his hips to aid her questing fingers.

'I want to know,' she answered softly, shaking her head. 'I will not die without knowing.'

Her hand squeezed his shaft. 'Show me,' she demanded.

'If you keep doing that,' he groaned, his voice hoarse with need, 'you will learn only what it means to have your hand covered in a man's seed.'

'Show me,' she repeated finally letting go of his cock and leaning back down towards him to press a soft kiss on his lips. 'Please Gabriel. I do not want to die a maid.'

The Viscount shut his eyes briefly, knowing he was lost. Then with a growl, he relented, pulling her head down to reclaim her mouth. This time his tongue plundered hers as he carefully shifted her onto her back. As soon as she was beneath him, he put one knee between her legs and tearing himself away from her lips, manoeuvred himself down as far as her breasts, already pink in the candlelight from his fondling. With one last glance at her glazed features, he bent his head and took one rosy nipple into his mouth, causing her to cry out and grip his shoulders. He flicked his tongue first across one nub, then the other until Hope was writhing beneath him, twisting her head restlessly from side to side.

Heart thudding as though this was his first time, Gabriel lifted her skirts, exposing her to his heated gaze. There was no time to make sure she was ready for him, they could be discovered at any time, and now for some inexplicable reason that had nothing to do with Hope offering herself to him, Gabriel was determined to make her his. Entirely.

His hand sought and found her shadowy centre, and without taking his eyes off her face, he slowly slid a finger into her tight heat. Dear God, she was wet. She would need no priming. He slid another finger alongside, sinking both deep into her tight sheath in readiness for his entrance. In answer, her eyes flew to his, and she gave a gasping moan, thrusting her hips up towards his questing fingers, her knees falling open instinctively. 'Please,' she whimpered.

Gabriel needed no further urging. Rising up, he positioned himself above her. 'Are you sure love?' he questioned through gritted teeth, the effort of holding himself back almost too much.

Hope lifted her hands to cup his face. She could feel the tip of him between her legs, hard and throbbing against her entrance. 'Show me,' she whispered again and lifted her hips, inviting him in.

With a harsh groan, Gabriel plunged deep inside her tight warmth. All thoughts of taking his time were lost in the desperate need to feel her heat surrounding him. Dimly, he heard her cry out, felt the slight resistance to his thrust, and panting, he began to pull out then forced himself to hold still. Had he hurt her? He bent his head to stare down at her dazed features, the strain of remaining unmoving with her tight warmth wrapped around him an agony he could hardly endure. 'Do you want me to stop?' he whispered harshly. Hope gazed up at the face above her. Even now, he was giving her a choice. Her eyes closed and she accepted the truth.

She loved this man. She loved him enough to give herself to him in what might be her last act on earth.

Smiling, she shook her head, and reaching her hands around them to grasp his taut buttocks, pulled him down towards her. With another groan, Gabriel threw his head back and thrust hard and deep. Hope moaned, at first simply revelling in the feel of him stretching and filling her. But as he continued to slide in and out of her in an inexorable rhythm, she began to meet him thrust for thrust until she was arching her hips upwards, almost mindlessly pursuing the throbbing pressure that was building, building, building ... until abruptly the pleasure intensified as she cascaded over the edge, crying out as wave after wave of sensation engulfed her. Dimly, she felt his thrusts increase their tempo until with a low gasping moan, he thrust into her one last time before losing himself to oblivion.

They were both dirty, battered and bruised and lying on a cold hard floor. And Gabriel had just experienced the most powerful climax of his life.

CHAPTER 20

'*R*ight then, Percy, you give me a leg up, and I'll scope out the lay of the land, so to speak.'

'That wall's got to be six foot high,' protested Percy, 'We've already tried to do this at Redstone House Sir, and you can't deny it didn't end well.'

'That was a deuced window,' huffed the Reverend. 'Entirely different. If I can get on the top of the wall, I can pull you up, and we're in.'

'What about Freddy?' The Reverend paused, clearly having forgotten about the foxhound who was busy snuffling around in the underbrush.

'He'll just have to wait for us here. Come on then, Percy lad, stop dallying. Hope may well be in there somewhere, and it's up to us to get her out.' He waited impatiently until, with a weary sigh, the curate got down on his hands and knees. 'The ground's cold and wet,' he complained placing his hands gingerly into the dirt.

'It's the middle of deuced winter, what did you expect?' was the unsympathetic response. 'Right then, don't move.' The Reverend's first attempt to climb on his curate's back ended up with Percy spreadeagled in the dirt with Freddy capering around in excitement.

'Tare an' hounds,' the large man grumbled. 'This is harder than it looks.'

'We've had this conversation before,' retorted Percy, spitting out some obnoxious brown substance tangled in the leaves. 'And now my cassock is ruined.'

'You needed a new one anyway. In all honesty, Percy, I've been meaning to have a word. I'm all for a vow of poverty, but when it means going into the church looking like the village beggar, then it's time to put your hand in your pocket.'

The curate climbed crossly back to his feet and leant forward in an effort to brush some of the dirt off his robe.

'You might be right on this occasion though,' the Reverend conceded after a moment, eying the wall doubtfully. 'Mayhap if I give you a bit of a lift, you can have a look what the drop's like on the other side.'

Percy sighed as his superior bent down cupping his hands together creating a step. 'Come on then, lad, get a move on, this is not doing my back any good at all.'

Tentatively, the curate placed his foot into the Reverend's hands. 'Just give me a minu…'

His words trailed into a startled yelp as Reverend Shackleford heaved upwards, launching the terrified curate into midair. Half a second later, Percy landed back on the wall with a loud thump, legs and arse facing his superior.

To be fair, the Reverend was not entirely without sympathy and his demand of, 'What can you see?' was said with a definite wince.

For a few seconds, the silence was interrupted only by a strangled wheezing noise due to Percy having the wind completely knocked out of him.

'We haven't got all day,' added the Reverend, his commiseration evidently short lived.

'Freddy,' wheezed Percy a few seconds later. 'I can see Freddy.'

'What the deuce do you mean you can see Freddy? Have you been drinking the communion wine again, Percy?'

'He must have found a way in,' rasped the curate. 'Can you help me down, Sir?'

'That mean's there's an opening,' mused the Reverend completely ignoring Percy's legs waving frantically just above him. 'You stay there,' he ordered, 'while I go and investigate.'

'Don't leave me here ... no Freddy, this is not a game, bad dog.' Percy's words were interspersed with growls and yaps as the excited foxhound decided to play nip the curate.

'Thunder an' turf, Percy, would you believe there's a gate,' came the Reverend's enthusiastic voice from about ten yards to the right. Seconds later, the large man was back. 'Right then, let's get you down,' he declared, taking hold of the curate's feet.

'No, wha ... *stop* ...' Percy got no further as Reverend Shackleford gave his legs a good shove catapulting the curate headfirst into the shrubbery.

Seconds later, the Reverend reappeared on the other side of the wall. 'Clever dog,' he murmured, mussing the foxhound's head affection-ately. 'What the deuce are you doing down there, Percy?'

∞∞∞

The doorbell was answered by an ancient butler much like Bailey, the elderly retainer her husband refused to get rid of in their London town house. The sight heartened the Duchess, as she believed it demonstrated a similar kindness in Admiral Atwood. Although to be fair, he hadn't shown much in the way of compassion towards his nephew.

'Is the mistress of the house at home?' she enquired, taking care to keep her voice a combination of politeness and imperious demand. 'Please inform her that the Duchess of Blackmore is here to see her.'

The butler stared silently at her, and for a second, she wondered if he was deaf. 'I said...,' she started again, only to stutter to a halt as the ancient servant simply turned and shuffled away. Grace stood irresolute at the door, unsure of what to do next. This wasn't going exactly as she'd planned. She assumed the fact that the butler had left the front door open indicated his intention to fetch Mrs Atwood. Hesitantly, she stepped into the shadowy hallway. Looking around, she could see only one or two candles lighting the gloom, despite the lack of sunlight. In her experience, such a lack indicated only one thing.

The Admiral didn't have a feather to fly with.

Why though? As the new Viscount Northwood, he clearly had access to a large fortune. To her knowledge, the Estate was not short of funds. Why else would the Admiral and his obnoxious offspring have sought to put an end to Gabriel?

Anxiously lingering in the hallway, she began removing her gloves, mainly to give her hands something to do. After five minutes passed without either the butler or Mrs Atwood making an appearance, her nervousness began to turn to irritation. Indeed, she was just about to march towards the door she'd seen the butler disappear through, when a woman materialised in the gloom. So sudden was her appearance that Grace stepped back involuntarily, half believing the figure a ghost.

There was a short silence as both ladies stared at each other, then, 'May I ask what you are doing here, your grace?' So, this was Admiral

Atwood's wife. She was a small woman, who Grace guessed had once been beautiful, but now her features were gaunt, and her gown hung off her thin frame. Clearly her life had not been a happy one.

Grace took a deep breath. 'I am here to make enquiries about your nephew, Mrs Atwood,' she stated firmly.

There was a pause as the chatelaine of the house stared at her, evidently nonplussed. 'Gabriel?' she questioned finally. Grace nodded. 'The very same,' the Duchess responded, trying to keep the impatience out of her voice.

'Gabriel Atwood is dead. He died in Spain. It is common knowledge, your grace. I am surprised you were not aware.'

'He was believed so, it's true,' answered Grace carefully, 'but I have it on good authority that Gabriel, in fact, survived...' She paused and took another deep breath. 'In fact, I have reason to believe that Viscount Northwood may well be in this very house.'

'The present Viscount Northwood is indeed resident in this house.' The loud masculine voice came from the top of the stairs, and Grace looked up startled, her heart speeding up rapidly. The man was undoubtedly Admiral Benjamin Atwood, and as he descended the stairs, she could see he was in no better state than his wife. Curiouser and curiouser.

Grace backed up closer to the front door. She finally began to see how foolish she'd been to come here alone. She had mistakenly believed that her title would provide her with the protection she needed, but truly she should have known better.

The Admiral reached the bottom of the stairs without taking his eyes off her. As he got closer, she could clearly see the resemblance to Gabriel.

'What brings you to the belief that my nephew is still alive?' he asked coldly, 'And why the devil would you think him here?'

Heart beating suffocatingly, Grace swallowed and drew herself up. It would not do to show any weakness.

'Your nephew, the rightful Viscount Northwood, is indeed alive,' she declared in a voice that was every inch a duchess. 'And I know this because he came to see my husband who I'm sure you are aware is the Duke of Blackmore. The Viscount's intention was to seek my husband's aid in foiling a dastardly plot to murder him in cold blood and seize his inheritance.'

For a few seconds, she wondered if she'd gone too far, then to her surprise, the Admiral laughed. 'Then where is he?' Benjamin Atwood demanded, still chuckling. When Grace didn't immediately answer, he sneered. 'Mayhap your grace has drunk one too many glasses of sherry,' he suggested, 'or perhaps given your delusions, your husband should be looking to lock you away. For your own safety naturally.'

He had stepped nearer to her as he spoke forcing Grace to slowly retreat, her fear mounting. The Admiral spoke like a man who simply had nothing to lose. His impertinence showed complete disregard for her standing, and too late, she remembered her husband's dry comment that she was far too like her father for her own good. Evidently, he was correct. There was no doubt in her mind that she'd made a mull of the whole thing and was now in the suds.

Doing her best to stifle her alarm, Grace stared coldly back at the man in front of her, finally realising that he too had the same unkempt look as his wife. His clothes were tattered and none too clean, and more importantly his face had the hectic look of someone either half sprung or sick as a cushion.

Admiral Atwood was clearly a man in torment.

'I do not know for certain that Gabriel is here,' she commented warily after a second. 'However, it *is* certain that he was taken against his will, and my sister with him, not two days ago, by a bunch of gallows birds who were in the pay of your son Henry.'

'Henry has him?' The look of horror on Benjamin Atwood's face was entirely unfeigned and persuaded her that, on this occasion at least, the Admiral was not party to his son's heinous plan.

She opened her mouth to speak, but the Admiral's wife got there first.

'*No,*' she hissed, striding over to her husband. 'That is a *lie.*' Her face was twisted, and spittle flew from her lips as she spoke. 'My son would never harm his cousin, *never.*'

Grace stared at the furious woman. Here then was her true danger. She thought briefly back to little Peter. Never underestimate the loyalty of a mother to her child. Clearly Mrs Atwood had not known that her son had harmed his cousin, not once but twice. While Grace had no doubt that Henry Atwood's intention was to finally do away with Gabriel once and for all and possibly Hope with him, it was becoming increasingly apparent that neither of his parents had been aware that their nephew was very much alive before she'd enlightened them. Mayhap she could use their ignorance to her advantage.

'If Gabriel is not here,' she risked, 'then it is certain he and my sister are being held at Northwood Court.'

Caroline Atwood continued to shake her head, glaring at Grace, her entire body exuding resentment and animosity. The Admiral, on the other hand, appeared to have somehow caved in on himself and now simply looked wearied unto death.

She took a deep breath and focused her attention on the broken man in front of her. 'Were you aware that Henry attempted to murder Gabriel in cold blood while they were in Cadiz?' she questioned bluntly. He did not need to answer, his eyes clearly told her that he was, but everything about him now indicated overwhelming regret.

Not so his wife.

'How dare you come here with your vile accusations,' she raged, storming up to Grace and taking hold of her arm.

'Remove your hands from my person *immediately*,' returned Grace in the coldest voice she could muster.

'Or what?' Caroline Atwood shot back savagely. 'What are you going to do, *your grace?*' Looking into the woman's furious eyes, Grace was truly afraid for the first time. She glanced over at the Admiral who simply stood there, almost trance like.

Her heart beating frantically, Grace attempted to twist away from the woman's vicelike grip, but despite an impression of frailty, Mrs Atwood was strong, and she was unable to free herself.

'Does the Duke even know you are here?' the vile woman questioned Grace, eyes narrowing in the sudden realisation that the Duchess may have come here without her husband's knowledge.

'Her husband may not be aware of his wife's impulsive actions, but I deuced well am.'

Percy had clearly not succeeded in discouraging the Reverend from his partiality for dramatic entrances.

And truly, Grace had never been so grateful.

∞∞∞∞

Once they'd left the inn, with the horses newly fresh, Nicholas and Malcolm made excellent time, arriving at Northwood Court well before lunch. The day was cold and blustery which kept all but the most determined firmly indoors. From the admittedly small section they could see from their vantage point aside a crumbling part of the wall surrounding the estate, there did not appear to be any movement inside the house, but the Duke was of the opinion that the lack of activity did not mean that Gabriel and Hope were not being held inside.

They had no way of knowing whether their messages had reached the intended ears of Adam and Roan but were nevertheless hoping that additional aid was on the way. However, whether help was coming or not, both men knew they would have no choice but to act once a suitable opportunity presented itself.

So, they waited and watched.

CHAPTER 21

*H*ope lay curled up in Gabriel's arms and wondered how she could feel so absurdly happy given their horrific circumstances. She recalled Temperance, always the most gregarious of her sisters, describing the act of love between her and Adam as being, 'wondrous beyond anything she'd ever experienced.' Right up until half an hour ago, she'd simply thought her sister moonstruck. Indeed, Hope truly believed Tempy's pursuit of the Earl of Ravenstone to be shockingly beyond the pale. But that was thirty minutes ago.

Now, here she was lying on a cold hard floor with a man she'd known only weeks, and for the moment, nothing mattered but the two of them. Naturally, she was pragmatic enough to know that her euphoria would not last, but for now, she kept the fear at bay by focusing entirely on the man in whose arms she lay, and more scandalously, on the delicious sensations he'd evoked within her.

Gabriel for his part felt no euphoria. Indeed, his feelings could be more accurately described as dread, the like of which he'd never suffered before. Making love to Hope had taken him to heights he'd previously only dreamt of. But not only had it intensified the strong feelings he already had for her, but also the terror of losing the woman he'd realised was the love of his life.

Now, more than ever, he was determined to put an end to his bastard of a cousin. But more than that, he finally had something to live for. Something beyond a title and the bricks and mortar that went with it. Indeed, he now truly had a reason to survive beyond the length of time it took to make Henry pay for his heinous crimes.

And it terrified him.

Stroking Hope's hair, he pressed a soft kiss onto her forehead. 'We need to rearrange ourselves,' he murmured reluctantly. 'Should Henry become certain that we're more than simply acquaintances, he will seek to use the knowledge to his advantage.' Sighing, Hope lifted her face to his. 'I wish we could stay like this forever,' she whispered sadly. Gabriel's answer was to bend his head and place another kiss on her lips. 'Me too,' he breathed, 'but I think our stomachs would eventually have something to say on the matter.'

In answer, Hope's stomach gave an obliging growl, and Gabriel gave a low chortle. Reluctantly disentangling them both, he helped her struggle into a sitting position. 'Truly, it's not just my stomach that's aching,' Hope grimaced softly, 'it seems as if every bone and muscle in my entire body is rising up in protest.'

'Well, I would have preferred our first intimacy to have taken place in more salubrious surroundings,' Gabriel commented ruefully, sitting up beside her with a groan of his own.

'Starting with a bed?' teased Hope.

'Oh, definitely a bed. And mayhap some flower petals decorating the pillows?'

'Roses,' decided Hope, rearranging her bodice into some semblance of modesty. 'I believe rose petals would smell divine.' She gave a small laugh and looked over at Gabriel. 'I fear in our current state of déshabillé though, a hundred rose petals would make not one jot of difference.'

Gabriel grinned back at her, his heart swelling with love and pride at her unwavering spirit. 'Then mayhap we should…' He was interrupted by the sound of a key being turned on the other side of the door. Hope's eyes widened in sudden fear, and Gabriel gave her fingers a quick reassuring squeeze before climbing quickly to his feet. Fortunately, they were no longer in a state of undress, and the Viscount was able to regard the slowly opening door with a relatively impassive expression. He was not surprised to see all three of Henry's henchmen in the open doorway, nor the fact that two of them were carrying pistols pointed directly at him and Hope. Clearly, his cousin was taking no chances.

What did surprise him, however, was the sight of the third man carrying a tray. 'Don' try any bloody funny business,' the ruffian ordered, hurriedly placing the tray onto the floor and backing out. 'An' don' eat it all at once' The last sneering comment was made just as he slammed the door shut and turned the key.

Gabriel strode over to the tray. On it were two glasses of water, bread, cheese and what looked like some kind of meat. He turned back towards Hope who was staring at him … well … hopefully.

He bent to pick up the tray and returned to his position next to her, placing the feast between them.

'Wait,' he warned when Hope made a grab for the nearest piece of bread. 'The fare may well be laced with poison or some such. I would not put it past my cousin to take the easy way out.' Hope stared at him in frustration. She was so damned hungry.

'At least let me try everything first,' he added at her anguished gaze. Leaning forward to give her a quick peck of sympathy, he picked up a piece of bread and tentatively put it to his mouth. Five minutes later, he'd tried everything on the tray and seemed to be feeling no ill effects. Hope had never taken her eyes off him the whole time.

Although he wasn't entirely sure whether her close regard was due to concern for his wellbeing, or simple longing to put something in her mouth after so long, she actually reminded him of their family dog Freddy.

He smothered an ill-timed chuckle and waved his hand towards the food. 'I'm still here, so go ahead and eat, love.'

Hope fell upon the food like someone starving which she undoubtedly was. For himself, Gabriel ate sparingly. He had become accustomed to sporadic and meagre rations whilst making his way home through Spain, and his appetite had not yet fully recovered.

When every crumb was devoured, Hope sighed and patted her belly. 'Here we are in mortal danger, our lives in the very balance ... and never have I enjoyed such paltry fare so much. It was better than the finest banquet.' She gave an unladylike burp and reddened in the candlelight. Unable to help himself, Gabriel laughed, causing her to flush even further.

'My love, your face now matches your hair,' he teased. Hope made to cuff him impishly, but he caught her arms and pulled her to him. 'Would that we had the time for me to cause you further blushes,' he murmured, his lips a mere inch away from hers.

Despite their ongoing peril, Hope felt an answering tingle between her thighs. Her gaze clung to his, and her pulse quickened at the intensity in his eyes. The moment stretched, and she had no ready quip. At length, he bent his head and covered her lips with his. But where before his kiss had been all consuming, this time it was soft, searching and filled with so much promise. As they broke apart, Hope knew that if they managed to survive, Gabriel had claimed her as his own. Indeed, even if they perished this day, the Viscount had unquestionably conquered her heart.

Gabriel rested his forehead against hers, and she stroked her hands over his broad shoulders.

'We need to come up with at least some kind of strategy, however vague,' he advised wearily. 'It's my belief that Henry is lulling us into a false sense of optimism in an attempt to get as much information out of us as possible. But make no mistake, he will not allow either of us to leave this house or indeed this room, alive.' Hope made to speak, but he softly pressed his finger against her lips.

'When Henry arrives, let me do the talking, love. He knows nothing about your family's connection to the Duke of Blackmore, and we must keep it that way lest he panic and rid himself of us sooner. At the moment, he does not expect any immediate interference. The longer I can keep him talking, the more time we are giving Nicholas to come to our aid.'

'You think he will come then?' whispered Hope, uncertainty lacing her voice.

'You think your sister would allow him otherwise?' quipped Gabriel.

Hope chuckled softly, the first hint of optimism stirring under her fear.

'Do not allow Henry to draw you out,' the Viscount continued. 'He will...'

Gabriel's words were cut short as they heard the key turning in the lock again. Looking up as one, they watched as the door slowly opened.

∞∞∞∞

Grace had never seen her father pointing a pistol before. Indeed, she didn't even know he owned one, given that he took the Lord's commandment, *Thou shalt not kill* to encompass all living things. Even as far as refusing to hunt though he owned a deuced foxhound. Naturally, he did not extend this edict to others lest he be forced to live the rest of his life on rabbit food. Carrots were all well and good, but much better served on the same plate as the rabbit.

The perversity of her parent was without question but nevertheless, though she was entirely certain he would not use it, Grace was beyond thankful to see him pointing the weapon steadily at the Admiral and his wife.

'Don't move,' the Reverend ordered in his *slippery slope downstairs* tone of voice. 'Percy, have a look to see if they have a cellar or at least a deuced room with a lock.' The curate who'd been hovering anxiously behind his superior, hobbled forward, and Grace wondered what calamity had befallen the small man this time.

'Father, Hope and Gabriel are not here,' the Duchess informed the Reverend, hastily stepping away from the wild-eyed Caroline Atwood. 'In my opinion, neither of Henry's parents were even aware that Gabriel was still alive.'

'Hmph,' was all the Reverend commented without taking his eyes off his quarry. Grace hurried over to him. 'We need to get to Northwood Court as quickly as possible now we've ascertained that they aren't here.'

'Are you absolutely confident of that Grace?' her father questioned.

'I am certain. There is no doubt in my mind that neither the Admiral nor his wife are responsible for Gabriel's and Hope's kidnapping.' She looked back at the obnoxious couple who hadn't moved. 'At least one of them is guilty of attempted murder, of that I have no doubt, and they are most assuredly both cowards...' She paused before continuing in a lower tone, 'And I believe that Mrs Atwood is more than a little addled.'

'There's a small cellar with a lock and key.' Percy's jubilant tones inter-rupted Grace as he limped back into view.

'Right then, lead on Percy,' Reverend Shackleford ordered. 'Let's waste no more time on these unpleasant individuals.' He stepped closer to the Admiral and waved his pistol threateningly. 'Your disgraceful activities are finished, Atwood. Your wife may well be dicked in the deuced nob, but you have no excuse for the way you've treated your nephew.'

'Let me help,' the Admiral commented in a low anguished voice, entirely ignoring his wife's indrawn gasp of outrage.

For a second the Reverend thought he'd misheard. 'I think you've provided more than enough help, you blackguard,' he sputtered after a second.

'Your actions are beyond despicable,' Grace added icily. 'You are truly a loathsome little man with absolutely no honour, and I for one hope you swing for your part in this.'

The Reverend looked over at his daughter in astonishment. Truly he had no idea his eldest could be quite so violent.

'Move,' he ordered, waving his pistol around threateningly.

The Admiral held out his hands in entreaty. 'Please,' he murmured brokenly. 'What I did was unforgivable I know, and I did it to my own flesh and blood. I have no excuse, but I... I was desperate.'

'Desperate enough to have your nephew murdered for his money,' spat the Reverend, his voice radiating disgust.

The Admiral shook his head. 'I... I'm dying,' he rasped.

Reverend Shackleford raised his eyebrows. 'Forgive me if I don't shed any tears,' he responded, realising as he spoke that the Admiral's wife was now regarding her husband in shock. Clearly, she didn't know, though he couldn't imagine how she'd missed it. He'd seen livelier corpses.

'I have syphilis,' Benjamin Atwood admitted brokenly. He looked down at his wife. 'Fifteen years.'

'That ... that woman in Belgium,' breathed Caroline, forcing back a sob. The Admiral closed his eyes. He hadn't realised she'd known about Marie. 'That's why you never touched me again.' Her voice became stronger, and she almost shouted the word *touch*.

'Now just a deuced minute,' Augustus Shackleford interrupted, anxious to head off any violence. 'Nobody here wishes to know about your habits in the bedroom.'

'I couldn't risk passing it on to you,' the Admiral responded, ignoring the Reverend's comment. He did not add that the only woman whose bed he even now yearned to be in was long dead.

Benjamin Atwood looked over at the Reverend. His gaze was that of a man who cared not whether he lived or died. Clearly the price of what had been done to his nephew, however desperate the Admiral had been, was far too high for the man to live with.

'Please,' he repeated desperately, 'let me help.'

'Benjamin, no,' cried out Caroline, her skeletal hands grasping hold of her husband's arm.

Admiral Atwood continued without looking at his wife.

'I cannot allow Henry to commit any further atrocities,' he continued hoarsely, 'God knows he's led me by the nose long enough.'

Caroline Atwood, pulled at his arm, hysterical sobs now shaking her thin frame. 'How could you say such a thing about your own son?' she shouted. 'Henry would never hurt Gabriel, *never*.'

Admiral Atwood looked distastefully down at the frenzied woman hanging on to his arm. 'If you believe so, why haven't you encouraged a move to Northwood Court?' he demanded. 'Why have you been content to stay here burying your head in the sand and living like a pauper?' He shook off her hand.

'You know our son's nature as well as I do,' he continued. 'That's why you've stayed well away. Doing so means your conscience remains clear.'

Before either the Reverend or Grace could react to the Admiral's words, Caroline gave a shriek and launched herself at her husband. 'You're a liar,' she screamed, attempting to gouge out his eyes.

'Tare an' hounds,' muttered Augustus Shackleford, turning hastily towards Grace who was just as dumb struck.

Caroline Atwood's strength belied her feeble appearance and within seconds, she'd knocked her husband to the floor, where she continued to pummel him with her fists as the Reverend, Grace and Percy looked on in horrified disbelief.

Fortunately, there was one member of their party who was not entirely rooted to the spot. Freddy, who'd been watching the proceedings with tail-wagging interest, needed no further urging. Barking furiously, he tore across the hall, immediately drawing the fighting couple's terrified attention. Scrambling apart, they scooted backwards while Freddy sat directly in front of them and simply growled low and menacingly.

'I think now would be a good time to lock them up, sir.'

∞∞∞∞

'There are recent hoof prints around the entrance to the Court,' Roan commented as he strode back to the waiting men. 'By my estimation, they have been there no more than a pair of hours.'

'Then Gabriel and Hope are in there?' Adam questioned with a frown.

'Naturally there is no certainty of that,' responded Nicholas, 'but we are out of options, gentlemen and must act soon if we are to find either of them alive.'

Both Adam and Roan had arrived within half an hour of each other. Although he said nothing, in the Duke's opinion, both men looked exhausted having clearly ridden hard to arrive in time to lend their aid. While Nicholas was beyond grateful for their loyalty, he nevertheless couldn't help but silently wonder whether they had any fight left in them.

'I suggest Nick and I find somewhere round the side of the house to sneak in,' proposed Malcolm. 'I doubt there will be many servants milling about. If Atwood has even the remotest sense of self preservation, he will have cleared them all out, at least for the day.' He paused, then grinned. 'Adam and Roan, what say you both walk in through the front door?'

∞∞∞

'You can't lock us up in here,' protested Caroline Atwood, as she and the Admiral were herded towards what looked to be little bigger than a large walk-in cupboard.

'It's roomier than a deuced coffin,' Reverend Shackleford retorted.

'Please, you'll need my help,' cried Benjamin Atwood, frantically trying to convince them one last time. 'Let me talk to my son. He'll listen to me. I swear I will be able to dissuade Henry from seeking Gabriel's death a second time. And believe me, this time he will be certain to finish the job properly.'

To the Reverend's surprise, Grace placed a hand on his arm, staying his action.

'What makes you think you'll have even the slightest effect on your revolting offspring's murderous tendencies?' she questioned the Admiral coldly.

'Because I know why he's doing it,' pressed Admiral Atwood urgently. 'I know why he so desperately wants Gabriel dead.'

'So, you're telling me there's more to it than the fact he's been drawing the deuced bustle too freely and now doesn't have sixpence to scratch with?'

194

The Admiral nodded and glanced over at his wife who was glaring at him in loathing. The Reverend realised it was only the low warning grumbles of the foxhound stopping her from launching herself back at him.

'Tie my hands,' Atwood continued. 'Strap me to the back of the carriage if you must, but please, let me help you prevent further bloodshed.'

Grace looked over at her father. 'I think there is far more to this than we suspected. Mayhap we should take him with us.' She shook her head and regarded the weeping Admiral with distaste. 'Whatever happens now, he is finished. Nicholas will never allow him to walk away from justice.'

Reverend Shackleford frowned wavering.

'Don't you leave me in there on my own you … you *bastards.*' Caroline Atwood's sudden shriek decided him. Primarily because the Reverend suspected her husband might not even survive to be brought to trial if he was locked up for more than five minutes with the screaming harridan in front of him.

CHAPTER 22

$\mathcal{T}$he first man through the door to the cellar was the one Hope thought of as the leader of Henry's three accomplices. Once he'd ascertained that the prisoners were not hiding behind the door, he stepped aside, hanging a lantern on a hook to the side of the entrance, and Henry Atwood sauntered in.

'I trust you are feeling a little more replete than when you arrived at my house?' he enquired with mock concern. To Gabriel's dismay, he directed his question to Hope.

'I have eaten my fill,' stammered Hope in reply after a hesitant look at the Viscount.

'It is not your house,' pitched in Gabriel through gritted teeth, determined to bring Henry's attention back to him. 'It has never been your house.'

'I beg to differ cousin,' Henry drawled, his voice not quite concealing an undercurrent of rage.

'In truth, this house belongs to neither of us. Though I believe my claim to it is stronger than yours.'

'What the devil are you talking about?' growled Gabriel, fighting to stay calm.

'This house belongs to my father as the next in line to the Northwood title. Then, on his death it will pass to me as the eldest son.'

'That may have been true if you'd succeeded in finishing me in Cadiz,' Gabriel shot back savagely, 'but as you can see cousin, I am very much alive.'

'Let's not go down that route again,' retorted Henry with mock weariness. 'You are well aware that neither you nor your companion will leave here alive.'

'Then why feed us?' burst out Hope unable to stay silent any longer.

Henry Atwood chuckled and shrugged. 'Simply this. I wished my dearest *cousin* to be thinking about something other than his stomach when I broke the news to him.'

'Broke the news about what?' bit out Gabriel. 'That you're a murderous thieving cowardly bastard? Believe me, *that* I already knew.'

Henry's chuckle died, and he took a deep breath, clearly trying to get himself under control.

'Did you know my father and your mother were very close once upon a time?' he remarked mildly. Gabriel frowned at the sudden change of subject. 'What of it?' he questioned with a shrug.

Henry grinned again, his good humour restored. 'Did you never wonder why it took sooo long for you to be conceived?' he pressed. I mean, your dear mama was quite long in the tooth when she finally became pregnant with you. And when you were born, mere months after me... well we were the spitting image. Everyone said so.'

Gabriel stared back at his cousin's smirking face, sudden bile rising into his throat. 'Spit it out, Henry, for pity's sake,' he ground out, wanting nothing more than to wipe the smug grin off his cousin's face.

'We're brothers,' Henry shouted out gleefully, evidently unable to hold his revelation back any longer. '*Lady* Northwood was my father's whore, and you, the high and mighty Gabriel Atwood are my father's by blow.

'In other words, dearest brother, you are a bastard - in name as well as nature.'

Gabriel opened his mouth to argue, then shut it again, his heart slamming nauseatingly against his ribs.

It was true, the deepest darkest part of him knew it. It explained so many things. His father's estrangement. His complete lack of interest over anything his son said or did.

And Gabriel's closeness to Benjamin Atwood. He felt a small hand slip into his as his world crashed slowly around him. Staring at his grinning sibling, he shook his head automatically.

'So, you see, neither your pretend father, nor your *real* father gave a rat's arse about you.'

'Then why kill me?' questioned Gabriel huskily after a few moments. 'Why not just take what was yours?'

'My dearest father,' Henry answered, 'or should I say *our* dearest father. He refused to denounce you. He said there was no proof, and the resulting scandal would taint the family name forever.' Henry shook his head and scowled.

'The doddering old fool preferred to leave his bastard in possession of the title rather than securing it for his rightful son and heir. I *begged* him, fiend seize it, I *pleaded* with him.' He laughed harshly. 'I even threatened to tell my mother, but he said he'd cut me off without a penny if I said so much as a word.'

Gabriel felt Hope squeeze his hand, offering what comfort she could. He dared not respond but simply stared at Henry, waiting.

'I knew it was up to me. Obviously, my first attempt to get rid of you was a bit of a disaster, but I think I could be forgiven for acting a trifle irrationally given that I'd only just found your whore of a mother's letters in the old man's desk.' Henry grimaced at the memory. 'And then, when my father packed me off to sea, I thought my life finished. How wrong I was.

'First of all, I met this fine fellow.' He nodded towards the grim-faced man standing silently beside him. 'And then, every time I was on leave, I set about spending my father's fortune. Every opportunity I had, I gambled it away and enjoyed watching every penny go down the drain, until the old man finally faced disgrace and ruin.

'Until the fool had no choice unless he wanted to put a gun to his head.' Henry stopped and smirked at Gabriel. 'He's too much a coward to do himself in. I knew he'd rather see his bastard dead. But even then, I had to do the blasted deed. Far, far away from his pathetic, sensitive eyes.'

Finally, Henry Atwood ground to a halt, and the only sound in the room was his panting. It was as if his violent tirade had exhausted him.

Gabriel was still. If his hand in hers had not been so warm, Hope would have thought him a statue. Then slowly, he slipped his hand away and began to clap, slowly, insolently. 'If it was decreed that the title go to the man with the most vivid imagination, then you would win Henry, hands down,' he drawled. 'But as always, you flunked it, didn't you, just as you've flunked everything else in your life. You couldn't even commit a decent murder.'

Hope's eyes flew to Gabriel's in panic. What the deuce was he doing? In answer to her unspoken plea, the Viscount took her hand again and squeezed briefly without taking his eyes off Henry Atwood's twisted face.

But if Gabriel had been hoping to goad Henry into doing something rash, he was disappointed. His brother drew himself up and shook his head. 'You may rest assured I won't fail again.' His voice was calm, as though the last few minutes had not taken place. 'I did not want you to go to your grave ignorant of your true position. The last time I was forbidden to tell you. But that was before my father became nothing but a pathetic tosspot, interested in nothing but the bottom of a bottle.

'In truth, it's so much more satisfying this way. I simply wanted to ensure you knew everything before I tell John to shoot you both in the head.'

Staring at the man he'd known for all his life as his cousin, Gabriel finally realised he was entirely unhinged. Henry's hatred would never abate because he would never accept that it was only due to a quirk of fate and the simple fact that Benjamin Atwood had been unable to keep his hands off his brother's wife that he, Henry Atwood, was not the true heir to the Northwood title.

'Leave Miss Shackleford out of it,' entreated Gabriel, knowing he only had seconds in which to save Hope's life. 'She's a nobody. Let her go, and she'll simply run, not daring to tell anyone what she's seen. Who would believe a penniless chit anyway over the next Viscount Northwood?'

Henry's eyes narrowed, and Gabriel realised with a sinking heart that he'd overplayed his hand. The intensity of his appeal had given away the fact that he had feelings for his companion.

Slowly, Henry grinned. 'Oh, this is priceless,' he crowed with a low chuckle. 'John,' he beamed, turning to the taciturn man at his side, 'shoot the woman first.'

'*No*,' yelled Gabriel, dropping Hope's hand and stepping protectively in front of her.

Henry Atwood laughed out loud, slapping his thighs in delight at Gabriel's instinctive reaction.

White-hot fear gripped the Viscount and along with it a fury that made him abandon all reason. Pushing Hope firmly behind him, he stepped forward with a snarl.

Just as the doorbell clanged.

Henry stayed his henchman's hand, waiting to see if the caller went away. When the bell rang again, this time for longer, he scowled and turned to pull open the door. 'Stay here and watch them,' he ordered before stepping through, slamming the door behind him and turning the key.

∞∞∞∞

Roan and Adam waited impatiently at the main entrance. 'How long do we give the bastard before we knock his bloody door down?' growled the former sea captain.

'Remember our role is to keep the son of a bitch talking,' warned Adam, 'however much we might want to draw his cork. We dare not act recklessly until we know for sure where he's stashed Hope and Gabriel. He has at least three thugs at his beck and call whose where-abouts are equally uncertain.'

Roan nodded his head. 'Hot headed I may be, but not entirely bacon-brained,' he commented before adding a rueful, 'unlike our wives, on occasion.'

The two men grinned at each other in perfect accord. A few moments later, Adam was just about to give the doorbell another tug, when they heard footsteps approaching from inside.

Both men took a deep breath and waited as the door was slowly pulled open.

The man on the other side was clearly not Henry Atwood. Both his manner and his attire, not to mention his doubtful hygiene declared him one of the thugs Adam had mentioned.

'Pray tell your master he has callers,' Adam ordered in his most aloof condescending tone.

'Master's not 'ome,' was the sullen response as the man began to close the door in their faces.

'You misunderstand me,' Adam added coldly, sticking his foot in the door. 'I did not ask whether Henry Atwood was at home. I simply asked you to inform him that we are here to see him.' He paused and looked down his nose at the bogus footman. 'And while you're about it, you might well consider having a bath.' Roan fought to hide a grin as Adam affectedly pulled out a kerchief from his pocket and held it in front of his nose.

There was a pause as the man wrestled with what he should do. Then, 'Who shall I say is callin' on 'im?' His agitated response was that of someone who'd had very few dealings with the *ton*.

'You may tell him that the Marquis of Birmingham wishes to speak with him. Perhaps you will also enlighten him as to why you are leaving a peer of the realm loitering on his doorstep.'

Thoroughly cowed as Adam had intended, the man hurriedly stepped back and allowed them to enter. Then, with an awkward bow, the ruffian turned and all but ran towards the back of the house.

The two men stood silently, using the time to examine their surroundings. On any other occasion, Gabriel's home would be considered quite delightful.

Moments later, Henry Atwood finally appeared. Flanking him were two of his ruffians. The man who'd answered the door and another, even more brutish. Both Roan and Adam were in no doubt that these were the bastards who'd abducted Hope and Gabriel.

'How can I help you, my lord?' asked Henry obsequiously. 'Are you lost perchance?'

Roan eyed the despicable individual who'd done such dreadful things to a gentleman he'd only recently had the great fortune to call friend. The resemblance was indeed remarkable, but the man in front of him was merely a pale imitation of Gabriel Atwood. In truth, on seeing the evil bastard for the first time in person, Roan was having a difficult time holding to Adam's command.

'My carriage struck a rock some two miles back,' declared Adam coolly, his tone every inch that of a bored aristocrat. 'I would be in your debt if you could send one of your men post haste to the nearest town to secure my companion and me alternative transport.' He looked haughtily around the hall before returning his wintery gaze to Atwood. 'In the meantime, if your chef would provide us with a small repast, I would be most grateful. We shall wait in the drawing room.' The Earl paused, staring down his nose at the master of the house who was even now turning an interesting shade of puce. After a space of a few moments, Adam quirked an enquiring brow and spoke again, his voice a few degrees chillier.

'Perhaps you would direct us to your drawing room, preferably one with a large fire in it.' He shuddered theatrically and began removing his gloves. 'The weather has been excessively inclement lately.'

∞∞∞

Nicholas and Malcolm made their way along the edge of the wall until they reached a section that had succumbed to the elements. Clambering over the scattered rocks, they continued along the boundary, this time on the inside, taking care to keep close to the cover provided by the shrubbery. In the distance, they heard the doorbell clang insistently and glancing at each other, shared a knowing grin. 'Aye, I'd give a lot right now te see Adam in all his pompous glory,' chuckled Malcolm.

'Let's hope Roan doesn't ruin the charade by laughing,' the Duke commented drily. He parted an enormous rhododendron and pointed to a large orangery. 'There,' he decided. 'It's around the side of the house so we're unlikely to be spotted crossing the lawn as long as Adam keeps Henry Atwood talking in the hall.

'Hopefully, we'll be able to break a windowpane to get in.'

'Gabe'll not love ye for damaging his property,' warned the Scotsman.

'At least he'll be alive to ring a bloody peal over my head,' responded Nicholas. 'Come on.'

The two men raced across the lawn towards the orangery. The myriad windows reflected their every movement giving them the uncomfortable feeling of being watched by someone inside. Once against the dubious protection of the building, Nicholas hunted for a door. 'No sense in breaking a window if some idiot has left the entrance unlocked,' he murmured, finally spotting two large doors in the French style. Unfortunately, after trying both handles to no avail, the decision was made for them. 'There's a key on the inside,' he observed, pressing his head against the glass above the lock.

'So, breaking and entering it is,' mocked the valet with a sigh.

Quickly picking up a small rock, Nicholas glanced around, then swiftly struck the glass and cautiously pushed the shards into the room. Then reaching carefully over the jagged edges remaining around the edge, he turned the key and opened the door.

'Ye missed yer vocation, clearly,' commented Malcolm with raised eyebrows at the speediness of their entrance.

'I always imagined being a knight of the road,' quipped the Duke as he stepped inside.

'Too soft for such a profession since becoming a land lubber,' scoffed the valet behind him. 'Ye'd not last a pair of hours standing and delivering.'

Both men chuckled softly as they made their way between overgrown bushes that may or may not once have been orange trees. On reaching the door into the main house, they paused. Faintly, they could hear Adam's nasal tones talking down to someone. 'Let's hope it's Atwood,' murmured Nicholas as he eased open the door.

CHAPTER 23

'I'm not entirely convinced old Admiral Atwood didn't feed us a complete bag of moonshine,' grumbled the Reverend as their carriage bowled along the road towards Northwood Court.

'Mayhap you're right,' admitted Grace, 'but could we take that chance? I was of a mind to quiz him while we travelled, but it's a dreadful crush in here as it is with three adults and a dog. And while we sincerely hope his intentions are honourable, his past actions give no assurance of that, and goodness knows what a desperate rogue such as he will do if he's determined to gain his freedom.'

'I'd like to see him get away from Freddy,' huffed her father.

'He's hardly likely to escape from a trunk,' interrupted Percy disapprovingly. 'Indeed, I'd be surprised if he's able to walk when we set about freeing him.'

Grace sighed. 'You are right, of course, Percy. Your censure is well deserved, but in truth, I did not know what else to do with him.'

'It's no more than the blackguard deserves,' defended Augustus Shackleford, 'and anyway, he's got plenty of padding on top of my unmentionables. Indeed, I wouldn't be surprised if he's dozed off already. I can't imagine he's had much sleep over the last few years, married to that deuced baggage. If it was me, I'd be concerned she intended to murder me in my bed.'

'If it was you, Father, she undoubtedly would have,' countered Grace drily.

'So, what's our plan?' demanded Reverend Shackleford, deeming it an appropriate time to change the subject.

'I have no idea,' admitted Grace, shaking her head. 'I suppose it depends on what we find when we get there. It could be that Nicholas and the others have already put an end to the whole smoky business and we discover Hope waiting for us. On the other hand…'

'On the other hand, we might arrive to an empty house aside from two corpses,' declared the Reverend sorrowfully.

'Father, please,' protested Grace. 'Must you be so Friday faced? I have every faith in my husband. Nicholas will even now have taken charge of things. He will not allow any harm to come to Hope or Gabriel, surely you believe that?'

Augustus Shackleford sighed. 'I want to, Gracie, I really do,' he muttered, 'but the Almighty has already given me far more than I rightly deserve, and I fear payment may be due any moment now.' His pessimism was so out of character that both Grace and Percy stared at him in concern.

'Sir, I do not believe the Almighty keeps a weights and measures account of our blessings,' responded Percy earnestly. 'It is enough to simply believe that he will aid us in this undertaking as he has on all the other occasions.

'By the time we arrive we can hope that his grace has everything in hand. But should our assistance be required, we will do our part, confident in our Lord's approval.'

The Reverend nodded slowly, his demeanour brightening. 'You are right, Percy. I really should listen to you more often.' He leaned forward to pat the curate affectionately on the shoulder. 'I sometimes forget that now and again you're more than just a chuckleheaded windbag.'

∞∞∞

Nicholas stole towards the voices with Malcolm on his heels. The corridor they were in was wide, giving a good indication that it was in regular use. There were several doors leading off, but the two men paid them no heed, except to watch for the possibility of someone exiting one of them unexpectedly. Their intent was simply to get as close as they could to where they believed Henry Atwood to be without being spotted. Once there, they would assess the situation.

They finally came to the end of the corridor which they could see from their vantage point opened out into a large entrance hall. Nicholas risked a quick glance around the corner of their hiding place and noted that Atwood had two men flanking him. He nodded, satisfied at the odds if indeed there were no other ruffians in Henry's pay lurking about the house.

Pulling back, he whispered his discovery to Malcolm. 'I dinna think they'll be his only support,' the valet murmured. 'There's no sign of Hope or Gabriel, so it's safe to assume he's got another of his cronies guarding the pair.' The Duke nodded. 'But if so, it's unlikely the man will be in a position to join any fight, at least not immediately, which gives us valuable time to disarm these three idiots.'

'Aye, that's true, but we canna risk the prisoners' lives if the bastard decides to eliminate that threat first.'

Nicholas nodded again, thoughtfully. 'I believe it's a risk we'll have to take,' he decided at length. 'The longer Adam keeps up the charade, the more likely that Atwood will smell a rat.' He shook his head. 'That said, if possible, we must refrain from using pistols. Any sound of gunfire will alert our third man which could spell disaster for Gabriel and Hope.'

Malcolm reluctantly bobbed his head in agreement and waited as the Duke risked another glimpse.

'If you would be kind enough to step in here, my lord,' Henry was saying. 'I will have a fire built up immediately.' Nicholas watched as Adam and Roan were ushered towards a room which he could tell even from his distant vantage point had not been used in months.

'Get ready,' he murmured over his shoulder to the Scotsman.

'I'm not sure this is suita...' The rest of Adam's comment was lost as Henry Atwood shoved the Earl hard, taking him by surprise. By the time Adam recovered his balance and swung round, the door had been slammed in his face.

'Fiend seize it, *now*, before he gets that door locked,' Nicholas ground out, moving quickly to take advantage of Henry Atwood's preoccupation. The two ruffians were not so easily surprised, and as the Duke and Malcolm sprang from seemingly nowhere, after being initially startled, they quickly readied themselves for a fight. Not so Henry. Their sudden appearance caused him to fumble and drop the key he'd been holding. Cursing, he bent to pick it up just as Adam and Roan yanked open the door and burst forth.

Roan, clearly more accustomed to fisticuffs in a harbourside alley than at the Corinthian Path, indulged in no battle niceties but immediately used his foot to kick Atwood backwards. 'He's yours,' the former sea captain shouted as he ran to join in the fight with the two kidnappers, one of whom had pulled out a pistol. Using his momentum to knock the gun out of the ruffian's grip, Roan immediately drew his free hand and planted the man an enthusiastic facer. The thug went down as if he'd been poleaxed with his companion joining him a second later after a fervent clout on the back of his head from the butt of Malcolm's gun.

Seconds later, Adam dragged a struggling Henry Atwood towards his companions. 'Don't think you'll get away with this,' he sputtered.

'Where are they?' Nicholas demanded icily, completely ignoring the lick spittle's bluster.

'You'll never find them,' sneered Henry, 'not if you look for a month of Sundays, and if I don't return soon, my man will kill them.'

'So, they're not dead yet then?' commented Malcolm mildly. 'Lucky for ye laddie as I'm sure you'll not be wanting yer ballocks handed to ye on a platter.'

Henry blanched and looked wildly between the four men. There was no indication that his two henchmen would be coming round any time soon. The coward realised he was on his own.

'Swear you'll let me go, and I'll tell you where they are,' he burst out, making no effort to conceal his desperation.

'How about you tell us where they are, and we'll see that you don't end up with the morning drop,' offered Roan.

'You think I want to spend the rest of my bloody life in Newgate limbo?' Henry spat, the horror of being buried alive in London's most notorious prison clearly giving him a belated backbone. 'I'm not telling you anything until you promise to set me free.'

'I think Viscount Atwood might have something to say about that,' Adam growled.

'Tie all three bastards to the bannister,' Nicholas ordered Malcolm before bending down to stare icily into Atwood's terrified eyes. 'And if you so much as make a single move to warn your associate that we're here, you won't actually get the opportunity of a trial,' he grated, 'because I will personally cut your damned throat.'

Five minutes later all three were secured. 'Mayhap we should split up,' suggested Roan. 'There can only so many hiding places in one house.'

'What if it's a priest hole,' Nicholas replied in exasperation. 'They were traditionally very well hidden. We truly could be looking for days. There's no way Atwood's man will wait much beyond an hour before he guesses something has gone awry and cuts his losses.'

'He may decide to simply scarper, leaving them both alive,' Roan commented without much hope.

'I canna see the murdering bastard doing such a thing,' responded Malcolm shaking his head. 'At the vera least, he'll not want to leave witnesses. The rest of us have nae seen the man, so couldna identify him if we tried.'

'Did you hear that,' snapped the Duke, turning back to Henry. 'Your paid thug will undoubtedly leave you to swing.'

Atwood shook his head confidently. 'John will *never* betray me.'

'Ye seem certain of that, laddie,' said Malcolm. 'Well, ye can rest easy while we be putting your conviction to the test.'

Twenty minutes later the four men reconvened having had no luck locating the priest hole. 'If Gabriel was bloody well here, he'd be able to tell us where it is,' muttered Adam, running his hand through his hair in frustration.

Atwood was seated where they'd left him, now openly grinning.

'Are you averse to torture?' grated Roan, fighting the urge to draw the bastard's cork.

Nicholas swore. 'We don't have time to wait for these two sleeping beauties to wake,' he growled.'

'Running out of time, your grace?' crowed Henry becoming more confident by the minute.

'Someone gag that son of a bitch,' the Duke bit out, clearly fighting to keep his temper in check. He closed his eyes wearily for a second.

'We've got to look aga…' he started as the unlikely sound of footsteps approaching the front door caught his attention.

'Who the devil's that?' questioned Malcolm.

'Don't let them ring the damned bell,' hissed Adam, 'the bloody clanging is loud enough to wake the dead.'

Nicholas strode quickly to the main entrance and threw open the door before anyone had the opportunity to take hold of the bell rope. To his complete astonishment, a shapely form mumbled incoherently before throwing herself into his arms. With a loud grunt, the Duke stepped back, seeking to avoid falling ignominiously on his backside on receipt of the sudden weight.

Incredulously, he looked over the head of his sobbing wife to her father who was puffing up the steps behind her, followed more reluctantly by Percy.

'What the blazes are you all doing here?' Nicholas bit out, trying to contain his anger. 'The only one deuced well missing is Freddy.'

'Don't you worry, your grace,' wheezed the Reverend cheerfully. 'Freddy's here. He's currently in the carriage guarding Admiral Atwood.'

'Do you know where the priest hole is hidden?' Nicholas questioned Benjamin Atwood without preamble once the man had been freed from the trunk and brought inside. Clearly in pain, the Admiral did not immediately answer the Duke's question as his eyes sought out those of his son. Though unable to speak, Henry's gaze glittered with unmistakeable hatred as he stared back at his father.

'I don't know where it is,' responded the Admiral, finally tearing his gaze away from his son's blatant loathing. 'I never came here after Gabriel's mother died.'

'Your trollop, you mean,' spat out Henry from behind the gag.

Adam raised his eyebrows. 'Clearly, your mouth-securing methods require a little work,' he murmured to Roan.

'Unquestionably a lack of practice,' came the grim response.

'What does he mean by *your trollop?*' barked Nicholas to the Admiral who by this time was swaying on his feet.

'Would it be an idea to get him a chair?' asked Grace with a small cough. Her voice was so diffident, that she drew incredulous looks from both her father and her husband. Indeed, it couldn't be denied that her subservient tone was entirely dissimilar to her usual inclination. However, once she'd been assured of her husband's continued health, Grace had deemed it wise to avoid raising his ire even further given that his *health* most definitely extended to his temper.

Glaring at his errant wife, Nicholas grabbed a chair and commanded the Admiral to sit on it. 'Speak,' he ordered, clearly coming to the end of what little patience remained.

'Gabriel is my son,' whispered Benjamin Atwood brokenly, 'and Henry knows it.'

There was a deafening silence as the implications of the Admiral's words sank in.

'Thunder an' turf,' breathed the Reverend first.

'Does Gabriel know?' demanded Nicholas wondering how the hell they were going to break it to him.

Nicholas bent over their chuckling prisoner and dragged down his gag. 'Does Gabriel know?' he ground out.'

Henry laughed out loud, almost choking on his mirth. 'He didn't take it well,' he mocked sadly.

'I'm finished with him,' declared the Duke in disgust, standing back up.

'So how the deuce did you think you could help?' demanded Grace, momentarily forgetting her decision to remain submissively in the background.

Admiral Atwood looked up at her, his face strangely serene. 'Like this,' he murmured, suddenly reaching inside his coat and pulling out a pistol. Before anyone could react, he abruptly stood, calmly pointed the gun at his son and fired, before turning the pistol and using the second barrel on himself.

CHAPTER 24

Gabriel could see their gaoler was becoming increasingly skittish as the minutes went by, mainly because the man kept glancing over his shoulder towards the door as though somehow his checking would materialise his employer out of thin air.

Both Gabriel and Hope remained standing, but the Viscount dared make no sudden movements on account of the pistol still pointing steadily at them. John made no attempt at conversation, but in the flickering light, Gabriel could clearly see the sweat begin to gather on the thug's brow and feared that sooner rather than later the man would risk Henry's wrath, shoot them both and be done with it. He was trapped, every bit as much as they were, with no one knowing his whereabouts except his master and two associates.

Silently, Gabriel calculated the distance between them and their abductor. Could he cover the ten feet separating them before the man had time to aim properly and shoot? If he did so, he would undoubtedly be risking Hope's life as well as his own. Drawing the ruffian's fire towards himself would most certainly leave Hope's life forfeit if John managed to get off a lucky shot.

His thoughts went round and round in his head and meanwhile he was well aware that his companion was also becoming increasingly distressed.

Hope did not dare move. She felt as though she was in some kind of hellish realm with the flickering light from the lantern on the floor competing with the lamp hanging from the wall. Shadows danced and weaved with the flames causing their assailant to come in and out of focus in an almost demonic fashion. Trying her best to stifle her rising hysteria, Hope glanced over at Gabriel who clearly could not risk taking his eyes off their gaoler. She dared not even squeeze his hand lest it take his attention away from the pistol pointing straight at them. Her heart was thudding erratically, increasing in tempo along with her panic. Dear God, they were both going to die. She wasn't ready to die…

Suddenly, shockingly, there was a muffled gunshot, followed almost immediately by another. John started slightly, but for a couple of seconds did nothing. Then, clearly coming to a decision, he gave a telling half step forward and raised his arm slightly.

Heart slamming, Gabriel knew he had to act, but before he had chance to move, the most deafening noise he'd heard in his entire life suddenly shook the chamber they were in.

'WE'RE DOWN HERE, HEEEELP…'

Fortunately, despite almost having an apoplexy, Gabriel had in fact heard Hope shout before, though he didn't recall it being quite so ear splitting. Not so their gaoler. As the thunderous racket reverberated around the chamber, he instinctively began to crouch, clearly thinking something calamitous was happening. The Viscount needed no further urging. Letting go of Hope's hand, he sprang forward, taking the henchman entirely by surprise. As the ruffian began to lift his hand defensively, Gabriel knocked the pistol out of the man's hand and drawing back his arm planted a facer that would have made Gentleman Jack proud. Indeed, his punch was so hard, their assailant sailed backwards and crashed against the door, his head hitting the wood with a sickening thud.

Gabriel stood over the brute's prone body panting and shaking his throbbing hand as Hope sobbed softly behind him. Then bending down, he checked for a pulse but found none. Unbelievably, their gaoler was dead.

Turning round, he strode back over to Hope. 'Is he...?' she wept.

'Shhh,' the Viscount soothed, gathering her into his arms. As she calmed, he kissed her lightly on the lips and leaned back. 'It's not over yet, love,' he murmured, stroking her hair. 'We still have to get out of here, and right now we have no idea whether that gunshot was delivered by Henry or those come to rescue us.' He grimaced and stepped back. 'But whatever happens, we cannot remain entombed down here with a dead man.' He glanced back at the body on the floor and spied the pistol laying two feet away.

He grinned slowly. 'And now we have a weapon. Let's give Henry Atwood the reception he deserves.' Dropping another light kiss on her forehead, he went to pick up the gun. 'On my say so, could you do that err... thing you do with your voice again, my love?' He went to position himself by the door, so did not see Hope's mortified flush.

Turning back to her he quirked a brow and added drily, 'Just one more thing before you wake every ghost within a three-mile radius. Do you think you might refrain from shouting except under the direst circumstances once we are wed?'

∞∞∞∞

The stomach-churning mess in the large entrance hall would undoubtedly take an entire army of servants to clear up, but the Reverend's sheepish comment of, 'Mayhap we should have checked the Admiral for weapons before we stuffed him in the trunk,' was paid no more than a passing heed. They were all far too afraid that the noise of the gunshots had alerted the remaining henchman to their presence, leaving them minutes at best to find Gabriel and Hope.

'Mayhap Freddy can find them,' faltered Grace in panic.

Before anyone had chance to answer, they heard an incoherent shout.

'That's Hope,' exclaimed Reverend Shackleford. 'I'd know those prodigious vocal cords anywhere.'

'Which way did it come from?' demanded Nicholas urgently. The rest shook their heads and the Duke briskly ordered everyone to remain still and listen. Two minutes later there was another muffled shout.

'This way,' the Reverend announced, letting go of the foxhound who took off with a single bark.

Freddy led them all down a hitherto unnoticed passageway which culminated in a small study. Without hesitation, the dog stood in front of a panelled wall wagging his tail enthusiastically. The shout came again, this time more urgent.

'Tare an' hounds,' groaned the Reverend, 'Hope's being murdered as we speak.'

Nicholas, Adam, Roan and Malcolm began examining the wooden squares covering the wall. On the face of it, each one looked the same until abruptly Adam gave an exultant shout. Pressing something, there was a click and a door shaped section of the wall swung open.

'About bloody time,' muttered the Scotsman as they crowded round the entrance to a steep flight of stairs.

'Grace, remain up here in this room' ordered Nicholas, making no effort to soften his words. His wife opened her mouth to speak, then shut it again as her father threw her a cautionary look, before dragging Freddy away from the opening. 'Be careful,' was all she said in the end as the Duke began carefully descending.

'Roan, with me,' he ordered softly. 'Adam, Malcolm, guard the top of the stairs. If the bastard manages to get past us, it'll be all down to you two. Protect Grace first and foremost.'

'Steady on,' mumbled Reverend Shackleford a trifle indignantly. Percy simply hovered at the door, wringing his hands.

Seconds later the two men were at the bottom of the stairs, Just as Hope's shout came again, this time with only a door muffling the deafening cry.

'God's teeth,' muttered Roan looking incredulously at the Duke who raised his eyebrows in return. 'Get ready,' Nicholas murmured and silently began turning the key while Roan stood sideways at the entrance gripping his pistol in preparation.

'After three,' whispered the Duke, without looking up.

Seconds later he shoved his foot against the door, slamming it open. In the same heartbeat, Roan stepped forward, pistol first, only to come face to face with Gabriel Atwood who was pointing his own borrowed weapon directly towards the former sea captain's face.

For a second, nobody moved, then a relieved grin slowly suffused the Viscount's face. 'What the bloody hell took you so long?' he drawled, lowering his pistol. 'Any more of Hope's entreaties for help were like to render me deaf as a post.'

∞∞∞

With the demise of both Henry Atwood and his father, it wasn't too difficult to ensure there was no scandal. Few people cared about the imprisonment of two anonymous cutthroats and certainly no one took note of a bizarre story involving a kidnapping by a man held in such high esteem. Indeed, the Admiral was buried with full military honours along with his son Henry.

The official account was that Benjamin Atwood had refused to believe his nephew dead. He'd been absent from London for several months desperately searching for Gabriel, determined to find him and bring him home. During his father's absence, his devoted son Henry remained ensconced in Northwood Court, a diligent custodian of the Estate.

Naturally, the Admiral eventually located his nephew, wounded and left for dead by the French, and after diligently nursing him back to health in a secret location, valiantly attempted to bring him back to England. Sadly, Benjamin Atwood lost his life after being struck by a mast during a violent storm that almost destroyed the fishing vessel on which they'd secured passage.

Henry Atwood, on hearing of his father's tragic demise, and subsequently mad with grief accidentally fell down the stairs and broke his neck. The Admiral's widow Caroline Atwood, on learning that both her husband and son had perished had taken herself off to a convent where she undertook a vow of silence.

'And if they believe that bag of moonshine, they'll believe anything,' was Reverend Shackleford's muttered verdict. His opinion was of course shared by those few who knew both the Admiral and Henry intimately, but no one cared enough to throw a rub in the way. Indeed, it was generally considered the whole Atwood family were slightly dicked in the nob and best left to their own devices.

Which suited the newly restored Viscount Northwood entirely.

And not only Lord Northwood. In Augustus Shackleford's opinion, which he enthusiastically shared with Percy over a few celebratory glasses of brandy, the Viscount's ability to carry off a good cock and bull story made Gabriel Atwood a perfect addition to the family.

There had been a brief hiccup in his burgeoning relationship with Hope when Gabriel deemed it only honourable to inform everyone involved in the whole smoky business that Henry's revelations had revealed him to be the Admiral's by blow. However, he was told in no uncertain terms by both the Duke of Blackmore and the Earl of Ravenstone to remove the poker from his arse and get on with it.

Roan of course had relished enlightening the Viscount of his own less than respectable upbringing, and finally Reverend Shackleford had cheerfully informed Gabriel that as long as he cared for Hope, was in possession of plenty of blunt, and a good pair of ear plugs, then her father had no objections.

EPILOGUE

*E*ntirely unused to being the centre of attention, Hope stood uncomfortably silent while her younger sisters argued over whether the addition of a sprig of honesty would add anything to her ensemble.

Patience was of the opinion that the whole affair was an entire waste of a day, citing the fact that she'd already been forced to endure three of her sibling's weddings and asking why Hope couldn't simply have eloped to Gretna Green like Ada Leigh and John Gaynor in the village.

Chastity was of the opinion that the addition of any more flowers would not actually render Hope any less homely and instead result in her looking like she had a garden on her head, while Charity pointed out that the inclusion of honesty was a trifle hypocritical given that in her view Hope had most definitely fabricated an entire Canterbury tale when recounting the details of her unexpected courtship with Lord Northwood to her sisters.

Prudence said they made her look as if she'd just been dug up.

The arrival of Grace and Temperance, both now happily enceinte, put an end to the quarrel as the Duchess was holding the most beautiful garland of gladiolus flowers, while Temperance smilingly carried a matching bouquet.

'They represent hope and strength,' Grace said, placing the crown on her sister's auburn tresses, 'and goodness knows you've shown more than enough of both recently.'

The delicate blue was a perfect foil to Hope's red gold hair and for a few seconds her sisters were speechless, until Prudence announced that they were a definite improvement as the bride no longer looked as though she'd been dead for a week, merely a couple of days.

Before anyone got chance respond to this exaggerated observation, Faith arrived, flustered and agitated before leaning dramatically against the door.

'What's wrong?' asked Hope anxiously, half expecting the groom to have backed out at the last minute.

'Nothing at all,' responded Faith with forced gaiety. 'What could possibly be wrong?'

Not trusting her sister's denial for one second, Hope handed her bouquet to Patience and put her hands on her hips. 'What's father done now?' she demanded.

Grace and Temperance exchanged frowns. Whatever calamity had transpired, they certainly had no knowledge of it, and Hope's heart gave an uncomfortable lurch.

'Is it Gabriel?' she asked. 'Has he cried off?'

'Of course not,' answered Faith indignantly. 'What on earth made you think such a thing?'

'Tell me what's happened,' Hope commanded.

'Very well,' Faith relented. 'Just ... well ... *please* don't shout when I tell you.'

Hope felt sick as she stared at her twin, eventually giving a small nod.

Faith sighed, then taking a deep breath, she whispered, 'The Queen is here.'

'What do you mean the Queen is here?' yelled Hope. 'Which queen?'

'What do you mean which queen?' returned Faith frantically flapping her hands at her sister to lower her voice. 'There's only one deuced queen - Queen Charlotte.'

'Why is she here?' cut in Grace, her calmness effectively cutting off the rising hysteria.

'Apparently because Gabriel's uncle was such a hero,' Faith stammered. 'She wants to pay her respects to the families of those sons of England who've paid the ultimate sacrifice in the war against old Boney.'

'His demise can hardly be blamed on Napoleon Bonaparte,' scoffed Temperance.

'How did Napoleon kill Gabriel's uncle?' queried Chastity frowning.

'I heard father talking to Percy about him having the *French box*,' piped up Prudence.

'Prudence' chided both Grace and Temperance at the same time.

'Is that a type of coffin?' asked Charity.

'Did he bury the Admiral alive in a French box?' persisted Prudence macabrely.

'For pity's sake, stubble it,' snapped Grace, finally coming to the end of her patience.

She looked over at the bride's white face and lowered her voice.

'This is a great honour, Hope, and I am entirely certain it will make your special day even more memorable.' She ignored Patience's ill-mannered snort and ploughed on.

'Tempy and I have no choice but to leave you now. Our place is with our husbands and...' she faltered, briefly revealing her nervousness before determinedly continuing, 'You, my darling, will concentrate solely on your day. Leave her majesty to us.'

With that, she took Temperance's arm and marched her clearly reluctant sister to the door.

'Did Napoleon put a poisonous snake in the French box?' Prudence yelled just as the door slammed shut behind them.

And so, there was a fourth wedding in Blackmore in almost as many years, though this time everyone in the village agreed that they'd certainly not seen this one coming.

Nor had they imagined in their wildest dreams that the Queen of England might attend, and her unexpected appearance would undoubtedly be talked about for many years to come, though not necessarily for the reasons one might think.

Indeed, most of the villagers believed it had been the extra glass of port that had prompted Reverend Shackleford to ask her majesty to dance, although no one could have imagined he would be quite as nimble at the Scotch Reel as he subsequently proved, or that Agnes Shackleford would turn out to have such a possessive streak...

THE END

The Reverend and the rest of the Shackleford family return in *Patience: Book Five of the Shackleford Sisters*. Now available on Amazon

Turn the page for more...

KEEPING IN TOUCH

Thank you so much for reading *Hope,* I really hope you enjoyed it.
For any of you who'd like to connect, I'd really love to hear from you.
Feel free to contact me via my facebook page: beverleywattsromantic-
comedyauthor
or my website:
www.beverleywatts.com

If you'd like me to let you know as soon as the next book in the series
is available, copy and paste the link below into your browser to sign
up to my newsletter and I'll keep you updated about that and all my
latest releases.

https://motivated-teacher-3299.ck.page/143a008c18

And lastly, thanks a million for taking the time to read this story. If
you'd like a sneak peek at *Patience* Book 5 of The Shackleford Sisters,
turn the page...

PATIENCE

*W*ith her four older sisters now married, it's Patience Shackleford's turn to take charge of her younger siblings' education. But given that Patience's most prodigious skill is lock picking, any abilities she passes on to her younger sisters are unlikely to provide any assistance in the drawing rooms of the genteel, especially as she has no interest in either high society, or horror of horrors... marriage. Indeed, her father the Reverend Augustus Shackleford is firmly of the opinion that the less society knows about his fifth daughter the better...

When Grace and Temperance, now married to influential members of the ton, offer to take her in hand and bring her out, both Patience and her father are entirely horrified. For once in total accord, they endeavour to hatch a plan to somehow avoid the upcoming Season.

But that's before a chance meeting with the enigmatic and undeniably handsome Marquis of Guildford when Patience discovers that lock picking is exactly the expertise he happens to be looking for...

CHAPTER 1

*M*aximilian Wolverton, the tenth Marquess of Guildford watched as his great grandmother's favourite diamond and sapphire necklace was paraded around the ballroom.

His outward demeanour was entirely impassive as he pretended to sip his champagne with practiced boredom. In truth however, the luke-warm liquid would never have made it past his clenched teeth.

This was precisely the reason he'd chosen to attend his first ball in nearly three years. In fact, the necklace was actually the second trinket he'd spotted that should have been locked in the Wolverton coffers but was instead being worn by a member of the *ton*.

'Guildford, we haven't had the pleasure of your company in an age. Are you perchance intending to favour us with your presence this Season?' The female voice tittered directly into his right ear.

Closing his eyes briefly, Max made a valiant attempt to swallow his ire. He could not afford to alienate any ambitious mothers seeking a husband for their daughters in the forthcoming Season's marriage mart, however much he despised the whole debacle.

Now he was assured things were every bit as bad as he'd feared, he would need to court their favour, especially those whose offspring came with a large dowry. In truth, the larger the better, given that he was currently penniless.

Swallowing his ire, Max turned towards the speaker. 'Lady Bellamy,' he purred, bending low over her proffered hand, 'how delightful to see you again.'

∞∞∞∞

'Percy, there's no doubt in my mind, none whatsoever, this is totally and utterly an … an … *unequivocal* disaster.'

Without waiting for his long-suffering curate to reply, Reverend Augustus Shackleford collapsed into the vestry's only chair. 'Why, *why?*' he beseeched, raising his eyes heavenward giving Percy a good indication that the question was not directed at him.

Sighing, the curate got up off his hands and knees and placed the half-cleaned sconce carefully onto the table. 'Has something happened, Sir?' he asked warily, entirely sure he didn't wish to know.

'You may well ask Percy, you may well ask,' the Reverend groaned sinking even further into his chair. 'You would think that considering all the good I've done, the Almighty might see fit to allow me a modicum of peace.' He glared at the curate as if somehow it was all the small man's fault. Having been down this path many times, Percy merely regarded his superior dubiously and waited.

'My two eldest, most *meddling* offspring have suddenly come up with the preposterous idea of taking her in hand and finding her a…' The Reverend stopped and closed his eyes, clearly overcome by the calamity of … whatever it was. Not knowing what else to do, Percy stepped forward and awkwardly patted the large man's back. 'I'm sure it can't be that bad, Sir,' he murmured, utterly sure that knowing the

Shackleford family, it very possibly could. 'What on earth has happened to vex you so?'

Reverend Shackleford gave a despairing moan and followed it with a heavy sigh. To the curate's alarm, he actually looked on the verge of tears.

'It's Patience,' he managed finally. 'They want to find her a deuced husband...'

∞∞∞

'Blast and bugger their eyes,' Patience muttered yanking viciously at the apple blossom that shielded her from any prying eyes. She thought back to the events leading up to her current position high up in an apple tree on the edge of the vicarage's overgrown garden.

The day had started so promisingly. She'd managed to convince her father and stepmother over breakfast to give her leave to take her sisters and brother to the Easter Day celebrations in the village. Once she'd obtained their permission, she'd gone on to suggest that she remove her younger siblings from the vicarage extra early to allow her father to focus all his energies on the spiritual mentorship of his flock on such an important day.

So persuasive was her argument that she succeeded in making herself appear noble and self-sacrificing. In truth, she simply wanted to avoid Percy's interminable Easter sermon. The year before, it had lasted well over two hours, despite being read by her father at breakneck speed.

Of course, Reverend Shackleford was perfectly aware of the true reason for his daughter's sudden altruism, but conscious that Patience could elucidate for hours to get her own way if needs be, he chose to surrender to the inevitable.

There was also the added incentive that she'd undoubtedly go ahead and do it anyway with or without his permission, and at least by conceding to her request, the Reverend could preserve the belief that he had at least a modicum of control over his determined daughter.

Patience on the other hand, didn't waste time wondering why her father had agreed, it was enough that he had.

It was precisely as she was leaving the breakfast table that things had rapidly gone to hell in a hand cart. She'd been busy filching some sweet rolls to eat later when a missive arrived from her sister Temperance.

As Tempy had only months ago delivered of a baby boy whose lungs Patience was convinced already made him eligible to be a future town crier, she did not pay attention as her father began reading the message out loud. It was only as he faltered after a few moments, leaving a silence thick with unexpected dread, that Patience looked up from her pilfering with a frown. Indeed, the look of sheer horror on her father's face caused her to swallow with sudden anxiety as she glanced around the hushed table.

But it was her stepmother Agnes's unexpected wail of despair that truly made her heart plummet down to her sturdy boots, though she still didn't fully understand the reason for it until the matron followed it up with a shriek of, '*Do* something Augustus. If they so much as allow that hoyden within a hundred miles of a London Season, Anthony will be spending the rest of his days as a … a…' She paused to let out a sob before finishing in an appalled whisper, 'a … *vicar.*'

Ignoring her stepmother's histrionics, Patience snatched the letter from her father's hands to read its contents for herself. It was far, *far* worse than she could ever have imagined.

In it, Temperance announced her husband, the Earl of Ravenstone's intention of sponsoring Patience for the coming Season. The letter declared in no uncertain terms that their mother - God rest her soul - would turn in her grave if Patience was allowed to roam wild for much longer. (The words she *actually* used were, for the most part, not commonly favoured by ladies, and certainly not ladies married to titled gentlemen.) The letter finished with the avowal that both she and Grace intended to take it upon themselves to find their younger sister a husband.

As soon as possible. Before they were all ruined.

Well, she didn't actually *write* the last sentence, but Patience had no doubt that that was her meaning.

Ignoring her stepmother's dramatic collapse onto the chaise longue where Prudence was enthusiastically shoving salts up her nose, Patience lifted her eyes from the letter and allowed her horrified gaze to meet that of her equally horrified father.

The Reverend's pallor was such that Patience was left in no doubt of his genuine terror at the thought of his first wife's youngest daughter being paraded before the *ton*. For a moment she hadn't known whether to be relieved or slightly affronted, but then reality kicked in. Her father had every right to be alarmed.

In truth, Patience, more so than any of her sisters, was entirely unsuited to wed especially a man of considerable means, which was clearly Grace and Tempy's intention. Indeed, the last man who'd attempted to get within thumping distance only ever did it once, and Patience's reputation in the village had reached an all-time low after the incident with old Bernard's pig pen. And those individuals didn't have sixpence to scratch with.

No, Patience decided as she sat defiantly in her tree, if there was to be a fifth Shackleford wedding, it was most definitely *not* going to be hers.

Patience - Book 5 of The Shackleford Sisters is now available on Amazon.

ALSO BY BEVERLEY WATTS ON AMAZON

The Shackleford Sisters
Book 1 - Grace
Book 2 - Temperance
Book 3 - Faith
Book 4 - Hope
Book 5 - Patience
Book 6 - Charity
Book 7 - Chastity
Book 8 - Prudence
Book 9 - Anthony

The Shackleford Legacies
Book 1 - Jennifer
Book 2 - Mercedes
Book 3 - Roseanna will be released on March 27th 2025

The Shackleford Diaries:
Book 1 - Claiming Victory
Book 2 - Sweet Victory
Book 3 - All For Victory

Book 4 - Chasing Victory
Book 5 - Lasting Victory
Book 6 - A Shackleford Victory
Book 7 - Final Victory

The Admiral Shackleford Mysteries
Book 1 - A Murderous Valentine
Book 2 - A Murderous Marriage
Book 3 - A Murderous Season

Standalone Titles
An Officer and a Gentleman Wanted

ABOUT THE AUTHOR

Beverley Watts

Beverley spent 8 years teaching English as a Foreign Language to International Military Students in Britannia Royal Naval College, the Royal Navy's premier officer training establishment in the UK. She says that in the whole 8 years there was never a dull moment and many of her wonderful experiences at the College were not only memorable but were most definitely 'the stuff of fiction.' Her debut novel An Officer And A Gentleman Wanted is very loosely based on her adventures at the College.

Beverley particularly enjoys writing books that make people laugh and currently she has two series of Romantic Comedies, both contemporary and historical, as well as a humorous cosy mystery series under her belt.

She lives with her husband in an apartment overlooking the sea on the beautiful English Riviera. Between them they have 3 adult children and two gorgeous grandchildren plus a menagerie of animals including 4 dogs - 3 Romanian rescues of indeterminate breed called Florence, Trixie, and Lizzie, and a 'Chichon" named Dotty who was the inspiration for Dotty in The Dartmouth Diaries.

You can find out more about Beverley's books at www.beverley-watts.com

Printed in Great Britain
by Amazon

57993078R00136